WRONG MAN RUNNING

WRONG MAN
RUNNING

Alan Hruska

This first world edition published 2011
in Great Britain and the USA by
SEVERN HOUSE PUBLISHERS LTD of
9–15 High Street, Sutton, Surrey, England, SM1 1DF.
Trade paperback edition first published
in Great Britain and the USA 2011 by
SEVERN HOUSE PUBLISHERS LTD.

British Library Cataloguing in Publication Data

Hruska, Alan.
   Wrong man running.
   1. Public prosecutors – Fiction. 2. Rape – Investigation –
   Fiction. 3. New York (N.Y.) – Fiction. 4. Suspense fiction.
   I. Title
   813.5'4-dc22

ISBN-13: 978-0-7278-8027-7 (cased)
ISBN-13: 978-1-84751-346-5 (trade paper)

All Severn House titles are printed on acid-free paper.

Severn House Publishers support The Forest Stewardship Council [FSC],
the leading international forest certification organisation. All our titles that
are printed on Greenpeace-approved FSC-certified paper carry the FSC logo.

Typeset by Palimpsest Book Production Ltd.,
Falkirk, Stirlingshire, Scotland.
Printed and bound in the USA by
Sheridan Books, Inc., Chelsea, Michigan

The Second Victim

Helen Cassenov crossed West 112th Street on a moonlit night, untroubled by forms lurking darkly in alleys. Shadows impersonating people, she thought, reminding her of the University administrators she contended with every day. Laughing to herself, she hastened her step. A dark-haired, spiky woman of forty-six, she drew energy from her belief that she was smarter than anyone she knew, which included most everyone else on the Columbia faculty.

Many opportunities were given Helen to reconfirm this conviction, such as the University function she'd just attended. Indeed, the after-dinner remarks, as she observed to the starchy young man sitting next to her, were fatuously long-winded. And now, much to her annoyance, she'd been delayed returning to her apartment until well past midnight, by which time the building staff had already gone home.

Helen let herself into the lobby. It had, she said later, unlike the open street, 'a certain *sans merci* feel, as if there were something disturbing there, "palely loitering".'

She lived alone and preferred it, although the choice wasn't entirely hers. Her penchant to find flaws, expressed with a wit that cut deeply, defined her own greatest flaw. She knew lecture halls, fawning students, academic politics and disappointing men. She had no experience of handguns.

With one thrust in her face, she underwent a progression of unfamiliar sensations, culminating in sheer terror. Then, the jolt up her spine as she dropped to the tiles, on her bottom, legs splayed.

In the murky lobby of her building, at the mailboxes, where failing bulbs were rarely replaced quickly enough in her opinion, a ski-masked man who knew her name, who apparently had been lurking there, waiting for *her*, now grazed the top of her head with the barrel of the weapon.

'Think of it this way, Helen,' he said, in a voice electronically altered. 'In an hour or two, this'll be over.'

She fully grasped the psychology of terror; she taught it. And though she'd never personally experienced it before, she knew exactly what she would do: whatever this man asked.

Which meant, at first, picking herself up, her handbag, her handkerchief, getting into the elevator with him, dazed but functioning. On the ascent she thought, this can't be happening. Then, what a naïve, stupid thing that was to think. She caught him being interested in her clothing – her nubby black shantung jacket, white silk blouse, long black skirt, black stockings. Her skin tightened. A scream wailed inside her head. On the landing of her floor, rows of doors shone impassively. There were families sleeping inside. She believed, if the scream leaped out of her head, began bounding audibly down the hallway, the first one to die would be her.

Holding her keys, she stubbed one at the lock, then looked at him helplessly. He grabbed them, opened the door, shoved her inside, kicked the door shut, seized her hair and pushed her head forward. Howling silently with pain, she let herself be yanked by the hair into the thinly carpeted hallway of her home, past walls lined with books, streaks of light from the street, clumps of shadows. In her living room, he released her hair, took possession of the sofa and made her stand.

It took some moments to control her trembling.

'How do you know me?' she said, throat dry, voice croaking.

'Come to this spot' – he tipped the gun barrel downward – 'and kneel.'

I'm not here, she thought, nodding dully, stumbling toward him, doing what he said.

Then he laughed, which, as an amplified sound, seemed preposterously melodramatic. 'You're already angry. Furious at this invasion of your privacy. I'm imagining how it'll be when we get started on your clothes.'

'Oh, Jesus.'

'Describe yourself,' he said.

'*What?*'

'It's not complicated, Helen.'

'Goddamnit! Who the hell are you?'

'Would you like to live?'

'Describe myself,' she repeated dully. 'I'm older than you.'

'Are you?'

'I'm not . . . sure.'

'And?'

'I'm a professor of—'

'Describe your body.'

Still on her knees, she looked up at him. *'Oh, please leave, leave this apartment.'*

The gun – its cylinder attachment, a silencer – pushed at her cheek.

'It's ordinary,' she got out. 'I'm short.'

He cupped her breast lightly with his free hand. 'You're very thin.'

'Please, don't.'

'Was that a whimper, Helen? From you?'

'Please!'

'I will hurt you. It's an inevitable part of this . . . process. But there's an inverse correlation between the degree of your cooperation and the pain you will feel. Do you understand that?'

'I'm not stupid.'

'You will be soon.'

'What does that mean?' she snapped.

'In pain, everyone's stupid.'

She brought her hands to her face, as if warding him off.

'You have boundaries, you're telling me,' he said in an amused voice.

'I can see your eyes,' she said, dropping her hands, desperate and showing it. 'They're a bit glazed.'

He laughed again. 'And you're, what now? Diagnosing me?'

'I'm a doctor. Maybe you knew that.' She peered up at him. 'Perhaps you suffer from blackouts? Fainting spells?'

'Oh really!'

'These are symptoms.' She was blurting. 'It's my specialty. Could explain a lot here.'

He yanked her hair again, then fisted it. When she screamed, he stuck the gun in her mouth and the silencer tore at her palate. 'There's only one thing you need to know about me,' he said, the gun further bruising her.

She made a noise in the back of her throat.

'It's what would I rather be watching? The back of your head blown off, with the pattern that makes on the walls and the ceiling? Or maybe it's you opening yourself up. Mentally, physically. Depends on you, doesn't it, Helen? So be inventive. You understand?'

He removed the gun barrel to allow her to answer, but she could say nothing. She couldn't speak. He pinched her chin hard between his gloved thumb and forefinger and tilted her head back.

'Yes,' she blurted out.

'You wish to please me?'

'Yes.'

'So say it, Helen.'

'I wish to please you.'

'Good choice. So let's begin. And when I say open . . .'

'Yes. I know . . . what you want.'

ONE

The file arrived, carried in personally by Hedda, my secretary, a kindly middle-aged reed of a woman from Barbados. 'Sex crime, Ricky. From Frank.' She used his first name and mine. We were informal here. Frank Seaton, the District Attorney, encouraged it, perhaps as an antidote to the autocratic style with which he actually ran the office. And for Hedda to deliver the package with an expression like that – raised brow, lips puckered as if savoring pickles – someone had to have made a point of it.

Probably Frank himself. In a hand I knew as well as my own, he'd scrawled 'Eric Corinth' across the top of the file envelope. I had a chance only to glance at the contents: a rap sheet, photos of a line-up, and a police report – a 'DD5' in NYPD lingo – of a victim interview.

Frank had been New York County District Attorney since before I started law school. In fact, he taught a class I took at law school, NYU, and he tapped me to be his research assistant. Fifteen years later he had me working for him as Chief Assistant. And one of the first curveballs he aimed at my skull was this case.

I had ten matters even more urgent to deal with. They chewed up that day and most of the next. I didn't get to the DD5 until wolfing down a tuna and tomato on rye at my desk the following evening. I almost coughed up the sandwich when I saw Helen Cassenov's name.

The general idea is, before grinding up some poor bastard in the machinery of the system, prosecutors, like me, are supposed to be objective. In fact, we aren't, especially when it comes to the prosecution of violent crimes. And while considering a rape case involving a personal friend wasn't a conflict exactly, it sure as hell felt wrong. Even apart from the question of objectivity, it felt intrusive. Frank should have known it would. As well as tear me apart.

Helen had been interrogated the same night she'd been attacked. Cops assigned to the Special Victims Squad of the NYPD had barged into her room at the hospital. Questioning started routinely. A woman referred to as Lieutenant Spaeth, a detective, recited the circumstances of the inquiry, including where they were, Helen's name and her position as a chaired professor of psychiatry at Columbia University Medical School. Definitely not routine was the fact that the main body of the report was a virtual transcript. Lieutenant Spaeth was apparently a stickler of some sort, but it wasn't clear to me why she had taken Helen's words down verbatim.

Normally, Helen's tone fit her looks: nothing sweet in that beauty and plenty of wounds. I could imagine the edge with which she dealt with Spaeth's questions.

'Could you describe what happened tonight?'

'Lots of things *happened* tonight.'

'The reason you're here.'

'I'm *here* because I've been raped.'

'I do know. Would you prefer doing this later? The doctor says you're not in shock. Obviously, the sooner—'

'Now! Do it! Ask!'

'Could you just tell me what happened, please?'

'You want every little detail, do you?' Helen's outrage flared from the page.

'We want to catch him and stop him.'

'Yes, good. You do that. This guy's in a ski mask, OK? Downstairs, waiting – *for me* – he says to take him to my apartment. With a gun in my neck, that's what I do. *OK?* He says, strip, I strip. He says, show, and I show him. You following this? You'd like a picture drawn, maybe?'

'Did he assault you, physically?'

More silence. Then, the professor biting her words off: 'How would you rate . . . the insertion of a gun barrel into the anus? *That* qualify? *That* physical assault in your book, Lieutenant?'

Helen's description of the assailant wasn't helpful. 'Caucasian. I think, although, damnit, with that mask and gloves, I can't be absolutely certain. Tall-ish, I should say, with a one-sided walk. But, I suppose, anyone could do that. Brown eyes. Yes, I know – contacts are possible. What else was he wearing? Exercise gear. Navy blue. Stuff you can buy anywhere. Gap sort of stuff.'

'Anything else?'

'Yes. He picked me. It was not random. And I will tell you, he would have pulled that trigger. This man is dangerous. He liked what he did to me, and he will do it again. Perhaps even to me, unless he's prevented. I need protection.'

End of report.

I sat there a long while.

Helen and I were not intimate friends but a lot more than casual. She was once married to a guy, Roger Hazzard, who had since became presiding partner of my former law firm. At a firm dinner dance years ago, I happened to be seated next to her, and we ended up talking non-stop through the evening, oblivious, unpardonably, to everyone else. Her peeve that night was her husband whom she divorced soon afterwards. Hazzard apparently thought I had in some way contributed to the break-up, since our relationship soon cooled, although, in fact, I had defended him. In all events, since then, Helen and I had often invited each other to dinner parties in our homes, and we met several times every year for lunch. Somehow, that first night, I'd inched under her shell, and she mine. I guess she let me because she felt she could trust me, and it was mutual. Most people having shells understand that the harder one makes it appear the softer one is beneath it. So I had some idea what this night of terror must have done to her. I couldn't speak, or think of anything else, for more than an hour.

Eventually, I looked at the photos of the line-up. For years, defense counsel and the media have clamored for videos of line-ups, and the DA's office has refused to make them. For obvious reasons. The data confirm the unreliability of the whole process. The line-up they did here showed why.

The guy Helen identified – a shaggy, hatchet-faced ex-offender named Sikes – anyone would have picked out as the suspect, since he was the only one who didn't look like a cop. And I could all too easily imagine a jury empathizing with this guy. He'd been dragged in, thrust on to a stage under glaring lights, blinking and frightened though trying to look bored, made to stand there feeling naked, his accuser hidden behind a one-way glass. *I* empathized with him, even though I knew he was a creep. The experience would have dehumanized a hero.

By now Sikes had been arraigned but not yet indicted. I shot another look at his rap sheet and took a walk. The DA and senior staff occupy offices on the eighth floor of 100 Centre Street, using a separate entrance on the south side of the building, called One Hogan Place. All the views from these offices are south or east. I traveled to an empty conference room having windows looking north; the four bridges up the East River, the uptown skyline of the city. I kept being drawn to that view – leaning into the window's embrasure, thinking about the oddness of even being there, let alone now, sitting in judgment on some twice-convicted rapist they'd picked up in Hell's Kitchen. Prosecute? Let him walk? What? Three weeks before, the view from my private law firm office uptown had been even better, the issues simpler, and I worked in a place I genuinely loved. Then, I'd radically changed my life.

Frank Seaton was about to be named Chief Judge of the State of New York. His proposition to me was that I serve several months as Chief Assistant DA, then take over his remaining term as DA on an 'acting' basis. Then run for the office.

Not totally insane for a guy like me – an over-achiever, nearly forty – or I wouldn't have taken the bait. I'd been an Assistant

DA for three years, then gone off to private practice in an old-line firm, took bar association posts, joined *pro bono* boards; the usual path of a driven careerist. I'd also been pushed into dozens of TV interviews by both Frank and some senior partners of my firm. If I were going to make any sort of political move, I was about the right age. So I had the profile, but did I really have the desire? The need? I knew where it could lead. New York District Attorneys had become Governors, Senators, even candidates for President. And even before I'd been sworn in, the beat reporters had gotten the scent.

You'd think I was made for it, having grown up poor in a company shack in some backwater Illinois steel town. The problem was, two months into the job, I arrived at the realization it wasn't for me. I'd done the trial work before, the prosecutions, but administrative work in a government office is a swim against the tide of bureaucracy. The fact is I wasn't very good at it. And the one thing I hated worse than watching myself yakking on television was thinking about being watched doing it by people I knew. Also, the power, or the prospect of it, did nothing for me – at least nothing positive. I remembered that wonderful scene in one of the Anthony Powell novels where Widmerpool confesses to Nick Jenkins that the love of power he learned he had as a colonel during World War I inspired him to stand for Parliament. I learned the opposite. I figured I'd do the best job I could for two, maybe two and a half years, then retire with some dignity before the election.

I should have known myself better. I'd never taken politics seriously, much less politicians. They always reminded me of the kids in school pumping their hands in the air for attention. Every time I hear the governor on the radio making a 'public announcement' at taxpayers' expense, I feel that I'm listening to a satire on self-promotion. Yet sometimes, in the heat of quixotic idealism, I think I can march right in and shake things up. It always gets me in trouble.

Two minutes after I got back to my office, the door flew open. Frank. He loved coming in this way. His preference would have been the accompaniment of a brass band. And the welcome of a standing ovation. See, he's made for this life. A natural pol. He just waited too long to make a run at the governor's office and got boxed out. Still, the chief judgeship wasn't popcorn. And he loved this show of condescension, coming to see you in your office, rather than summoning you to his. Looking like he was slaving away at night in shirtsleeves, just like one of the troops. It was part of his pretense of being a regular guy. But there was real humanity in Frank, too. Holding this job for more than twenty years hadn't totally erased it. Maybe that's why he'd gotten boxed.

My office had one big leather chair, and he settled into it. Big hair, shock of white, big flushed beefy face. 'Whatta you fucking around for, Ricky?' He reveled in the accent of Queens. 'You've been squattin' on this Sikes matter almost two days. See, here we don't have that luxury.'

'I know, Frank.'

'So what's it to be?'

'Let him go,' I said.

Surprise made his lower lip curl. 'Really?'

'Yeah. That's what I think.'

'Unit Chief wants to prosecute. Mancuso. Good man, Mancuso. Twelve years, he's headed Sex Crimes Prosecution.'

'I worked for him,' I said. 'Before. In Frauds.'

'So you did.'

'As if you'd forgotten.'

He laughed. *'As if you'd forgotten,'* he mimicked. 'Why is it, every time, with you, I feel like I'm talking to a character in a Henry James novel?'

'You'd like what? South Illinois?'

'You could use that, Ricky – a little of that wrong side of the tracks. I'm talking politically.'

'We going to talk about Sikes?'

'Of course we're gonna talk about Sikes,' he said. 'Shit. So, whatta you saying? You're sure he's not the guy? You're not sure, but we don't have enough to convict?'

'I don't think he's the guy.'

No humor now, no playing around. 'Cassenov ID'd him, picked him out of a line-up. Body type, walk.'

'She never saw his face,' I said. 'Or heard his real voice.'

'He's a sex offender. Multiple arrests, two convictions.'

'Which is why the police picked him up.'

'They want to prosecute,' said Frank.

'Cops always want to prosecute. Which is why it's not their decision.'

'Whatta you going on, Boy-o?'

'Sikes is a jerk. Crude. Beats women up until they stop fighting. The guy who did Helen Cassenov tortured her – mentally, even more than physically. What he wanted was to humiliate her. To bring down a smart, superior woman. I think she's right when she says he chose her. Harold Sikes doesn't have the wit for that. Much less for the kind of dialogue that went on during this scene – as she described it.'

'Could have been her translation,' Frank noted.

'Could have been.'

'She's a woman quite possibly given to self-glorification. And Sikes – well, people change. Refine their technique.'

I laughed. 'From slam, bam to the Marquis de Sade? Don't think so.'

'You got any more?' he asked, with sharp appraisal.

'Yeah. I got more. Another rape.'

'Oh, really?' But now he didn't look surprised.

'Woman banker. Investment banker at Goldman Sachs. Name of Diane Nethersong. Early thirties, rising fast. Sexually tortured for two hours. Same M.O.'

'Why don't we have this case?'

'Because it happened in New Jersey.'

He got up. 'I'll tell Mancuso.'

'Frank?'

'Yeah?'

'Why'd this even come to me? It's a routine matter. Mancuso makes these decisions every day.'

He gave me the same kind of look I remembered from law school. Then jabbed a finger at his brow. 'Yours – that mind of yours – used to be pretty sharp. Just wanted to make sure a Wall Street practice hadn't turned it to mush.'

I followed him to the door.

'You knew Helen Cassenov was a friend of mine.'

'I met her in your home, Rick. She's a very beautiful woman.'

'And?' I said.

'And what?'

'The fact that I knew her – that didn't give you pause?'

'About putting you on this?' Temper flashed. 'Whatta you think, it should have?'

I shrugged. Before I could answer he turned abruptly and left.

Another thing at which Frank excelled and I didn't: dodging questions with questions. Another reason I wasn't suited for his job.

TWO

I rented a two-bedroom on Central Park West, in the upper nineties. I hated being there. It wasn't the apartment itself. Most people would kill for it – high floor, glorious view of the park. I hated being what 'there' represented: one half of a failed marriage.

Relationships pose problems for me. Not the entering-into part. I love women, love their company. But long term, they haven't worked out. After my divorce, they didn't work even in the short term. I was still too much in love with Ali, my ex-wife.

Ali and I had ended up wanting different things. I wanted there to be no barriers between us. My romantic conceit was that this was possible between kindred souls. Ali suffered such devotion for nearly fourteen years before the screaming started. What she needed were barriers. Or, to use her favorite word, endlessly repeated: '*space.*' In the beginning, she would have laughed at a code word like that.

We met near NYU where Ali was in the graduate school of education. One of the Village cinemas was running a revival of Ingmar Bergman films, and, on the line for *Smiles of a Summer Night*, she was standing in front of me, unaccompanied, mostly hidden by a scarf, four layers of clothes, and a parka. Still, I recognized her.

'I'm not normally this shade of blue,' I said when she looked back at me. 'I'm just freezing my ass off.'

She smiled and turned away, but I said, 'You do your homework in the Law School library.'

A second backward glance, this time over her shoulder. 'Is that supposed to be remarkable?'

'A bit. Since you don't go to the Law School.'

'You checked?' she said, now swiveling to confront me.

'I did, actually.'

She laughed, frosting the air, but having quite the opposite effect on me.

Be cool, I thought, glancing behind me at the growing line. *Make it less personal.* 'You know why they keep us standing out here?'

'So they can clean the theater?'

'They could've cleaned the theater five times by now.'

'We're meant to be shilling for the movie?'

'Exactly,' I said. 'And for this movie, it shouldn't be necessary.'

'You've seen it?'

'Four times.'

'Three,' she said, pointing to herself.

Now or never, I thought. 'I'm Rick.'

She took my hand in her mitten. 'Ali.'

'When we get inside,' I said, 'if they ever let us inside, may I buy you some popcorn?'

Her lips pursed with surprise. 'We're moving pretty fast here.'

'Right. I was thinking dinner. But then I thought . . . insufficiently audacious. Why not jump all the way to popcorn?'

'You always talk like that?' She flashed a look of reproval. 'Insufficiently audacious?'

'I've a range.'

'I see. You're a lawyer . . .'

'Not yet,' I said, reminded of something. 'Do you like Trollopean names?'

'Ohmigod,' she said, mockingly. 'He reads Trollope.'

'I do.'

'So you mean like, the real estate agent named Julia Fee?'

'Exactly. And the head of Price Waterhouse.'

'His name was Fee, too?' she said.

'No. Spotchek.'

'You made that up!'

'Absolutely not!' I said. 'The man was the senior partner for years.'

'I'll bet you haven't heard of the old football player named Bill Wham.'

'I have, in fact. He played for the Bears. And I once knew a lawyer named Hash.'

'I assume a bad lawyer,' she said.

'The worst. Beaten so often in court, the judges began calling him Into.'

'That,' she said, trying to keep a straight face, 'is a really bad pun.'

Sometimes it's the dumb things that tell you. The labels always stuck out from the neck bands of her blouses and sweaters. She never sweetened her tea but always her coffee. She not only loved bad puns – the worse, the better – she loved repeating them. 'I'm going to get my hair cut,' I'd say. 'Which one?' she'd ask. Always. Deadpan. 'I'm trying,' I'd say, when she'd ask me for a second time to do something. 'You sure are,' she'd reply. Off-putting in someone else, I'm sure. Not in her, at least not to me.

Funny, Ali wasn't my physical ideal. My physical ideal – for reasons I couldn't begin to understand – was a scrawny short girl with light hair and freckles. Ali was tall, dark-haired and pale. Nonetheless, as Keats said of Fanny Brawne: everything about her went through me like a spear.

On our second date, I told her I would always protect her. The words just flew out of me, an idea that surged up inside and expressed itself before I could give much thought to it. Then I did, and it still felt like the right thing to have said. We were in a coffee shop in the Village having BLTs. With her half sandwich poised in mid-air, her eyes suddenly shining, I wanted to cocoon myself around her and start the protection at once.

We got married while I was still a second year at law school. We were too hot *not* to get married. I know everyone self-justifies. I'm probably doing it. But I had no idea we were so different. If anything, it was then Ali who couldn't be parted from me. She came to the law library to study every day. On her field trips she called me three times a day. In fixing her schedule she made sure it dovetailed with mine so we could have maximum time together. Not that I resisted. I loved it. Ali could get kind of New Age sometimes about crystals, auras and herbs, but basically? We were both, I thought, equally, crazy in love.

She's had sex since with other men. While we were married, most likely. Certainly after. And you know what? I hated it; it threw me into terrible depressions, but I wouldn't have left her because of affairs. I loved her too much not to forgive her. In any event, after the last of too many unexplained all-nighters, and voicemails from nameless men, she left me.

Out of the blue, after our second child, she stopped deriving real pleasure from sex. Which may have been the reason she started having affairs, and why each ended noisily almost as soon as it seemed to have begun. I said to her once, pretty close to tears, 'Sex is a gift that people who love each other give to each other.' From her look, I was babbling. Sex had become a favor she bestowed – as infrequently and fastidiously as possible. I began hearing words like 'space' and 'boundaries' and 'co-dependency.' I was being bludgeoned with self-help jargon. And yet, still, when I see her, my blood rushes, goose bumps dimple my skin.

We have two great kids, girl and boy – hence the extra bedroom in my apartment. They weren't shattered by the divorce, even if my daughter, who is the elder, became a little distant for a time. This is Manhattan. They're in private school. Most of their classmates' parents are divorced. Pretty cool, actually. Double treats. Ali and I enacted no scenes. She still touched me with apparent affection. It would mystify most bystanders why we had split. I'd come away from that – that affectionate touching – like a wounded animal. But, of course, I wouldn't show it. I was much too sophisticated to show it. I just keened, in that empty apartment.

I had a date that night with a young woman I'd met in the practice. A lot has been written about this, the state of the nearly-forty newly divorced. It's bad enough having to present yourself all over again, and often, as a candidate for co-habitation, or even just sex. But now you also have unreeling in your head

– and, you know, in hers – all those scenes from movies and books: the newly met working so hard at it. You listen to yourself sounding like one of those characters. Before you know it, you're being bombarded by self-mockery and self-doubt. Or, at least, I was.

The young woman that night was Stacy Moskowitz from the Bronx. 'Riverdale,' she reminded me. Not beautiful, maybe, but she had dark, luminous skin. And if not brilliant, she was quick, lively. Working together as co-counsel two years before, we'd hit it off, the sexual attraction being so conspicuous and insistent we could laugh at it. The time hadn't been right then. It was now. Which made the laughter a bit strained.

We were concentrating on each other at a bistro off Columbus Avenue.

'We ought to talk about this,' I said.

'Yes?'

'I believe in talking things out. Saying what you mean. Laying it right out there.'

'Me too.'

'I think we ought to have sex. See where it takes us.'

'Obviously,' she said.

I gazed at her with admiration, not entirely used to this sort of forthrightness. There was, besides, something deeply appealing about her. And she dressed beautifully, draping her slender form in cashmeres and silks, revealing and concealing.

'I mean, I think we should start tonight.'

'Of course,' she said. 'It's like our what? Fourth date?'

Clever Stacy had bought a condo on West End Avenue almost immediately after law school. Today, she wouldn't have been able to afford it, which made her doubly proud. Only one bedroom, but a sizeable living room where, cloistered within the dark cotton tapestries on her walls, we plunked down on a many-cushioned sofa in dim light. Her kiss was a surprise. Bone-crushing.

'Won't be a minute,' she announced as she marched off to the bathroom.

In about five, she came prancing out. Absolutely naked. Enjoying my shock.

I was, by this time, sitting on the edge of her bed, a

four-poster affair with a patchwork quilt covering. She sat down beside me. Another bone-crushing kiss. We both undressed me, and she plopped down on her belly, as an invitation to caress her back and buttocks. 'Not much of an ass,' she said, without a trace of self-pity.

Then her phone rang. No hesitation. She sprang up and answered it.

During the next forty minutes, she took four more calls of varying duration, exhorting clients, chatting up friends. At the conclusion of the last, she held in her hand the manifestation of my arrested interest. 'Y'know,' she said, 'you may be a sexy-looking guy . . . but I can't do anything with this.'

One of those things. I wasn't going to call her again. Nor she me. Some embarrassments cannot be expiated. Only allowed to rest in peace.

THREE

I was in Rikers. Chief Assistants do not do this, go to the 'Rock,' as it's known, to interview suspects in jail. For one thing, pre-indictment defendants arrested in Manhattan, such as Sikes, almost never get sent to Rikers. They go to the Tombs at 100 Centre Street where they have twenty-four hours to be arraigned. After that, the DA's office has six days to indict under CPL 180.80 – what Assistant DAs refer to as 'making the 180.80' – or the defendant must be released and the complaint dismissed. Because the 180.80 period is so short, these prisoners are rarely moved from the Tombs until after they're brought before a judge to be indicted.

So what the hell was going on with Sikes? Rikers was a harsher environment. Certainly more desperate people there. Were they trying to scare him?

But there was another reason my going out there was exceptional. When Assistant District Attorneys want to see Rikers inmates, they normally have them shipped back to 100 Centre Street. That's more than a convenience. Corrections officers hate having ADAs on their turf. I was more concerned at the moment, however, about making waves over Sikes at 100 Centre than I was at Rikers, and the latter was actually easier to arrange for. I just needed a driver, which I got as a matter of course; moving him would require a security escort and a bus.

Sikes's court-appointed lawyer, who, naturally, would sit in, was a law school classmate of mine, Don Jaglon. I told him the truth. I was probably going to overrule opposition anyway, but I wanted more ammunition. He knew the risks. But we'd had good experiences, so he trusted me.

More than I can say for the cops.

Betsy Spaeth for one; Helen Cassenov's interrogator, and, apparently, lead detective on the case. Younger than I'd expected and a lot better looking. Her attitude, however, said, at this stage I was just meddling. Pity. She was the kind of young woman you sometimes catch a glimpse of; going the other way on the escalator, across a theater, passing on the street. Who fills your fantasies, and stops your breath.

In fact – and it just took me another second to realize this – I had seen her before. Gliding with just such self-assurance. On the reservoir track where I and maybe a hundred other regulars ran four or five times a week at about six thirty in the morning. She was a real steed. Ash blonde hair that had nothing to do with chemicals. Pale blue eyes. Cheekbones of Nordic perfection. Even the slight tilt to the high bridge of her nose and the fullness of her lips were, if imperfections, nonetheless assertions of class. Every man secretly coveted her. Must be an horrendous job disability, I thought, as I took a seat across the table from Jaglon and Sikes. But what in the world was a woman who looks like this doing in such a job in the first place?

Harold Sikes, on the other hand, looked as if, as a baby, his long thin head had been squeezed in a vice and made longer and thinner. Black hair sprouted every which way atop a very narrow cranium. He had been told by a lawyer he barely knew to cooperate with another whom he'd never met, who happened to be a prosecutor. Of a naturally paranoid disposition, he gave me a face – a dark, lined, brooding face – that fully communicated the contempt with which he held this advice.

'Morning, Harold,' I began, to which he just shook his head

morosely, with a dash of disdain, as if he knew something bad
about me that he might or might not choose to mention.

'You fuckers!' is what came out of his mouth. 'I'm gonna
sue you up the gingy hole. Whatta you think? You think you
can just pick me up every time some cunt gets nailed in this
city? This time I'm getting myself a real lawyer. One of those
sharks who works on – whatta you call it? – a contingency!
Sue you fuckers for fifty million dollars!'

I looked about the small windowless featureless room,
breathed in air tinged with industrial-grade disinfectant. 'You
were picked up, Harold, within three blocks of Professor
Cassenov's building. And she identified you in the line-up.'

'Then she's fucking blind. I don't know her. I never seen her.
And there was fifty thousand other guys within three blocks of
her building. Why the fuck didn't you pick them up too?'

Don Jaglon, short, large-nosed, well-groomed, tilted his head
a bit. 'No prints, Rick. We permitted DNA, fingernail, everything. No match.'

'Tell me, Harold,' I said. 'Why'd you go to New Jersey,
Thursday night, eight days ago?'

'What?' He looked totally confused.

'We have you on video boarding a train at the PATH tubes.'

'The fuck you have. I ain't been in New Jersey for six years.'

I glanced at Betsy Spaeth. Her attitude about me or this
meeting hadn't improved.

We were in the parking lot at Rikers before getting into our
respective cars. Briny, wind-whipped, desolate place. Only
government cars were allowed here. Private lawyers had to take
the bus. I said, 'I don't know why I should feel like, maybe, I
ought to apologize. I really did do what I thought should be
done. Was the right thing to do.'

People as angry as Betsy was usually can't talk. Not coher-
ently or below a scream. 'That was bullshit! That lawyer – no
DNA? There was no fucking semen!'

'I know,' I said, trying to make it sound calm.

'The last time we had this prick he walked, because someone
screwed up the evidence.'

'I know.'

'And we had a plant here!'

'Oh, Christ.' So that was the reason for Rikers. I was impressed. This woman really works it, I thought.

'What do guys like you *want*?' she seethed, with her light blonde hair blowing all over her face. Eye to eye, she was nearly my height. 'What is it? Just the power thing? Make all the right moves, low risk, until you slither up the pole? And what's the kick up there? The doorman's face in the morning? The air-headed star-fucking bimbos?'

'Nice meeting you, Betsy. Have yourself a lovely day, OK?'

'You goddamn coward. That son-of-a-bitch is going to rape five women before we can put him away.'

I was already in the car, and the driver, who had heard most of this, had started the engine. 'Let's go,' I said to him, wondering what was taking this woman so far over the line.

Stage directors say contradictory emotions aren't playable. I threw Betsy a look through the window meant to show both my sympathy with her ends and my opposition to her means. It just confused her.

Victims Three and Four

Caroline Lambeth arrived home after the *au pair*, Solange, had already put the children to bed. A sweet girl, Solange; she commiserated with Caroline for having just missed tucking the kids in. Caroline immediately went to their rooms, though she'd been running around, cramping all day, and was badly in need of a pee. Eddie, age four, was sleeping, covers off, mouth open, as he always did. Caroline watched for a moment, worshipfully, before pulling a blanket over his legs. In the nursery, Sarah, two, who had troublesome dreams, worked steadily on her thumb.

Caroline retreated to the sanctuary of her own bathroom. It was the only room in the apartment not renovated. Caroline loved the old fixtures, installed in 1912, sink, bath and tiles, hand-picked by the architect, as this was the original developer's apartment. She lingered for a moment at the mirror, her face appearing by lamplight even more tired than she felt. All these lines, unacceptable at thirty-five. Solange, ten years younger, had the face of a child. Caroline resolved to replace the light fixture that weekend.

On the toilet, skirt hiked, long legs tucked back, she gazed languorously at the new shower curtain, a Gauguin print, a present from the manager of the Metropolitan Museum shop. When she unspooled some paper, the shower curtain moved. Couldn't be, she thought with a chill. She laughed at herself. Then started screaming when a man in a ski mask came out of her bathtub holding a gun.

Solange burst in almost at once, and she too immediately began screaming. The man slapped Caroline, which made them both stop. He said, 'If you scream again, I'll bring the children in to watch.'

FOUR

A week after Harold Sikes was 'let loose upon the streets' (as, I imagined, Betsy would put it), two new rape victims were taken to New York Hospital. In point of fact, the attack on them had no more connection to Harold than had the incident involving Helen Cassenov. But another coincidence was damn troubling. Helen Cassenov had been a friend of mine for some years; Caroline Lambeth and I went back even further.

In my senior year at Yale, as a scholarship student, I took a variety of jobs, including running freshman orientation at Pierson, one of the residential colleges. Caroline appeared in the courtyard one late August afternoon, a skinny blond pony-tailed kid in Bermuda shorts trying awfully hard to look like a Yalie. She'd obviously matured considerably since then, but that's how I still saw her. We hit it off on first meeting, and have been checking in with each other ever since.

For days after being hospitalized Caroline couldn't talk. But her videotapes made any interview superfluous.

Caroline had just been promoted to a great job: head of the Department of Contemporary Art at Christie's. The announcement had caused a stir. She'd recently published a book on a popular subject – having it all – with a twist: after shedding your husband. Caroline also had two young children. To 'have it all' she left them to the care of a succession of nannies, whom she secretly, daily, policed in every room, with video cameras, equipped with sound.

Each night, although Caroline came home exhausted, she watched the daily 'rushes' – it seemed, despite the book, guiltily. Four nannies were fired, and never knew why. The fifth, a young Haitian woman, Solange Delfine, was brought to the hospital too. I learned about the videotapes in a note from Frank Seaton.

'You should take a look at this,' he wrote, sending the package to my desk. Not much warning.

My conference table came equipped with a TV and VCR. They'd been used in the past principally to see how the sound bites coming out of this building played on the daily news, which was the over-riding preoccupation of the Office. Even in this building, however, no one was likely to have witnessed anything quite like what was on this video.

I've never liked pornographic films. I'm not a puritan, but, in the ones I've seen, the bad acting makes them ridiculous. This tape, on the other hand, was altogether too real. Banality makes things look real. Evil is banal, as Hannah Arendt once wrote, and torture is the most extreme form of it. With an in-house video of degraded quality, the impact was horrific. Video artists know about this effect. It's why they use the medium. Thirty-five millimeter film vivifies, makes everything too pretty to be real. Shoot it grainy and blurred, and it looks like home movies, or the evening news.

The creep who did this seemed anally fixated. He liked putting women into contorted positions, the point evidently being to increase the humiliation and the hurt. Through much of this, with the women bent side by side on Caroline's king-sized bed, Solange uttered a low moaning torrent of indecipherable patois, while it is doubtful that Caroline fully realized what was happening. Her mind seemed to have cracked early in the first hour. Despite the acts being committed, she stared fixedly ahead as if drugged.

The rapist broke her with a threat to her children. Grabbing the material of her skirt, he directed her to describe the darkest, ugliest sexual images that had ever come into her head. Upon the merest suspicion she was holding back anything, he said he would put an end to the life of one sleeping child, and then start on the second. As she gagged out the words, he stripped and molested her, until her recitals became monotonic. And Solange, dragged into this, also stripped and abused, delivered her murmur of hate.

Watching made me physically sick. I made it to the men's room, threw up in a stall, rinsed out my mouth, washed my face, and stood looking at myself in the mirror. I remembered reading a statement by David Mamet that he was no longer a brain-dead liberal who believed people were essentially good.

I called Frank Seaton. 'They've picked up Harold again?'

'No,' said Frank. 'They're being more cautious this time. But now we've got two hours of the maniac – Harold or whoever – on "candid camera". Might be Sikes. Doubt it, though.'

'Who's on the case?' I asked, my nonchalance too studied to go unnoticed.

'You know Betsy Spaeth?'

I called personnel and asked for her file. Someone that hostile had to have something in her history explaining it.

Another file, on an ex-sex-offender named Lucien Mossbacher, had arrived while I was out to lunch. Betsy Spaeth called as I finished reading the last document.

'We had the guy shipped up here from New Orleans last night,' she informed me. 'Solange ID'd him this morning.'

'Shipped up? You mean you had him extradited?'

'That's right.'

'Who handled that?' I asked.

'I don't know. Some guy from your office.'

I thought it extremely odd that Frank hadn't mentioned this. 'Mossbacher – his was the closest M.O. you could find?'

She didn't answer right away. 'Not on the phone.'

'You have an office? I'll see you there.'

'It's a cubicle. Glass.'

'You have any interesting photos taped up?'

'I'll come to you,' she said.

'I'm at—'

'I know where you are.'

She arrived in ten minutes and looked a lot better than Frank in that chair. Betsy liked suits. I would say Armani, although I'm not an expert on women's couture. A gray tweed, a lime silk blouse. Not on a policewoman's salary, I thought. Which meant there was either a man in the picture or she had independent means. I found myself, despite everything, hoping it was the latter. As for the new suspect, I had reviewed his file and liked it no more than I had on first reading.

'Why Mossbacher?' I said. 'There are at least four other guys as close or closer – looks and M.O.'

Betsy wasn't interested in other guys. 'We found him first and got the ID. Sometimes you get lucky.'

'You got the ID from a woman who was still borderline hysterical.'

'She seemed calm enough.'

'How'd he get from New York to New Orleans that fast? There are no planes there in the middle of the night.'

'He could have driven.'

'Just barely,' I said. 'Maybe. Without sleep.'

'He slept on the plane, coming back here. Whole trip. You may be able to use that.'

'You've asked him about alibis?'

She looked at me with contempt. 'He's given us names, and we're checking them out. But the guy's a junkie. His alibis are dealers and street people.'

I'd been sitting behind my desk. I came around to the front and sat on the edge, right up close to her.

'What do you think, Betsy? Really? Is this the guy who raped these women?'

Her return glance was blank, without warmth. 'You got a victim ID, what the hell more you need?'

'It doesn't fit. The most you got on this guy is that, in one prior, he made the woman talk dirty to him for two minutes. At least four other guys fit that pattern. We dig deeper, we can probably find four hundred. And Solange would probably make positive ID of any male other than a midget.'

'She picked him out of a line-up.'

'Right.'

'There was nothing phony about that line-up.'

I pushed off from the desk and circled back to my chair.

'What are you doing?' she said, with a sharp edge. 'You pulling out again?'

'Right now, I don't have enough facts to be in or out. But let me ask you a really dumb and offensive question. Do you care? About whether Mossbacher committed these rapes? Or is it enough for you that he's done it before?'

With a skyward glance of impatience, Betsy got to her feet. 'I'll give you four hours. You disagree, we take it over your head.' She made for the door.

'I think you've answered my question.'

She swung around. 'You know . . .' She let out another exasperated sigh. 'I haven't. But I'll tell you this. These low-lifes who rape women? After the age of fifty, sometimes you can rehab them. Before then – creeps like Sikes and Mossbacher – they're going to do it every chance they get. And for every ten women they hurt, we're lucky if one of those victims has the guts to stay with a prosecution. Those are the data. You can look it up. So I'm not really interested in your thoughts about due process. You go tell them to Solange and Caroline and all the other women whose lives have been shattered by these sick bastards.'

She slammed the door as she left, and I sat there feeling envious. She could indulge her bias. I couldn't.

Later that afternoon, Betsy's personnel file arrived on my desk from Seaton, marked 'Strictly Confidential.' I had asked a clerk for this file; she had knee-jerked the request to Seaton which itself said something about Frank.

About Betsy – sometimes the most obvious guess is the answer to the riddle. And Betsy had made no effort to hide the facts. On the contrary. Her application for 'Sex Crimes' had listed the crime done to her as part of her qualifications.

At a prep school in New England, Betsy, then sixteen, was gang-raped by most of the lacrosse team during a party given in one of the dorms. She testified; the participants were convicted and expelled, but not one served a prison term of more than a few months. A note in her file cross-referenced a psychiatric report marked privileged and confidential. But the last paper, a memo by the Commissioner himself, stated that the results of that confidential report confirmed his view that she should be allowed to do the work she'd applied for.

I skimmed through the rest of the report. When only eighteen, Betsy began a three year hiatus between prep school and college, traveling abroad for a while before taking an apartment on her own in Madrid. There, she'd been arrested over a 'disturbance of the peace' with an older man, the charges then dropped as a 'family matter', the man turning out to be her father. At Brown, from which she graduated *cum laude,* she eschewed the usual women's sports, but earned a black belt in karate. She lived off-campus; again, alone. Then, she earned a graduate degree from John Jay College of Criminal Justice, where her studies concentrated on sex offenses. Of course it all fit. She had a reason to be angry and was.

Betsy being raped by a gang of boys was not a picture I wanted in my mind. But no matter how much more I could sympathize with her point of view, I still knew we had no case against Mossbacher.

She wanted to take it over my head, fine. I called her well before her announced deadline to let her know she should start marshaling her forces for appeal.

FIVE

It was my night with my kids. Ali and I had no fixed schedule for visitations, no fiercely litigated-over routine. Mainly I got them when it was convenient for Ali, which meant, when Ali had dates. So imagine what that felt like: picking up Molly and Sam, taking them back to my new apartment, thinking of Ali waiting for the guy who'd be spending the night, or the interesting part of it, in the bed I still stupidly thought of as mine.

So what? I lectured myself on the way there. Doesn't matter.

Another twist to the heartache, was all. Do your worst, I said to Ali's image in my brain. By now, I'm impervious. The doorman greeted me warmly. Was it that Christmas would be here in three months, and the envelopes still came from me, or was this old retainer able to see through my good cheer? I suspect the latter or, perhaps, both. Poker was never my game. I've heard it said that more lawyers live on East Seventy-second Street in Manhattan than in the entire city of St. Louis. This shouldn't be surprising. An inordinate part of the world's headaches and broken deals end up in New York. And Seventy-second Street is about the best most practicing lawyers can afford. The co-op I'd bought, between Lexington and Park, wiped me out. Every cent I'd saved had gone into that apartment, and now I was renting somewhere else.

Upstairs, Maria, the maid, was just leaving – a friendly middle-aged Argentinean woman whose salary I paid – and the kids were waiting. Sam, just six, was already wearing his backpack. Molly, a more dignified eight, was doing homework at the dining room table, but that was a cover. Her backpack was as ready as his. Neither carried clothes, just school stuff and special treasures. My apartment housed their separate complete wardrobes, toiletries, toys, etc. Shuttling between East Seventy-second and Central Park West, my kids were self-sufficient at both ends.

Sam put his arms up for a hug and a kiss. He got big ones. 'Let's go, Pops!' I'd no idea where he picked up expressions like that. Until then, I'd been 'Daddy'. Sam was the beauty, blessed with his mother's fine bones, and, less strikingly, the honey brown hair I had as a child. He affirmatively liked having two homes. But while it augmented Sam, it seemed to diminish his sister. Molly resembled me in that respect as well as in her features, but had the auburn hair and cool demeanor of her mother. 'Hi, Dad.' A peck.

Ali came out of the hall from the master bedroom. Took my breath away. Still. Every time. New black dress. Serious décolletage. Killer upswept coif. Pearls I'd given her for our tenth anniversary.

'Who's the lucky guy?' I asked. I often did, rarely getting the satisfaction of an answer.

'Don't!' she said. Another peck. The children got more lavish send-offs. 'One program tonight. Sam's still on the penicillin, which is in his backpack. And Rick, remember: Molly's got to be at Spence early tomorrow.'

'It's a simple question,' I said.

And got a frown. 'Kids, Daddy and I have something to talk about, OK? You can have five minutes of TV.'

They scampered off to their respective rooms and videos.

She turned to me. 'Bob, OK?'

'Bob? What Bob? There are millions of Bobs. The city is lousy with Bobs.'

'Oh, Jesus!' she said. 'Bob Hayden.'

Not a surprise. But it made me reach for an antacid. 'Great,' I said sourly. 'How trite is that?'

'I thought you liked him.'

'He's very charming. I liked him fine when he was married.'

'His wife died.'

'What a shocker,' I said. 'She was twenty years older than him. And he's what? Twenty-five years older than you?'

'OK, Rick.' Clasping her waist, elbows pointed at me. 'How cruel should we make this?'

'Not at all. I'm off. You have a wonderful evening. You and *Bob.*'

'You know your problem?' she said.

'Really disliking conversations that begin that way?'

'You can't conceive how any woman could possibly not want to be with you. You've just had it too easy. You're this great skier, great tennis player, you've got this funny, wry, detached manner that fools people into thinking you're cool, in command. But the truth? You're the most thin-skinned guy I know. In fact, what are you doing in the DA's Office, Rick? What are you going to do in the first big case when the press starts ripping you apart? Talk about sensitivity to rejection!'

'Is that what we were talking about?' I asked in my best impersonation of a wry detached manner.

'In effect.'

'You'd prefer someone stronger. Bob, for example.'

'For example. Yes.'

'Well, it's grand that you have him, then.'

Her face got tense, even as her voice lowered. 'He'll protect me,' she said.

It didn't take me long. Less than a second, I'd say, to see our life pass before me. An old sensation of imminent blackout came and went. Damn good thing, because I then grasped a surprising but distinct possibility – that Ali had never loved me. It had been there to be seen, I'm sure. It was likely what gave rise to the barriers. I'd simply never before allowed myself to take it in.

'Want to see him?' she said fiercely. 'He'll be here any minute.'

'See you, babes.'

The opening door bashed my toe. Held by the man of whom we'd been speaking, entering the room like raw weather. A bit taller than me, better looking than me, tanned, blue eyes, the kind of black hair that streaks gray impressively, and eyebrows so thick they appeared to be fake. The bastard had the looks of Ralph Lauren's star model. Casual, despite his millions; youthful, despite his age.

'Rick. Good to see you. I hear you've joined the other side.'

For Hayden, the government was not an ally. Several years back he'd been put through SEC and New York State Attorney General investigations which, after considerable cost, found him blameless.

When I said nothing, he did his thing, which was to give me a smile and consult his BlackBerry. 'One of my kids is in law enforcement.'

'That right?' I said.

'You started out that way, didn't you?' he said, glancing up briefly.

'Three years.'

'Must be an advantage, knowing the tricks of both sides.'

'Helps.'

Ali could see I wanted to get out of the apartment as much as Hayden wanted me to leave. She re-gathered the children and brought them back to the front door as Bob stood there emailing and I looked away. 'You'll remember about taking Molly to school early tomorrow?'

'Got it,' I said.

'Great. See you, guys.'

'Bye, Mom! Have fun!'

'Bye, Moms.'

It was ridiculous how much Sam's even-handedness pleased me.

SIX

Molly and Sam called the West Side 'the underground city'. I haven't even the slightest idea how that got started. Nor did Ali, although she guessed it came from some book or television program. It bothered me we didn't know. The kids themselves had long since forgotten. They just liked the sound of it; and renaming places was their way of feeling in control. The Safari Playground, for example, they called 'Hippo Park', and Trader Joe's ice cream parlor on Broadway became 'Sweet Shots.'

What struck Ali about the neighborhood was the irony of my living there. 'Think about it,' she'd said when I'd moved in. 'I'm a lib-lab Dem, a natural West Sider. But I end up on posh East Seventy-second. You, on the other hand, Heartland to the core of your being, settle into the Upper West Side. The Upper Nineties no less. With all the book people and artists, and marchers for causes.'

'You're out of the loop, darling.'

'You're going to tell me they've all moved down to Tribeca.'

'East Village,' I said. 'Williamsburg, Dumbo.'

'Not the rich ones, surely.'

'Especially them.'

'Oh, my,' she said. 'Have I really missed entire migratory cycles? You see what I've been telling you? This "Momma Bear" life has addled my brain.'

'Not funny,' I said.

'I know. Sorry. And I am grateful – so very, very sincerely grateful – for this apartment. Bless you. For your generosity, for being you, for—'

'Stop it. Please.'

'Worse?'

'Infinitely.'

'Can't seem to hit the right note, can I?'

'There is none,' I said. 'Let me assure you, in this situation, there is none.'

'Right. I *got* that. I *have*. *Will* do better!'

Not, however, by dating Bob Hayden.

Ali was right when she said I'd first liked him. Difficult not to, given his considerate manner and not inconsiderable achievements. Born rich, he was left penniless while in college. His mother, a doyenne of New York society, had exhausted their estate on the directorships that gave her that status. Bob got his start with his wife's money. But he expanded her small fortune by developing hotels, then office buildings, and, most recently, radio stations and for-profit schools. Reportedly, he'd amassed what the Texans call three 'units' – three hundred million dollars. You wouldn't know it from his lifestyle. Bob had a narcissistic streak, which was expressed in the cut of his clothes and of his hair, as well as the training regime he imposed every morning on his already lean frame; but he lived much more simply than his money would have allowed. And his venture into private schools in the city, though a sideshow for him, was a great boon for Ali. I grew not to like him when I realized how much he liked her. Or at least coveted her. In my eyes it brought out all manner of negative traits about the guy I hadn't previously noticed. When Ali and I split, however, I hadn't thought of Bob Hayden. Now I could complete my waking nightmare with his face.

Not good. But I had the children for the night. I was temperate enough in my agonizing to know I should not let it drain the joy from my time with them.

Sam took his own bath. He demanded a story, however, which I read with pleasure. Also, afterwards, a chess game. He was a demon chess player, a real prodigy. The one flaw I saw in my otherwise perfect son, however, was his reaction to losing. I'd once won, probably an accident. Big mistake. Storming from the table, he refused to speak for hours. I thought, wait until he's ten before you allow yourself to win again. And then, trying to win would doubtless be futile.

With Sammy straining over the board, I got a few 'Y'know' this's and 'Y'know' that's, as he related the news of the day.

The game had been set up in his bed, which was the fold-out sofa in the living room. After he announced he'd checkmated my king, my happy son, at home and at ease, fell right to sleep.

With Molly it was a different story. Above the top shelf of her bedroom closet, reachable from a built-in ladder, a loose panel concealed a cavity in the wall which the prior owner had probably used to store valuables. An eight-year-old girl, who felt at home here, would have found it by now and used it herself. Molly had done neither. That *I* had moved here did not make it *her* home. It was I, after all, who had abandoned her home, or so it seemed. And she was still testing me.

We were on the loveseat in her bedroom. She'd hit a dead spot on the schedule of her TV week. 'Y'know at dancing school . . .' she started.

'Yes?' I said.

'There was this boy . . .'

'Oh, yes?'

'Y'know what he did?'

'Not unless you tell me, no.'

'He tried to pick up my skirt.' She gave me a hard look to see how I'd take what she said. 'He didn't see anything, though. I was wearing white tights, and who cares about that!'

I thought of all kinds of things I could tell her about boys her age. I hadn't forgotten what being that age felt like. But I could visualize a look of puzzlement deepening on her face. Too much information. I didn't think it was the dancing school incident that really troubled her, anyway. It was why her mom and dad weren't living together. She seemed to want to probe any disturbance in her life for elements of the cause of that greater disturbance.

We had tried to explain it to them: Mommy and Daddy loved them very much and still loved each other but had decided to live apart because we wanted different things. Net, net, sugar-coated. Sam was mystified but practical. Would his new apartment have TV? A chess set? Could he bring Spider-Man and his other plastic super heroes? Molly's silence on the subject was a lot worse than tears. One shrink told us not to worry. Another urged four sessions a week, at two hundred dollars a session, for the foreseeable future. Doubtless Molly would be helped by talking about the subject with the right person, but I didn't trust either of those guys for that role. Or myself.

'Y'know,' I said. 'A really modern dad might have some other ideas on this subject. But my advice? Next time some boy tries to do that, just slap his face.'

Her eyes widened. 'Really? Hit someone?'

'Absolutely. For what he did, it's the appropriate response. And if anyone asks? Just tell 'em it's what your daddy told you to do to fresh boys, and your daddy is a G-man.'

'You'll lock 'em up!'

'Won't have to. You're going to punish them yourself.'

She brightened with her new sense of empowerment. Which made me feel that on this question, at least – modern convention to the contrary notwithstanding – I'd given the right advice.

Then she said something devastating. 'Did mommy tell you? Yesterday I fainted.'

SEVEN

I got Ali on the phone as she arrived in her office. I didn't bother with, 'How was last night?' Or, 'Why couldn't I reach you at home this morning or on your cell?' Just, 'Why didn't you tell me Molly had had a fainting spell?'

I could hear her exhaling with impatience. 'Because the doctor – Spivak – said it was probably nothing. Because I knew you'd over-react.'

'You know my history,' I said.

'Exactly.'

'And you told that to Spivak?'

'Of course. He says your condition is probably an emotional disorder.'

'*Emotional disorder?*'

'Well, psychological disorder. So he says there's not likely to be any inherited influence.'

'He says *what*? He's diagnosing me by telepathy? Who is

this guy? Why aren't we still using the other guy – what's his name? Tannenbaum?'

'I prefer Spivak. And it's not as if he's unconcerned. He says
we'll have to keep a close eye on this. And the school's been warned.'

'It happened at school?'

'Yes.'

'And? What was going on? Was there any apparent cause?'

'Well.' I had to wait through her pause. '*Apparently.* Someone was teasing her about an incident at dancing school.'

The line went dead. I was standing on Fifth Avenue, outside Spence School where I'd just deposited Molly for the day. Other parents streamed by, no doubt wondering about this guy, me, who seemed rooted. By guilt. Because I thought Spivak, or whatever his name was, was wrong. I felt Molly had, compliments of her dad, a very bad inherited gene.

I suffered from blackouts as a child and still had them from time to time. They came on, as did Molly's, with emotional stress, but that didn't make them, in my humble opinion, a 'psychological disorder.' Many specialists had so labeled them, but that, to me, just exposed the limits of their expertise, and the best of them would agree. 'Psychological disorder' was the dumping ground of conditions whose cause the profession had yet to identify specifically, or cure. Now, it seemed, whatever it was, I'd given it to my daughter, which plunged me into a despair that felt like a migraine and probably marked me. At least two mothers approaching picked up their pace and went by very fast.

I got to my own office by ten a.m. When I hadn't heard from Betsy Spaeth by eleven, I called her.

'You may have been right about Mossbacher,' she off-handedly informed me. 'We have another lead. A strong one.'

'Good,' I said, stifling amazement she'd concede having been wrong, even though she spoke as if it meant nothing. 'You'll call, then, when you have something for me.'

'Sure thing.'

As I started to put down the phone, I heard, 'Oh, and—'

'Yes?'

'Next time you want to know something about me? Just ask, OK? Don't read my file. That's real unfriendly.'

I silently swore. Who the hell had told her? 'Less embarrassing for us both, I thought.'

'It's a two-way street, you bastard.'

'Be my guest,' I said.

And, hanging up, regretted the invitation.

After three minutes of bouncing around on my office laptop, it informed me that I was not an 'authorized person' so far as my own personnel file was concerned. That meant that Betsy wasn't either, but she could probably wangle a peek without making waves, whereas I probably couldn't. Asking for her file was marginally OK. Asking for my own would look highly suspicious.

So I went directly to the source. Rap sheet data bank. Connecticut. There it was. It had caused me a problem years ago, when I'd applied for admission to the Bar. I'd overcome that through the kind intercession of a senior partner of my firm who had vouched for me with the Character Committee. But it was still there. No more erased from the record than from my mind. And no less a subject of regret.

We thought it a clever way to meet girls. Challenge their field hockey team, and spot them ten goals. We knew nothing of the finer points of the game, but we never lost. Different school nearly every other weekend. Our junketing team developed a reputation – more for off-the-field athleticism than on.

When we went to UConn, I met Sue Ann Gillespie, their all-state goalie, with bright, obviously bleached, blonde locks flying. I got this amazing image in my mind: a blonde head of hair and a black pubic bush. I was nineteen. A nineteen-year-old boy who doesn't think mainly about sex? There's probably something wrong with the way he was made. Far better, though, had I only just thought about it.

For an athlete, Sue Ann could sure drink. She put me under the table before I even got started with what I'd considered to be the more serious and appropriate purpose of the evening. So I invited her down to Yale for the Colgate weekend. In the

Pierson courtyard, the men's field hockey team set up tankards of Sea Breezes that were eighty per cent gin. Massive party. Everyone sloshed. Sue Ann and I were in my narrow steel spring cot, and I was blind drunk, but I still remember every detail. It was hot. Suffocatingly and insufferably hot. 'Shower?' I said. Sue Ann agreed. 'Right, sport.' She had mysteriously taken to calling me 'sport.' But a shower, once mentioned, was irresistible. It meant taking our clothes off. No problem there at all.

'I knew it,' I said, dazedly.

'What?'

'I absolutely knew it from the first.'

'What, for crissakes?'

She caught me staring.

'Jesus, sport,' she said, in a tone of disgust.

Stark naked, we bashed recklessly into the hall, mindless of the fact that Colgate weekend, minor insofar as football was concerned, was also Parents' Weekend, no doubt so chosen to get more fannies into seats at the Bowl. As Sue Ann and I stepped into the john, someone sounded the alarm, 'Parents in the dorm!' We were oblivious. I held the shower door open, turned on the stream, and we moved ourselves under it, allowing the door to swing closed.

After only a few minutes, I shut off the water, thinking we'd dry off and go back to bed. But we stood there silently staring at each other. For much too long, as it turned out. Somebody's mother came into the john, took possession of the adjoining toilet stall and began peeing. Sue Ann burst out with a laugh, we both suppressed giggles. There were sounds of violent commotion in the next stall. Then the shower door slammed open. A smartly coifed woman, panty hose awry, skirt still bunched at her waist, commenced screaming. Her screams followed us down the hall, lashing our jouncing behinds. By the time we got back to my room and into our clothes, the New Haven police had arrived. Not the campus police, who were sophisticated in such matters, but the city police.

Sue Ann was let off, fortunately. I was charged with indecent exposure, which, on the facts, was ridiculous. But it turned out that the husband of the screaming woman was a member of the

Connecticut legislature. Some Legal Aid guy advised me – badly – to cop a plea. What he didn't do was negotiate for that record to be expunged. Then it got worse. I was picked up again the following year. This time it was really stupid, and not even my fault. My roommate, who was captain of the track team, suddenly decided, on the way back from track practice, to stop the car and take a leak in the woods. Why he couldn't have used the head in the locker room at Coxe Cage, I'll never know. But after he'd been in the woods for about five minutes, I got out of the car and went to find him. A hundred yards in he was standing there, trying to reason with four young girls who, as it happened, had been passing by at the wrong moment. Somehow, when they reported it to the police, or their parents did, I got arrested along with my roommate as a 'wand waver,' to use the cop jargon. Given the earlier incident, I was advised – again unwisely – to take a plea bargain for 'indecent exposure' to stay out of prison.

It's funny, but when I left my firm to go to the DA's Office, neither incident entered my mind as a potential source of trouble. I'd probably filed the first away as the sort of memory one wishes never to be reminded of, and the second, as a ricochet off the first. But I'd found the records quickly enough. So must Frank have before he'd asked me to join him.

I thought, and then he starts throwing me sex offender cases involving women I knew. It made me very uneasy all day. Not comparable, however, to what I felt when I got home.

The doorman was waiting. Luis. He'd only been at the building six months, but seemed like a keeper. Young guy, plump, wavy black hair, newly arrived from Chile. Ordinarily calm, that night he was excited, and worried about his job. Worried about *me*. 'They had a warrant!' he said. 'I called the super. He wasn't there. I called the building manager. He said, let them up. I went up with them, but I couldn't stay.'

I asked whether he had read the papers they had shown him.

'*Si, si*! I read . . . but. It looked very official. They said it was a warrant.'

I asked whether he happened to catch any names on the papers.

He hung his head and shrugged his shoulders. 'I saw, but . . .'

'Luis, don't worry about it. I know what this is. It's a joke someone's playing on me from my own office. You know I'm with the District Attorney's Office. I did this to some guy, now he's doing it to me. It's how we kid around. Sorry you got caught in the middle of it.'

Pretty lame, but it was the best I could come up with, and he looked as if he believed it. Almost.

Upstairs, I expected to open the door to a mess. Far from it. The same blandness of beige. Sofa and two upholstered chairs upright and intact. Drapes still hanging. Not a lamp overturned. It looked like an expensive hotel room the maids had made up. Decorator's taste. At the time I'd moved in, I'd cared about nothing, let alone interior decoration. I went into the bedrooms, opened the closets and drawers. Everything there, too, seemed to be as I'd left it.

What the hell was going on? Was Betsy Spaeth getting back at me in some weird way? She'd be able to get a warrant. Cops can move on their own; they don't always need an Assistant District Attorney. There are judges who will issue warrants on anything or nothing, like rubber stamps. The question was, having taken the trouble to get up here, why hadn't the cops conducted a real search? It didn't seem credible that they had, and then returned everything to exactly where they had found it.

The answer hit me in the face. They didn't have to disturb anything. They knew what they were looking for, found it quickly and left. Only, what the hell might that have been?

I called Frank, but he was attending a dinner that night and wasn't reachable. Or didn't want to be reached. Same thing. A bachelor for his entire life, he was now dating a thirty-year-old woman. After seven at night, forget it! Frank was in a different world. Even at political dinners.

I dialed Betsy's line. Same result. I decided not to leave a voice mail. I was just going to have to seethe over this until the morning.

EIGHT

I was in early, but Frank hadn't arrived. He'd been doing that recently, too; coming in late. At first, it was amusing. Not that morning. Nothing was.

And then, instead of getting a call-back from Frank, the guy I needed to talk to above anyone, I found on my private line the one guy in the world I wanted to talk to the least. 'I wouldn't bother you, Rick, but it's that important. Can we meet for a quick coffee at the Downtown?'

Entering the Downtown Association, a few blocks from my office, felt like time-traveling backwards at least one hundred years. Wood: dark, heavy and glistening. Retainers: geriatric and padding about. Robert Hayden himself was a throwback in his dark navy suit and Hermès tie, holding court in the front hall, greeting me as I walked through the door and introducing me to some older members who were on their way out.

'Damn good of you to do this, Rick'

'It's OK, Bob,' I said following him to the bar.

We took seats at a small corner table. That suit looked poured over his fit frame, the magic of bespoke tailoring. He scribbled our order on a slip of paper that a particularly ancient waiter materialized to collect. Otherwise we were alone.

'You didn't know my first wife,' Bob said.

'I thought Marie—'

'No,' he said calmly. 'I was married earlier, to a woman who died very young. She was a divorcee with a child, a little girl, Emma, whom I adopted.'

'She's the one in law enforcement?'

'No, no—'

'So you've two adopted children.'

'I do.'

He sat back, his weathered face creased with concern. 'Emma was raised mainly by my mother. You know who my mother was.'

'Chair of the Metropolitan Opera Company? For some years, as I remember.'

'The Opera Company, the Metropolitan Museum, New York Hospital, et cetera et cetera. Mother had a very full – and expensive – life.' He raised his implausible eyebrows as if to invite me into a private joke with a twisty punchline. 'I'm afraid neither of us did a good job with Emma.'

Then he leaned forward, studying me a moment, as if deciding how much more to tell me.

'Emma was a gifted child,' he said. 'Absolutely astounding grades on all the standardized tests. Abundant talent – writing, playing piano, composing – the kid was scary. I loved her from the first. As my own child.'

'Something's happened to her?'

'As a kid, still in high school, she fell in with an older man. Much older. He totally debauched her. We never caught the guy, but that's now irrelevant. Emma started running with a wild crowd, the worst element of the private schools. Sex parties, drugs. They even dealt them.'

'And now?'

'The blunt fact? She's a drug addict. Crack, heroin. Also – and this is the most immediate problem – a shoplifter.'

'I'm sorry.' What the hell can you say?

'She was picked up. Two days ago. Bloomingdale's.'

As I started shaking my head, he said with a sad smile, 'Don't worry, Rick. I'm not asking you to intercede at the DA's Office. I know you can't do that. What I'd be grateful for is if you could help me with the department store. To convince them to drop the charges. The fact is . . . she has a record. Other convictions.'

'For shoplifting?'

His BlackBerry on the table flashed red, and he consulted it quickly before thrusting it aside.

'Drug-related?' I asked. 'Possession? Dealing?'

'Prostitution,' he said, the hurt showing in the deep squint of his eyes.

Hardly unusual for a drug addict to resort to prostitution. But now I felt for this guy. He had the money, the position, power and *my wife* – but his kid was a junkie and a hooker.

I went back to the shoplifting. 'At Bloomingdale's – won't they listen to *you*?'

Hayden looked worn out. 'Not any more.'

Why did I want to help him? To show off to Ali? Probably, but there was more I couldn't get at. 'I'll have to see her,' I said. 'Where is she?'

'Rikers.'

I glanced at my watch. 'OK.'

'This is great, Rick. World class. I'll find some way to return the favor.'

Not, I thought grimly, the one way I'd like.

An Assistant District Attorney I'd handled some stuff with had the case. I wanted to see Emma Hayden; he couldn't care less. He had hundreds of cases. And a favor done for the Chief Assistant – who knows what that might get him?

So, back on the 'Rock'. Different room, same closed-in windowless feel to the place, same disinfectant smell. Emma was brought in, her eyes darting about, resting on me, and we were left alone. She plunked down on a steel chair at the opposite side of the table, and I rose slightly in greeting. She was emaciated but pretty, with dark curly hair, bruised sunken features and raccoon eyes. Heroin chic. Five foot three, maybe. Twenty-five. Arms like rods and needle-scarred to her stringy biceps. She didn't trust me one bit.

'I'm Eric Corinth.'

'I know who you are. You're the husband of the woman Bob's fucking.'

I try not to respond to obvious baiting. She studied me while I waited for her to get real.

After a difficult silence, she said, 'So?'

'You want help?'

She laughed somewhere down in her throat. 'I look like someone who doesn't need help?'

'I'm asking whether you want it.'

'Yeah, well, I'm not entirely self-destructive. Yet. Heading that way.' Her smile managed to be insulting. 'I'm in your hands, as it were.'

'You're not detoxing?'

'You kidding? Rikers? It's a fucking cornucopia.'
'If I help you, will you do something for me?'
'Where'd you like to stick it, sweetheart?'
'Why do you do that?'
She shrugged. 'You could come to my office. Eleventh Avenue. Forty-seventh to Fifty-first. My turf.'
'You work the streets. That's great.'
'No overhead,' she said, as if it were amusing.
'There's a guy I know, runs a rehab.'
She laughed out loud. 'Do-goody! You're a do-goody! Y'know how many rehabs I've done? I'm the fucking queen of rehabs. Look it up. Guinness Book. World's record.'
'You haven't met Angus.'
'Oh, I'd love to meet Angus. You get me outta here, honey – I'll meet Angus or anyone you like.'
'You get institutionalized, I help. That's the deal. Until Angus says you're ready.'
'Sure, baby. Your terms. Suits me fine.'

Back on Centre Street, no return call from Frank. I called the security office at Bloomingdale's, then went there with a big check from Bob. A few other calls, and Emma was sprung under the recognizance of Angus. I had little faith in the arrangement. Angus had had successes, but his rehab was a half block from Emma's 'turf'. When I met Hayden at the Downtown to get the check, Bob insisted on a quick drink at the bar, ordering a Pimm's cup for himself and a gin and tonic for me, the way I liked it: half jigger of gin only, big slice of lime, tall glass, tonic water up to the top. I'm not much of a drinker.
'I don't know how else to say this,' he said, at the same corner table we'd occupied that morning. 'So let me come right out with it. You're an amazing guy.'
'That right?'
'I'm serious, Rick. I *am*. You've got every reason to be pissed off at me, and you do me this huge favor. Ali walks – for no good reason, as far as I can figure out – and you let her take the apartment. You're a goddamn saint.'
I made a face at that, involuntarily.
'You know what I'd like?' he said.

'You'd like us to be friends.'

'Yes,' he said. 'I would. Blast right through the goddamn awkwardness of our situation.'

'Which is why you asked me to do you a favor.'

He laughed. 'Sharp, too.'

'I've got no quarrel with you, Bob.'

'Of course you do.'

'All right. I'd happily watch you drowning in a vat of Pimm's cup.'

He smiled. 'At least.'

'I'll get over it,' I said.

'You know,' he said, 'Ali still cares very deeply for you.'

And then I got up. I felt one of my spells coming on. I thought I'd leave before I hit him. It didn't help that the guy 'fucking my wife,' as Emma had so poetically put it, was a nice guy with his own grief.

NINE

Next morning, I arrived early again, but, this time, Frank had been earlier still. One of the secretaries handed me the note. 'Rick. Please see me in my office as soon as you get in. F.'

I'd had friendlier messages.

The offices of high government officials tend to be enormous. I think the purpose is not so much to induce anyone to seek these positions – getting power is inducement enough – but to instill a sense of government's majesty. Entering Frank's throne room, even I fell for it, and I'm a hardcore cynic. Carpets, drapes and upholstered furniture adorning excessive space created the intended illusion. Behind his outsized desk, Frank gave me a look that dispelled the charm.

'Why didn't you tell me you knew those women? Both of them?'

I hadn't expected hostility. 'Well . . . shit!' I paused, tried to put a smile into it. 'You knew I knew Helen Cassenov.'

'And the other one? The Lambeth woman?' His tone, still belligerent.

'I've been trying to call you for two days.'

'Terrific. You ever hear of email?'

This was beginning to annoy me. 'When you handed me the tape, I obviously didn't know it was Caroline. The fact I knew her as well as Helen – the *coincidence* of that hardly seemed important enough to write you memos about. And for that matter, why the hell is it?'

He looked ten years older. 'Rick, when I asked you to come over here, I knew about your escapades in New Haven.'

'Jesus fucking Christ!' I broke in. 'What the hell does that mean?'

'Calm down! It's on the record. Two convictions.'

'Why the fuck didn't you say something before I left my firm?' When he just closed his eyes in denial, I said, 'Look. I was nineteen. Not used to drinking, and very drunk. I took a shower with a girl. That's it. OK? You never do anything like that?'

'Not so I'd get arrested for it.'

'Right. That's the standard. Not what you do, but whether you get caught?'

'Always has been.'

'Let me tell you,' I said. 'What's more reprehensible . . . I went around with a group of guys in college, different girls' school every weekend, spinning lines and getting laid.'

'Good for you.'

'You got no problem with that?'

'Why should I?'

'But the other thing . . .?'

Frank shrugged.

'This is a little too hypocritical for me, Frank, coming from someone I'd thought of as a friend.'

'I am your friend.'

'Really?'

'Yeah,' he said. 'Really.'

'So is that how we're having this conversation? Or are you really also the DA?'

'Both.'

'Seems like you might be conflicted.'

'Seems like, yes.'

We both thought about that for a moment.

'You look at that second charge?' I asked.

'Yes.'

'I didn't do a goddamn thing. My roommate took a pee in the woods. Four girls, passing by, got hysterical. And I got caught up in it because of the first incident.'

'Bad luck.'

'No kidding. So why the hell are you taking either of these things as evidence of anything but my stupidity?'

'They have your ski mask, Rick.'

'My *what*?'

'Along with your navy blue gym suit, same kind the perp wears. They picked up both in a search of your apartment. The mask is now in a plastic bag. Minus a few strands they sent to the lab. Same ski mask out of which both Cassenov and Lambeth pulled a few fibers.' He looked at me with more severity than I'd ever before seen in his face. 'Says the lab.'

I don't know what I said, if anything. I know what I was feeling – like the scene had just turned surreal. I must have said, eventually, 'I don't believe it.'

Because Frank then said, 'I didn't either. But there's no mistake about these fibers.'

'There has to be.'

Frank slowly wagged his head, no.

'Her coming to my apartment at all,' I said, 'that was just spite.'

'No,' he said. 'Grunt work. They were looking for the mask, Rick. You bought yours with a card. And kept it, I gather, in the same drawer as the rest of your ski clothes, so it wasn't much of a challenge to find it.'

He got up, this large-headed, ruddy-faced man, went to the closet behind his desk and found a pack of unfiltered Pall Malls under a stack of files on a shelf. They must have been ancient. He offered; I declined and watched him resume a habit I'd thought he'd quit ten years ago. Then his tone changed for the better. 'What I said this morning to your friend, Spaeth, and her Squad Chief, was: *one,* it's a goddamn North Face ski mask

– *that* they told me themselves – something probably mass produced on some atoll in the Pacific. *Two,* there must be thousands of them and navy blue gym suits floating around this city. And *three,* while you were a notorious lunatic on the slopes, I didn't figure you for being a rapist.'

'Thank you,' I said, feeling a momentary waft of sanity.

'You're welcome.'

'And there's a fourth,' I said. 'I *don't* know the victim in New Jersey, Diane Nethersong.'

'Good. Four, then.'

'So that's it?'

He crushed out the cigarette. 'Not quite.'

We stared at each other through the smoke.

'They want you to take part in a line-up,' he said flatly.

I jerked back hard in my chair.

Frank asked, 'You have a problem with that?'

'You're goddamn right I've got a problem with that. Betsy Spaeth does a line-up, the guy she fingers gets identified every time.'

'I'll get someone else to run the line-up, then. She'll have nothing to do with it.'

I was shaking my head. 'It's not right, Frank. You wouldn't agree to this in my shoes.' I banged my fist on the arm of the chair. 'Damnit! What is this? A bad joke? Thousands of people know these two women. The additional coincidence of owning a ski mask – and you're going to put me in a goddamn line-up?'

'It will shut them up.'

'And cover your ass.'

'That's right,' he said.

'Forget it. Spaeth is crazy. Have you seen her file?'

'I've seen all of it.'

'You mean, the psychiatrist's report.'

'I mean,' he said, 'the Commissioner's own file on the subject, which includes the psychiatrist's report.'

'Then you know. She has a vendetta against anyone who has anything on his record that looks like a sex crime.'

He took his time. 'The psychiatrist drew a distinction between a woman, like Spaeth, who'd been victimized on a single occasion – which, he felt, would not necessarily get in the way of her performing the job – and someone repeatedly abused, as a child for example. Only the latter, he thought, would be unbalancing and disabling.'

'She shouldn't be working this case,' I said.

'Maybe not.'

'And anyway, how in the world did her application get bounced up to the Commissioner?'

Frank shrugged away his inability to answer. 'Probably because it was a unique situation.' Another shrug. 'After the line-up, maybe I'll take some steps to get her reassigned.'

'No line-up,' I said. 'No way.'

Frank heaved a great sigh. 'I'm afraid that's not how it's going to be, Rick.'

I looked at him as if I'd never seen him before. 'You're going to do this – put me through this – by compulsion?'

'I'm sorry, Rick. No choice. Burden of office. In the circumstances, there just isn't any option.'

TEN

Apparently, I had to be helped to my office. I'd blacked out leaving Frank's. Hedda, my secretary, with an expression of concern, stuck her head in. 'You OK, now, Ricky?'

'Absolutely Hedda. Everything's fine.' Obviously, it wasn't. The guy, *me*, given the job of prosecuting heinous crimes, was about to be branded as the psychotic who'd committed them. Nightmare territory. Way beyond anything I'd ever imagined.

What it meant to be charged – that I had a clear notion of. I thought of the impact on Sam, Molly, and on Ali, the disgust on the faces of everyone who knew me. And Ali was right. Being unfairly accused of anything drove me near crazy. And this charge was rape. No act was uglier. The smear would stick no matter what the outcome of a trial might be.

No one likes being the target of false accusations. But some of us are hypersensitive, and for that trait we can usually thank our parents. Mine had been dead for years – my father from a heart attack, my mother from Alzheimer's – but they'd been masters of the acid tongue. My father traveled a lot for a steel company headquartered in our town, Evanston, Illinois. My mother did church work. They were decent loving people in most ways, but my father, in his own mind, was never wrong. Nor, outside his presence, was my mother. So I was, invariably. And as an only child, I took the heat. All of it. Something bad happened, it was my fault. Often, no doubt, that was the case, but no one, not even I, could have screwed up *so* often. Especially after the steel mill closed, and we lived on odd-job wages and tips.

I remember one incident when I was about Sammy's age or a little older. My father had taken me to the hardware store. It was one of his infrequent weekends at home, and he thought we should do something together. Only he hadn't warned me of the plan, which was to convince the shopkeeper that the same hammer being offered for three dollars at his store was priced at two fifty at another we'd supposedly just come from. So I piped up, 'We didn't go to any other store.'

'Damn kid,' my father said. 'Suffers from spells.' Then he took me outside and slapped me hard in the face. 'Don't you ever contradict me in front of anyone again.'

I never did. Or forget being slapped in the face. The meeting with Frank felt a lot like the latter, but worse.

My dad called them 'spells'. What happens sometimes, when I get really pissed off, I black out, as I've said. Damned inconvenient. When I was fifteen, the family GP diagnosed my condition as a form of narcolepsy. 'Form of,' because high school kids don't get narcoleptic, if they're not taking drugs, and I wasn't. I wasn't epileptic, either; I didn't have fits. So finally everyone, but me, got comforted with the label, 'psychological disorder'. Throughout the country, there were maybe three other cases of what I had, and the others were more severe. For years I took prescription drugs – Ritalin, Prozac and other antidepressants – then, in law school, I stopped taking anything, and it got better. I've never blacked out at a trial, for example. It takes something extreme to bring it on. Like being accused of being a rapist.

I shook my head to clear it. *Get a grip!* I said aloud. It wasn't easy. Then I called two people who I thought might help.

Malcolm Spezio, my internist, intrigued me. Every doctor I knew held him in awe, yet he was uncommonly shy and unassuming. As he personally greeted me in his waiting room, I felt that shyness again, and the spindliness of his grip. Beanpole of a man, with a balding pate, he led me into his consulting room, actually apologizing for keeping me waiting five minutes. Of course, he knew my history. He'd been urging me for years to see someone who might help.

Malcolm occupied the corner room of a suite of Park Avenue physicians, all affiliated with New York Hospital and faculty members at Cornell Medical School. He took his seat behind a small desk, beckoning me to the leather chair in front of it. I'd already told him on the phone why I needed to crash his schedule.

'I've told you often, Rick, this is not my field.' He was seeing me out of friendship and courtesy.

'All right, but before you march me off to some brain surgeon – you have the records, the brain scans. I'd just like your take on the thing.'

'Well, let me ask you again. Are you still certain you got to your office on your feet? You weren't carried, or put in a chair?'

At my hesitation, he picked up a pair of glasses from his desk and stared at me through them. 'Less certain,' he concluded.

'It's a bit awkward to ask. To say the least. I think, if I'd been carted in, my secretary would have mentioned it.'

'And in any prior incidents – any recollection of being ambulatory? Fainting one place, ending up in another?'

I took my time. 'I can't swear that didn't happen, but I don't remember it happening.'

Malcolm got up, walked over to the window overlooking the avenue, and thought a moment. In his long white coat he was a stick figure, with a few wisps of hair standing out from the flat back of his head.

'There's no sleepwalking in narcolepsy,' he said. 'So, if you're moving about, the cause . . .' He turned back to me. 'I don't really want to guess about this, Rick. There's someone I know at Columbia who specializes in the area. I think you should see her.'

'Her?'

'Yes. Helen Cassenov. Do you know her?'

ELEVEN

I agreed to meet Carter Denison at the Merchants Club. The name of the institution gave a hint of its age as well as the occupation of its founders. Most merchants prefer being called something else – such as investment bankers – and that's been true for about a hundred years. Even more anachronistically, however, the club no longer catered to merchants of any description. Situated only three blocks from the courthouses on Foley Square, it was populated entirely by lawyers and judges (who, by other groups, particularly investment bankers, are often, ironically, denigrated for acting like merchants – of themselves).

I was lunching with one, a judge, my friend Carter. I had lots of acquaintances, relatively few friends. That day, after my meeting with Frank, I'd thought I'd just lost one. Carter happened to be the Chief Judge of the Federal District Court in Manhattan. Years ago we'd tried a reverse discrimination case together in Baltimore. My firm had given me leave to do it *pro bono*; Carter was then Associate General Counsel of the NAACP. We'd been close friends ever since. We had a lot in common, including the fact that we'd both worked our way through college and law school. His appointment to the bench came early. By an unusual set of circumstances, he later became the youngest Chief Judge in the history of the Southern District of New York.

With friends, a difference in race is obviously not a barrier. What I think interesting is how it becomes part of the bond.

Carter was a large man with a large, once-handsome, now fleshy face, light skin and gentle disposition. Years ago I met

Gene Upshaw, the Hall of Fame 'pulling guard' and long-time
President of the NFL Players' Union. Carter looked like him.
As if ready to put on the pads, as he once had for Princeton.
When you shook Carter's hand, you immediately knew two
things about him. He could crush your bones easily. And he
never would.

I laid out the problem over a pretty good buffet meal.

'My philosophy?' said Carter, finishing off the last food on
his plate. 'Pay the two dollars.'

'Don't fight about principle?'

'Not on this issue. There are issues you fight about. But you
pick them carefully. Average guy? Gets screwed three times a
day. You fight every one of those battles, you've got time for
nothing else. Pick your fights. Otherwise pay.'

We were in the main dining area, which was a large, white,
oval, high-ceilinged room on the second floor of a three-story
red brick Georgian building. Throughout the room, various
clusters of lawyers and judges communed about problems quite
possibly as serious as mine but not likely as personally
threatening.

'No small matter,' I said, 'going through a line-up.'

'Yeah, it is,' Carter said. 'I did it once. Sixteen I was at the
time. They nabbed me for swiping some videos. The clerk
couldn't ID me as it turned out, so I walked. The difference in
our situations? I had something to worry about. You don't.'

'Frank should know that.'

'He does. Of course he does. But he reinforces his reputation
for toughness by putting his own protégé in a line-up. And he's
probably a little pissed at you right now. Like Napoleon, Frank
likes his generals to be lucky.'

'Y'know, I was trying to remember, who was it, one of those
French existentialists, who said that the ultimate absurdity is
an innocent man trying to defend himself?'

'Camus,' said Carter, spooning sugar into his coffee. 'And
he was right. But get used to it. You want to be a public figure?
You're going to get blamed for lots of things you didn't do.
Didn't even think of doing. That's why sane men stay out of
the kitchen. It's no accident you're in this mess. You're just a
lot more conspicuous than the forty or fifty other guys who

own that kind of ski mask and have met or read about those two women. You need armor, man! Ego armor. And, Ricky, my friend. Got to tell you. I'm not sure you're sufficiently plated. That's a compliment, man. You're too fucking sensitive.'

I laughed; it seemed the only possible reaction. And I wondered whether Carter, in my situation, would follow his own advice. 'You ever hear anything about this woman, Betsy Spaeth?'

'Oh, yeah,' he said. 'I was getting to that. She came on the Force young, right after graduate school. Her first year, she collared so many of our people we thought we might be having a racial problem with her. A closer look indicated, no, just a terror on sex offenders, white or black, which was OK with my guys, so we let it go. She works for a Spanish dude, Vincente Chacon, who values her. Obviously, she's driven. And obviously, she's got her teeth in your ass. But she's not a total lunatic. You can talk to her. You may have to say it more often than you'd like, but she does listen, finally, and comprehend.'

'The way it looks now, she's ready to nail me for some dumb prank that happened twenty years ago and wasn't criminal then.'

'Right. That's probably her range. Sorry, kid. But you got to deal with it. Do the line-up. Then turn it on her.'

'You wouldn't get one of those high-profile criminal defense lawyers?'

'Jesus, man! That's the last thing I'd do. You want one of those egomaniacs showboating for publicity? And hiring one of those guys'd be like a confession of guilt.'

I must have looked pretty morose.

'Just do it, the line-up. Better than fighting about it. More options. Including, possibly, no one gets to know.'

'Pay the two dollars?'

'Right on, kid. Pay the two bucks. Like I said.'

Back at the office, I had four telephone messages. Ali's was the one I returned.

'Hi, honey,' she said. 'Thanks for calling back.'

As if I might not have. 'You OK?'

'Sure. Great. It's just, I use five babysitters, and tonight, when

I have this really key meeting, wouldn't you know, Murphy's Law, three of them have the flu, and the other two, including the day person, are committed.'

'No problem.'

'Really? You're the best. I know you just took them.'

'I'll pick them up usual time?'

'Actually . . .' She paused.

'What?'

'Molly may be coming down with it.'

'You want me to keep them there?'

'It won't be a late night. I should get home by ten thirty. And, if you like . . . you could sleep over yourself.'

I took a moment before asking. 'In our bed?'

Her pause seemed interminable. Her voice, finally ending it, was strained. 'I'm not ready for that.'

Odd locution. 'Meaning there's likely to come a time when you will be?'

A light breezy conversation had suddenly hit heavy breathing. 'I'm sorry, Rick. What I said about sleeping over was stupid and inconsiderate.'

'I thought it made sense, actually.'

'Rick, I still love you. I really do. As much as ever. But if we start sleeping together again, it would mean that I'd be right back where I began. In a situation that was causing me misery. And I've changed now. I've told you. I'm not the same person who accepted that situation.'

What situation? This was old ground, yet I never knew exactly what she meant. *Why* had she been in misery? What had I ever done that was so bad? Love her? I said as much.

At which she blew up.

'Oh, shit!' she said. 'Don't you listen to me? I have this feeling – I tell you my deepest thoughts, and you don't hear! It's like I'm talking to the insane. I explained it! How many times do I have to do that?'

I blew out my cheeks. Frustrating, this talking *at* each other. I gave it another few moments. 'I'll be there at six thirty. I won't be staying after you get home.'

'*Damn!* Rick. I'm sorry. You know I'm sorry. I wish it were otherwise.'

'Me too.'

'See you later?' she said hopefully.

'Sure thing.'

We hung up. I sat there feeling the disconnection. In happier days, I would have told her about the problems I was facing. Now she was almost alien to me. The person who had just been screaming at me was not someone I really knew.

TWELVE

I n the glare, under Klieg lights, on a riser-stage, I felt guilty and doubtless showed it. Which wasn't smart. Which was, obviously, the exact opposite of what I wanted to show. The other guys in the line-up, cops mainly, had no connection with this at all. They were there because of me. I was the suspect. They knew that, and it shamed me. So there I was, conspicuous when I wanted to blend.

I looked up at the observation window – an implacable oculus through which women would be staring at me. Shame built to anger; anger to rage. Being put there – humiliated unjustifiably – did damage to me. I did not black out. In a white-hot fury, I fought blacking out. But it still got to me, and that's lasted, like a rip in the gut that won't heal.

There was little comfort in the fact that Frank himself picked me up afterwards in the assembly room. 'Let's talk,' was all he said.

This was not what I wanted to hear.

The line-up had taken place at an NYPD building downtown, a few blocks from our office. The fall morning was bright and crisp, and, after we'd walked on to Foley Square, Frank suggested a quick cup of coffee.

It was about eleven o'clock. The coffee shop on the Square, where there used to be a Nedick's, was almost empty.

We took a booth in the back. Frank ordered a Greek coffee, the specialty of the house, and I did the same. Mechanically. I couldn't have cared less. Of course the news would be bad. Good news I would have heard at the station.

The night before, I'd had a fight with Ali. Really bitter. Having at each other in fierce hissing whispers so as not to wake the kids. She had gotten home from her 'really key meeting' – no doubt with Bob – an hour later than she had promised. Normally, her being late, no big deal. Now everything was a big deal. She had said to me in a hoarse scream, 'What do you want, Rick?' and I'd simply stared out over the apartment. Leaving, I had this raw feeling of having been used. Staring at Frank that morning in the booth, the feeling got a lot rawer.

'OK,' Frank said when the waiter left. 'It took as long as it did, because we went one woman at a time. Spaeth had no involvement. She was not even there.'

'She know about it beforehand?' I asked.

'Shouldn't have. No reason for her to. I set it up with Chacon, who also didn't show. He left it to others in the department.'

'Who called the women?'

'He did. I was clear on that.'

'This is a nightmare, Frank.'

He ceased any pretense to the contrary. 'I know.'

'You're going to tell me one of those women picked me out of that line-up. Identified me.'

Grim-faced, 'They all did,' he said.

I started laughing, before I bit down on my lip. 'This has a real dream-like feel to it. I must be very close to the last person alive who is capable of doing what was done to those women.'

'I don't seriously doubt that, Rick.'

'Tell me what they said. Was there at least some uncertainty?'

'No. None. Cassenov got you on the walk-in. I had to tell her to give it more time and be sure. She did, and she was. Lambeth picked you out in thirty seconds. Delfine took maybe five minutes. But she said she knew right away. She just wanted to be certain.'

'Unbelievable. Something's going on here I don't understand. None of these women saw the rapist's face. How *can* they be certain?'

'It's the way you stand, apparently. A little one-sided. And walk. Body-type too, I should imagine. Slim, long legs.'

'One-sided, you think?'

'Yeah. Kind of tilted.'

'You mean my right shoulder's down a bit.'

'Yeah!'

'Like, maybe, one-third of the male population. *Especially* if they've carried a briefcase for fourteen years.'

'Rick. Look.' The coffees came, the waiter again departed. Frank took a sip and began once more. 'I'm not going to prosecute you for these crimes. Quite apart from my own belief in your innocence, even these three IDs wouldn't stand up, given the earlier IDs Spaeth got. So, as far as that goes, you're in the clear. But . . .' His expression took on an aspect of pain. 'So far as the job goes . . .'

'It's over.'

'I'm afraid so.'

'Wow.' I knew this, but it still felt like a sucker-punch to the pit of the stomach. 'I left my firm, Frank. It was a place I really liked being. Burned my bridges there. Now – leaving after only two months . . .'

'I know.' He lit a Pall Mall. His hands were unsteady.

'This knocks me down pretty hard.'

'I know. I don't minimize it.' He sipped some more coffee. 'Maybe your firm . . .'

'Will take me back? I don't know.' Now I felt stupid. 'I've given my clients away.'

'There's no reason for anyone to know about this. No charge is involved. And when we catch the guy, if you're still interested . . .'

I broke this off with a sour laugh. 'You really have any hope of nailing this bastard? Much less in the near term?'

'If he does it again.'

'And makes mistakes.'

'That's right.'

'What about the Nethersong woman, the New Jersey case?'

'What about it?' he said.

'Are we working with them? Do they have leads?'

'The cases aren't necessarily connected.'

'Sophisticated assailant. Successful, attractive young woman. Humiliated, mind fucked for two hours. What the hell do you need to see a connection? Matching videos?'

'They have no leads.'

'Great.'

'I'm sorry, Rick.'

My laugh was softer but no less bitter. 'Anything like this ever happen to you, Frank? Some crazy out-of-the-blue accusation that has no relation to reality, yet sticks?'

He shook his head sadly. 'No. But I can understand what you're going through.'

'Oh, yeah? I'm not sure *I* can. I don't think the full implications of this have hit me yet.' I swallowed a bit of the sweet Greek brew. 'So.' I gave him a false smile. 'Think I'll go home and try to figure it all out.'

THIRTEEN

There's something peaceful about watching a room go from bright to dark in the space of an afternoon. I sat on my sofa which also served as Sam's fold-out. Along with the bed in Molly's room, it was the only furniture I'd taken any care in choosing when I moved in here. At about three o'clock, I got up to get a blanket. It wasn't a particularly cold day, and the windows were closed, yet I felt chilled. The next time I stirred, it was already dusk. Luis was buzzing from downstairs. 'Mr Corinth? Sorry to disturb you, sir. Three boxes are here. They're for you. I bring them up?'

Luis and the handyman carted them into the living room and left. I opened them expecting what I found. Frank had had my office cleared out. Was that an act of thoughtfulness, or the crude finale to a firing? Maybe Frank had been calling to explain it. Maybe others had called too, like reporters. Having unplugged the phone, I'd never find out, although too many people in the Office already knew what had happened. Of them, the number willing to retail this item to the press would not be small. It might even be all of them.

The buzzer, Luis again. 'There's a Miss Hayden who wants to come up.'

Not her, not in my apartment!

I said immediately, 'Tell her I'll come down.'

Emma, looking like Eleventh Avenue, was frightening the pedestrians on Central Park West simply by standing in front of the building. The ritziest upbringing, the best schools, and she had herself decked out like a prostitute with a drug problem, which, regrettably, was what she was.

'You want some coffee?' I said.

She shook her head, no. I noticed Luis noticing, and guided her across the street to a park bench a block away.

I knew why I didn't want her to come upstairs. Despite everything, she was too damn attractive. I was both an emissary from her father and age-inappropriate, but, insofar as resisting temptation was concerned, not the strongest guy in the world.

'So you broke the deal,' I said, sitting.

She gazed for a moment out on the traffic before perching at the edge of the bench. 'Yeah. Addicts do that. Very unreliable people, addicts. 'Course most people don't think we're people.'

'And why'd you come here?'

'To you?' Her lower lip pouted. 'Financing?'

'You've got me down as an enabler.' The night air had a snap to it, and I was wishing I'd put on more than a sweater.

'Well, I expected to work for it,' she said.

'Terrific.' I'd a pretty good idea what was keeping her warm, though she was on the lucid side of the high. It meant she'd be needing another fix within the hour.

'The thing about drug dependency?' she said. 'First you sell everything you own. Then you sell what you can steal. Then, of course, you sell yourself. Or maybe you start right off peddling pussy, since you know you're going to end up doing that anyway.'

'Emma . . .'

'Not interested, he says.' She looked away. 'I've got two great looking cats I could sell you.'

'Sorry.'

'I'd let them go cheap. You could resell them at a profit.'

'There's no market for used cats.'

'They're not *used*.'

'So what are you calling them?' I said. 'Pre-owned?'

'Rick, man! There's an offer on the table. I think you ought
to consider it seriously.'

'How'd you find out where I live?'

'Snooping.'

'I'm not listed.'

'You are . . . in Bob's address book.'

What I thought, and didn't much like.

'I flop at his place,' she said. 'Sometimes. Better than the
streets. Better than' – she flashed her eyes – '*grandma's.*'

What the hell did that mean?

'How 'bout I take you back to Angus?'

Her laugh was shrill. 'How 'bout you give me fifty for a
blowjob? Or we could just go upstairs and you could fuck me
all night. After I get my shit.'

'I know this is going to sound naïve. But, Emma, you're a
beautiful girl with a beautiful brain. Why don't you want a
life?'

'I do, baby, I do. Gimme a hundred, and I'll let you take
care of me.'

I wanted to – Christ, I really did.

'What I'll do – I'll take you back to Angus, that's the deal.
Or Bob's place, if you want.'

She got up with a pissed-off expression. 'You don't know
shit. Y'know! You don't know fuck.'

Probably right.

I watched her wobble away. Another frustration. I couldn't
help her any more than I could help myself.

FOURTEEN

I woke up famished the next morning. Hadn't eaten since
breakfast the day before. There wasn't much in the fridge.
The milk was fresh, I made sure of that for the kids. So I
ate some of their sugary cereal. A couple of eggs were OK.
Looking for coffee, I found a tea bag that wasn't ancient. Fine.
It was a much larger breakfast than I normally ate. Then I sat

there. Being out of work was a new sensation. It heightened
the unreality. What I was putting off doing was reading the
papers. The *Times* and the *Wall Street Journal* were sitting
outside my front door.
Finally, I gathered them up and brought them into my
bedroom. Flipped pages quickly. Nothing. Not a word about
my being fired. Of course, these were not necessarily the papers
that would carry such a story, if any would. I wasn't exactly a
celebrity. I threw on some clothes and, without shaving, went
downstairs and headed toward Columbus Avenue.
Another gorgeous day. Cool breeze, warming sun, everyone
walking with energy. I bought the *News*, *Post* and *Newsday*,
took them into the park, and riffled through all the pages. Again,
nothing. I thought, maybe I have some time.
Back upstairs I called Roger Hazzard who had recently
become the presiding partner of my old firm. He was in, and
took the call.
'Rog. You got a few minutes this morning? I'd like to come
in and talk to you.'
'How's eleven fifteen?'
'See you then. Thanks.'
I liked that. No false sentiment. No phony small talk. We'd
been partners. Been through the wars together. Creates a bond,
I thought, no matter what others might say. No matter what
resentments might have crept in, fact-based or imagined. This
might work, I thought.

It was absurd how good it felt to be greeted familiarly by the
security guards on the ground floor of my former office building
and let right up. As it used to be. As it still should be. At the
forty-fifth floor reception, however, the receptionist said, 'Mr
Hazzard will be right with you, Mr Corinth. He asked me to
ask you to . . . wait?'
Wait? He has to be kidding!
I'd of course waited in plenty of reception areas. But to be
treated as an outsider in what I still thought of as *my* firm? My
real office?
Our lawyers, staff, files and machines occupied the top ten
floors of the building. Each floor layout was different, each

elaborately planned to utilize every precious, and expensive, square foot. Forty-five was the main reception floor, designed for effect. Firm memorabilia, deceased partners in oils. Space age furniture in a vast airy expanse. Scope. Vision. Roots in the great dramas of the nation's history. Foreign branches plugged into the corridors of power in every major country of the world. At least that was the designers' idea. And I'd helped design it.

I stood at the window. My view. The one I used to enjoy from my old office. Uptown, Central Park, the Triboro Bridge. It had always been a measure of my personal journey, from poor, scruffy street kid, to the luxury of these trappings and the significance of the work.

A lot's been written about this kind of work and this kind of firm. Mostly, about how it crushes young lawyers and steals their souls. In the main, my partners and lawyer friends and my clients were decent people, with, as far as I could tell, their souls intact. Indeed, everyone knew who the exceptions were, and they were widely disliked. The books, the television series, the movies, seem generally to have been written by people who never worked at these firms, or did so only so they could write the books. The reality is, getting corporate and other institutional leaders to take your advice gives you more opportunity to do good for more people than a storefront practice. Of course it's up to you to take advantage of the opportunity.

And of course no one's a saint. Being decent doesn't stop some from being self-important and a pain in the ass. All the good feelings about coming up there, in fact, had dissipated by the time the great man communicated he was ready to be seen.

Obviously, I knew my way. The halls and passages of this place were as intimately known to me – and now as unwelcoming – as my ex-wife's body.

Hazzard had the largest suite, as befitted the presiding partner. Curious title. It came from the fact that he presided at meetings. Which meant whatever each occupant of the job could make of it. Since the firm was a true partnership, no one member had executive power. Any partner could be overruled, or voted out, at any time. Yet some presiding partners became pretty despotic. For Roger, these were still early days.

On that walk down the hall, I began thinking more than I had about Roger's coolness to me after my encounter with his first wife. It seemed absurd he'd still be bearing a grudge over something so trivial, and in reality unfounded, but I felt a sharp premonition he would. *Stop being so goddamn negative*, I thought. *He's not that petty, and he's been happily re-married for years.*

I liked his secretaries: one a gentle gay woman in her late forties who, I happened to know, had a long-time relationship with a woman much older than herself; the other, a stout fiftyish Brunhilde with a bad dye-job and a messy personal life. They were effusive, and real. One couldn't be so sure of the latter characteristic with regard to the guy on the other side of the door. But I opened it, hoping for the best.

'Rick.'

'Rog.'

We shook hands. He stayed behind his desk. I dropped into one of the wing chairs in front of it. I'd forgotten how large we'd made the presiding partner's corner office. As a member of the space committee, I'd even voted for it.

'What's up?' he asked. His accent was old Dutch New York.

'DA thing's not working out.'

'Ah,' he said. Didn't seem surprised. Didn't say something like, so soon? He just waited, as if in the enactment of this scene I had the next line, and he wasn't offering to be prompter.

Roger was a natural for his job. Any casting director would have picked him. Medium height, sleek face, pale blue eyes, just enough gray hair at fifty-two to pass for an elder statesman. He was a generalist, not a specialist, which was a throwback phenomenon in a world where almost every corporate lawyer did exclusively banks, underwritings, swaps or mergers and acquisitions. His style was to avoid confrontation. His standard advice to clients was 'do nothing.' It worked about eighty per cent of the time, and was generally received as wisdom incarnate. For anxious clients, Roger was the equivalent of Prozac.

Looking at his features now – the slightly beakish nose, the

sculpted lips reposed in self-satisfaction – I thought, not for the
first time, I know Roger's secret. He really didn't care that
much.
'It's a longer story than I'm going to bore you with right
now,' I said, and smiled. 'Some other time, if you like. But
Frank understands, and I'm out of there.'
Roger said nothing, and didn't bother to return the smile.
Again, it was probably more indifference than cruelty. With
clients, he would juice up his personality. With a former partner,
his throttle was on low.
So I said what I had come to say. 'Any problem about my
returning to the firm?'
Here he gave a faint smile, which made my pulse quicken
– with a jolt of resentment as to how much of my well-being
depended on this man's response. 'Perhaps you ought to wait
a while,' he said, his faint smile now frozen on false.
And the bottom dropped out of my life.
'Oh? Why's that?' I asked.
'Well . . .' He was beginning to look uneasy. 'Until things
cool a bit.'
'*Things?*'
'Rick, please.'
'Please *what*, Roger?'
'Perhaps I know more than I should . . .'
'Perhaps you should tell me what you *think* you know.'
He shut his eyes and opened them as if he were the one being
oppressed by this conversation. And then he sighed. 'It's bizarre,
I'm sure, absolutely freakish, but I'm told you're under suspicion
for crimes that everyone who knows you will know you couldn't
possibly have committed.'
I sat there for a while without speaking.
'And if you know that—' I started.
'We live in the world, Rick.'
'I would have expected more of you, Roger. More willing to
take a stand on your own judgment. For one of your own.'
'As for that, you did leave us.'
'I want you to tell me something straight up.'
'Oh?'
'That night years ago at the dinner dance . . .'

'I really don't think—'

'You know, I was on your side.'

'Rick, this is not a matter—'

'I said absolutely nothing to Helen that night I wouldn't gladly have said to your face. Except it would have embarrassed both of us for being so flattering.'

'I'm sure that's right.'

'So what are we talking about?'

'I thought we were talking about your request to return to the firm.'

'Which you're turning down because you're pissed off at me for something I didn't do a hundred years ago.'

He stood up. 'Let's end this, shall we? Helen slept with lots of men, besides you, Rick. This is simply not a subject—'

'*Sleep with her?* I didn't sleep with her! Jesus Christ, man!'

'I hardly expect you to admit it.'

'Listen to me, will you! I didn't do it!'

'Very well.'

'This is ridiculous. Roger! I'm not like that. Neither is Helen, for that matter.'

'There's no point, Rick. It's yesterday's newspapers.' He sat again and sniffed. 'And it hasn't anything to do with your returning, or not returning, to the firm.'

'Bullshit!'

'No need for that.'

'If it weren't for this grudge, which you've been harboring for – what is it – how many years?'

'And now I should just accept your denial?'

'If it were not for this . . . misconception—'

'There's risk to the firm.'

'A small risk. And you'd take it. You owe me that. What I've given this firm—'

'Then go to the firm. I can't stop you from communicating with the other partners.'

'All eighty-six of them.'

'It's your right.'

'And blow this up? Spread it further?'

Roger shrugged. 'Have we finished here?'

'Damnit, Roger! I did not have an affair with Helen.'

'Whether you did, or didn't . . .' He looked away. 'She wanted to. And I've seen you, Rick, with other men's wives.'

'That's unfair. I don't sleep with other men's wives, much less the wives of my partners.'

'They're no longer, my friend, your partners.'

FIFTEEN

Betsy Spaeth lived in a brownstone in Hell's Kitchen, between Ninth and Tenth Avenues. Sit on a stoop long enough in that neighborhood, especially on a warmish muggy night, one sees everything. Every form of life, some beyond one's imaginings. Doing pretty much everything. Drugs, of course. Wasted dead-skinned people crouched in shadows with their needles or pipes. Kids selling crack. All ages, both sexes, peddling sex. People hawking anything in fact: their watches, their mothers, other peoples' cars. People garbage-eating. I saw one animal of a man, lurking in doorways, get Maced twice. Women in scanties, bursting out of these, thrusting about in their clogs, looked like they were spraying him for sport. While all the dealers at the corner phones, too savvy to use mobiles, let loose their hilarity, like the ululations of hyenas. Yet there were families living here. There were art galleries, schools, plenty of food shops, restaurants. Intense smells of ethnic cooking layered the air along with the odor of dope. Several blocks away, the beautiful Worldwide Plaza, built only recently, was revitalizing the area. On the whole, however, it seemed a strange place for Betsy Spaeth to live.

She certainly hadn't expected me to be on her stoop at nine twenty-two that evening, and she wasn't pleased about it.

'You always work this late?' I said, rising to greet her.

She pulled back on the pavement, her lovely face looking strained. 'What the fuck!'

'My own day hasn't been much fun either. Want to compare notes?'

'I'm not with this, you intruding son-of-a-bitch. You want to talk, there's the telephone. Tomorrow.'

'Won't keep,' I said.

'Gonna have to.' Emphatically, trying to push past.

I blocked her path to the stairway. 'Lady, you've not only gotten me fired, you've rendered me unemployable. I've just gone from 'man on the rise' – *your* description – to a rape suspect. A goddamn pariah. My own firm won't take me back – which also means no other firm on the Street will touch me.'

'I didn't ID you in that line-up.'

'I know. And that's freakish. Those IDs are freakish.'

She looked me over for an instant, then sighed. 'I can't help you. Get a lawyer.'

'I don't need a lawyer. I'm not a goddamn rapist.'

'I want you to stand aside now,' she said with intent, 'so I can get into my building.'

'Listen to me for a moment. I want to talk to you. Not on the phone. My friend, Carter Denison, says that you're actually a person one can talk to. Despite all appearances to the contrary.'

'You know Carter?'

'Yes. He's a close friend. Maybe, at this moment, thanks to you, my only one. I want a chance to persuade you I could not possibly be the scumbag who is doing these things to women. That this is an absolutely ridiculous charge.'

'You're not being charged, as I understand it,' she said with apparent bitterness. 'And even if you could persuade me – although I don't see how that's possible, particularly tonight . . .' She broke off, and gave a harsh laugh. 'Look. This is crazy. I'm tired. I want to go upstairs. Will you please just leave.'

'Ten minutes. Give me ten minutes. You're not going to sleep right away. You're going to unwind. I'll help you. You've made a bad mistake about me. I want to give you a chance to undo it. Surely you're not afraid of me.'

She blew out her cheeks in exasperation. 'No, I'm certainly not afraid of you. I could probably break you in two.'

'I don't doubt it. Look. You and I barely know each other. By some really weird chance – I mean, from my standpoint, *really* weird – you . . . now . . . pretty much . . . have my whole fucking life in your hands. You understand?'

She said nothing.

'To salvage something – get back even part of what I had – I've got to move fast. I've learned that much from the damage-control artists. It can't wait until tomorrow morning, because tomorrow morning you're going to get tied up in twenty cases you'll think – rightly think – are more urgent than mine, and by then I'll be dead meat in the Street.'

She gave me an appraising glance.

'Let me be grateful to you,' I said.

She looked at her watch, shook her head with misgivings.

'Give me your jacket,' she said.

'What? You think I'm carrying a weapon?' I started laughing, but yanked off my jacket and handed it to her.

'I take nothing for granted,' she said while rifling through my pockets and feeling the lining of the coat. She gave it back to me. 'Now up against the railing.'

'Jesus,' I said, still laughing but complying.

'You'll probably like this part,' she said, feeling up and down my back and the insides of both legs. She started up the stairs, turned, looked down at me. 'Ten minutes,' she said, without any expression.

I followed, not really knowing what had flipped her, although I guessed it was my knowing Carter.

She occupied the top two floors of a five-story brownstone. I got no smiles from her in the tiny elevator; not even a glance, though a not unpleasant whiff of some unusual scent kept coming at me. She controlled the elevator with a key. There were stairs, and a triple locked door on the landing, but the elevator was an alternative, apparently for her use only. It opened into the bottom floor of her apartment, a long expanse of kitchen, dining, living spaces, with shiny hardwood floors, a brick wall, and a deck in back. Someone had spent a significant amount of cash putting in that elevator and decorating this place, which, again, given the location, was surprising.

'Drink?' she asked, opening the refrigerator.

'A glass of water would be great.'

I took an upholstered swivel chair. She sat on the sofa facing me, while placing our glasses of tap water and ice on a glass coffee table between us.

'Nice crib,' I said.

'Obligatory comment,' she said.

'True. But, in this case, warranted.'

'Prior owner. I think he saw it in a movie. What I cared about was that it was done. No work for me.' With a frown, she shifted her position on the sofa.

'Sorry.' I tried to get her to join my smile. 'I'm not going to do what I said, waste any of my ten minutes persuading you of my innocence. Because you already know it. You wouldn't have let me up here if you thought otherwise. No matter how easily you think you could throw me around the room with kung fu moves, or whatever it is they teach you.'

She looked bored.

'There are ways you can help me,' I said. 'Can we go back to the beginning for a moment? The search of my apartment?'

She took a sip of her water. 'I had nothing to do with that. We had fibers from the ski mask, checked out eight or nine brands. The lab confirmed it was North Face. Only a couple of outlets handle their stuff in this city. All credit card sales are recorded on their POS equipment. Your name coming up was the joker.'

'What about the gym suit?'

'Yours had been cleaned,' she said.

'So what?' I exclaimed. 'Still has fibers.'

She waved it off. Apparently fibers weren't what they'd been looking for. On the gym suit.

'And?' I said. 'You check out anyone else who bought that ski mask? Put anyone else in a line-up?'

'Didn't have to. After three positives on you.'

'In other words, you did me first?'

'That's right.'

'Whose idea was that?'

She shrugged. 'Not mine. Taken right out of my hands. I assumed by your boss.'

'You do some other guys now, you'll get the same results.'

'Not policy. Not after three positives.'

'False positives. Look,' I said, half way out of my chair, 'I was the only guy in that line-up who wasn't a cop. There was a bond among everyone there except me. I was the guy getting fingered. The odd one out. Everyone knew that, and I probably gave it away myself. I was really pissed off at having to be there.'

'No doubt.'

'So why don't you put some other guys through a line-up?'

'As I said. Policy. To protect the victims.'

'Bullshit. So as not to corrupt the evidence, is the real reason.'

She looked away.

'Betsy? Can I call you that?'

She didn't like it. 'You're a suspect,' she said. 'That's the point. I can't change that until . . .' She let it drift; the point was obvious.

'All right, then. How 'bout this? A simple phone call. It'll take three minutes, and restore some sanity to my life.'

She was shaking her head, no, already.

'Presiding partner of my firm,' I said. 'Guy named Roger Hazzard. He's an OK guy, if a bit paranoid, and just doesn't like confrontation. We play on that.'

'We?' she repeated.

'Yeah. All you've got to do is tell him who you are – that in itself will impress the hell out of him. Real life is something Roger gets very little of. Then say – and you can lead up to this however you want – that, in your judgment, there's about as much chance I committed these crimes as he did.'

'Whoa!'

A sense of humor, I hoped, lurked somewhere beneath that shell. 'So whatta you say?' I asked. 'Three minutes. Including the dialing. And you'd be telling him only what you believe.'

'See, that's the problem – or, at least, one of them. I don't purport to be an expert on people. You think you know someone – even someone you've known your whole life – you only *think* you know them. You don't *really* know them. You want me to make a judgment about you? Nice guy, couldn't possibly be a rapist? How the hell do I know? Same guy who's sweet to his mom and girlfriend one minute could be a homicidal maniac the next. Nature of the beast. And I don't mean only men.

Although men do seem to predominate in this category.'

I'd drifted, having no real expectation she'd give in. 'Funny thing is, what I said about Hazzard? It's probably right. Put that guy in a line-up with a bunch of cops, he'd get picked out faster than I did. He's even a bit one-sided like I am. Like most people are.'

This appeared only to annoy her.

'Don't you get it?' I said. 'There are literally dozens of guys, maybe hundreds, those women would have ID'd. Guys who knew them both. Don't you think it's just a trifle unfair that my life's getting trashed because of the accident of getting singled out first?'

She'd had enough. 'Unfair? You want to talk about unfair? You have any idea what I do all day?'

'I do. But here's the punchline on Hazzard. Helen Cassenov was his first wife. They hate each other.'

She took a moment to digest that.

'So . . . what are you saying? He did it?'

'Extremely improbable. But more likely he than I. He at least had a goddamn motive.'

I got to my feet, found a pencil and pad near her phone and scribbled my number. 'I don't have an office anymore. You can reach me at home.' I started toward the door next to the elevator which I figured opened on to the stairway.

'In case I change my mind?' Betsy said, with a trace of humor.

'Yeah,' I said, without much hope.

She looked at her watch. 'Exactly ten minutes.'

'I do try to keep my word.'

'Good trait. Got any more?'

I looked at her inquiringly. It was the friendliest thing she had said. 'An aversion to self-promotion.'

She laughed. 'In which case, you'd never have made much of a politician.'

'We'll never find out now, will we?'

'Guess not,' she said. And then, with surprising wistfulness, 'Maybe that is too bad.'

The Fifth Victim

'The good thing,' Doris Strickland would say, 'about having a law office in your own home is the commute. The bad thing? At night, you're the last one to leave.' Her office/home occupied a brownstone in Chelsea. On balance, Doris liked the arrangement.

At a relatively young age, she stood out among a dwindling class of high-profile individual practitioners. Her field was criminal defense. White collar, violent crimes, drug crimes, whatever. She had a staff of young lawyers and paralegals who were strictly employees – had no function but to support her. She did all the talking with clients and in court, and most of the thinking. For Doris, partnership in a big firm – which was offered periodically – was out of the question. She'd never 'played well with others.' Not even in the DA's Office, where she'd kicked ass for ten years.

Scott Barry, her most recent hire from law school, had been trying to impress her by staying late every night. She wasn't impressed – though, as she admitted to herself reluctantly, she liked him. If she hadn't had an abortion at nineteen, her kid would have been Scott's age now, probably with sandy hair and a bumpy nose like he had.

'Whatta you still doing here?' she asked him, on her tour through the first floor offices. Her own professional domain was the entirety of the second floor, and her living quarters occupied the third and fourth floors. Secretaries and paralegals had desks in the basement.

'The Cavanaugh case,' he said. 'Got an idea for an extra defense.'

'Oh, yeah?'

'Well, not really a defense. A factor on sentencing. Insider trading is a victimless crime. I mean, people got hurt because the company didn't release the info earlier – but they weren't hurt by Niall Cavanaugh, who happened to get the information earlier from a friend of a friend. I'm looking for cases on this.'

'Forget it. Go home. Or better yet, take out your girlfriend.'

'The point doesn't work?'

'Works fine. But I already know the cases.'

'Boy!'

'What?'

'You're depressing.'

'I should certainly hope so.'

Scott laughed. 'Anything else I can do?'

'Get the fuck outta here!'

'Yes, ma'am,' he said, threw some papers in a briefcase and headed toward the door.

'And Scott,' she said.

He lingered expectantly.

'I get it – you – don't worry.'

He left with a grin.

She toured the premises, turning lights off, a nightly ritual. She went out often enough, but preferred nights at home, preferably with company, although not of Scott's age, at least not in men. On the second floor she glanced briefly at her desk, remembered the local bistro delivery sitting in her fridge and headed upstairs.

A man in a ski mask, holding a handgun, was half-sitting on the edge of her sink, so casually and improbably that Doris thought she was having a hallucination. Then she went numb. Which was when he darted between her and the stairs. Doris said, 'Oh, shit,' before getting whacked in the mouth. He hit her with the gun barrel without preamble and when she got up, he hit her again. Then he dragged her, mainly by the hair, into the bedroom.

'Take it off,' he said. 'Everything.'

At her look of angry incredulity, he hit her a third time.

'More?' he suggested, watching her move slightly on the floor.

'No.'

'Let's make a game of it,' he said. 'All clothes off in two minutes. It's not as easy as it sounds. And if you don't do it, I'll hit you again, or maybe shoot you. Either works for me. It's a matter of impulse.'

He glanced at his watch and said, 'Go!' As she struggled with her buttons, he said, 'And once you're totally naked, we'll play real games.'

'Please,' she said, trying to get her blouse off.

'What?'

'There's no need for this.'

'But there is. Precisely for this. And there has been, for a very long time.'

SIXTEEN

Betsy's call came at mid-morning. I'd already run around the reservoir, showered, breakfasted, cleaned up the apartment, tried by keeping busy to forget I had nothing to do.

'Your friend Hazzard—' she began.

'You *phoned* him?'

'Waste of time. He's a lot slicker than you told me.'

'He'll cave.'

'I don't think so. He's already developed a patter.'

'Oh, shit! I know that mode. What is it?'

'Great regard for your abilities and character. Great sorrow you got stuck in a mess. But, for the good of the firm, until this blows over – and he's sure it will soon – so on and so forth.'

I'd been standing, excited by the fact she'd telephoned at all. Now I sank to the floor in a cross-legged sitting position. 'You were good to have made that call. I mean, damned good. I'm really grateful.'

'Well, it didn't work. Sorry. But there's something more important. Have you read the papers this morning?'

'No. Been saving them, actually. For something to do.'

'You better look. A criminal defense lawyer, a woman, was brought into the hospital last night. I just saw her. Same attacker, same M.O. Except her face was smashed in. This guy's turned truly violent. No longer just threats of nasty things he's going to do; he's started doing them.'

'Last night?' My brain was whirring. 'What time? When I was with you?'

'Close. Did you go straight home?'

'Absolutely,' I said, showing excitement. 'Straight home. You saw me. I was totally wasted. I'd been sitting on your stoop for hours.'

'There's a doorman in your building who can confirm your time of arrival?'

'Damn right. Luis.' Then I realized how this was sounding. 'Look, I'm sorry for that woman, I really am.'

'But if her misfortune could get a really large and ugly monkey off your back . . .'

'I wouldn't have made such a trade.'

'Yes, I understand,' she said. 'It's all right. Check with that doorman. Bring him in.'

'He'll be on late this afternoon.'

'Fine,' she said. 'By the way, you know this woman, is what she said. Doris Strickland?'

'*What?*'

'You do know her.'

'Of course I know her. Everyone knows her. She's one of the most prominent trial lawyers in the city. She's up for judgeship. Federal court. And she's beautiful.'

'Not at the moment, she isn't. How well do you know her?'

I felt a stab of suspicion. 'Why?'

'Never mind. Forget it.'

'What? You're still thinking: three women, he knows them all?'

'Should I be thinking something else?'

'Yeah, you should! In this city, there's what? Two thousand professional people *at least* who all know each other. And – wait a second. You gave me her name. You allowed to do that? Isn't there a rule?'

'There's an exception.'

'For suspects.'

'Right. Stay cool, Rick. We'll hope Luis will take you off the list.'

She'd called me Rick. Finally. Something.

She'd hung up. Then I did, but without otherwise moving.

There was something in the back of my head, this little nagging feeling of implausibility about Betsy. Which I attacked. *She slept on it, had a change of heart! Don't get paranoid!* And then a thought, a picture I'd been pushing down but now couldn't get rid of. Doris Strickland, another woman I admired, beaten and raped. The aftershock hit me in the pit of the stomach, thrusting my breakfast into my throat so fast I nearly didn't make it into the bathroom.

I considered, then rejected, the idea of getting Luis's home telephone number from the managing agent of the building. Don't make too much of it, I thought. You got home around ten fifteen. He saw you. Period. Enough said. In fact, I thought, instead of dragging Luis downtown, get Betsy to come by the building to take his statement.

I was beginning to feel tremendous relief. By four that afternoon, when the shift changed and Luis came to work, I'd emerge from this theater of the absurd piece. Frank would apologize and might well offer me my job back. It would appeal to his pride that he was a fair-minded man. Not necessarily loyal, as it had turned out. But fair.

Would I accept? Not a chance. And at four o'clock, I'd start reclaiming my life, either at my old firm or someplace as good. Maybe I could even help in the investigation. If this guy knew women I knew, there was a good chance I knew him.

I picked up the phone and, before I could reason myself out of it, called Ali at her office. Got put right through.

'Everything all right?' she asked, with a trace of alarm.

'Great. Something's happened. Not bad, don't worry. I'd like to talk. You free for lunch, by any chance?'

'I am, as it turns out, having just gotten canceled. But give me a clue. New girlfriend?'

I laughed. 'Not that kind of news. You have a boyfriend?'

'Yeah. Sam.'

'Good,' I said.

We met at Mario's, a Northern Italian *ristorante* in the West Fifties. A bit pretentious, but excellent food, the waiters yuppily garbed in gray shirts and black pants. Ali and I arrived at the same time, which was unusual. 'Ah, Mr and Mrs Corinth!'

How delightful! How we've missed you! What a pleasure to see old friends again!' The owner gave us his best and most private table. My choosing this place had been a stab at nostalgia.

Ali said, 'You think Mario's telling us he's pissed we haven't been coming here regularly?'

'Of course. He gave us this table on probation.'

'So let's make the most of it. Tell! What's the news?'

I told her the whole story. Every detail, including what it had felt like standing in that line-up. She grabbed my hand and listened with sympathy and reactions of horror.

'You know,' she said, when I got to the line-up part, 'you always liked Frank, and I never did. He gives you this "salt of the earth," "man of the people" façade, this "deep down, all I really want is to serve the public." It's bullshit. Deep down he's as self-seeking as any other pol.'

I told her about Luis, and she expressed her relief. I told her I'd decided to go back into private practice, and she seemed pleased. We'd reached that point, then, that we always reached. Sharing news, a third person would have said, gushing. Laughing a lot, touching each other. Real high spirits, on the bubble. Like we were the same as we had been. But, of course, we weren't the same. And all I had to do was reveal my hurt at that fact, or my resentment of her betrayal, and this bubble of conviviality would burst. So I didn't. I knotted the resentment in my chest and tried to ignore it.

'What about Roger?' she asked. 'Have you talked to him?'

I gave her a bottom-line summary of that chapter, including Betsy's report of her telephone conversation with Hazzard.

'He's just weak,' said Ali. 'When Frank comes around, Roger will.'

'If not, I'll make the rounds within the firm. Call a meeting. Or go elsewhere. Or, for that matter, start my own firm. Without this nonsense hanging over me, I can pretty much do anything I want.'

We had a fine meal and said goodbye on the street. She put her hand to my cheek and reached up to kiss me on the lips. Safely, in public. 'I still love you, Rick. I really do.' We were going in opposite directions. I watched her walk away. It's a word she uses, I thought. Love. Doesn't mean very much.

SEVENTEEN

I sat in the park for a while. Watched the leaves turn. Shockingly colored things flying the air on the tangle of branches. I watched the carriages and strollers pushed by mommies or nannies, tykes and tots bundled inside. Tiny faces smug with entitlement. Or screaming at slight inattentions.

And the mommies and nannies looked at me. How out of place a man is; my age, on a park bench, in the middle of the afternoon. How readable those thoughts!

Distractions. I was there, breathing the unusually clean soft air, glorying in this lovely Indian Summer afternoon, because I was about to free myself from a hellish problem, and because I wanted to relive in my mind every bittersweet moment of my lunch with Ali. I knew how pathetic this was, but the way I felt that moment, it was a good use of a park bench.

I had wanted to say to her, 'You came into my life, you filled it up, then you walked away. Things got a little tough, you walked away.' But I held my tongue. She had skipped into my arms in her light gray cotton tweed suit we had bought on sale at Bergdorf's, and the memory rush of that day, our making out in the fitting room, our literally dancing for joy on the streets, made the voicing of grievances inappropriate. Even huge grievances, like her splitting us up after fourteen years.

So we'd talked about the problem in my life that was about to disappear, and we'd talked about her work, which she did with excitement and evident gratification. She'd gotten her third promotion in little more than a year. Now, among other responsibilities, she supervised the running of three private schools. The company's mission – creating and operating for-profit specialized prep schools – fascinated the educational world. College admissions, recently announced for the first graduating class, were exceptional. It had helped that the president of the company, hand-picked by Bob Hayden, was a former president of Brown. Many entrenched interests wanted the venture to fail. The media was poised to strike either way. And Ali was in the middle of it. Reveling in it.

I was happy for her. Really was. Yet, I couldn't help thinking, was this another bubble? If it ultimately burst, she'd bear the brunt of the blame, since the principals of the three schools reported to her. And even if it succeeded, novelty didn't last long. In fact, were for-profits even a good thing? Not many parents could afford the fees, which were high. And for those who could, and whose children had the qualifications for admission, the non-profits had room. It was the non-profits that were losing out.

I'd said none of this either. Nor did I ask about her and Hayden. I watched Ali being excited, watched her feeling important, and was happy it made her feel good. I thought: I've been there. I know what this feels like. Heady stuff. And I wished she had already learned what I'd learned, which was it didn't amount to much in the end. What mattered in the end was what she had thrown away. What we once had. Corny as hell, because it was true.

I rang up Carter on my cell phone. Reached him during a recess. I felt the need of a friend. 'That problem I told you about? It's about to dissolve. In five minutes.' I filled him in. We rejoiced; it was terrific.

Ascending the park walkway up to Central Park West, I devised a modest plan. I'd be off-handed with Luis. As if my freedom and well-being didn't hang on what he said. From across the street and a block away, I could see his pudgy form out in front of the building, getting a cab for one of the tenants. When I felt my heart pumping at about twice the normal rate, I slowed my step. Took a few deep breaths. Waited patiently for the light. Walked half a block to the front entrance. Even greeted Luis casually and strode halfway inside before turning, as if it was an afterthought, and said, 'Oh, Luis. You remember when I came home last night?'

'Sure, Mr Corinth.'

'What time was that, about?'

'Oh, about midnight,' he said, smiling. *Smiling my life away.* 'Maybe half past.'

I returned the smile and tried to stop blinking. 'No, no,' I said. 'Had to be a lot earlier than that.'

He looked frightened. 'Whatever you say, sir.'

'No, I'm serious. You're off at midnight.'

'That's why I remember,' he said. 'Diego was late. I was waiting for him when you came. And he got here just after you did.'

'Luis, please, think! What you're remembering must be some other night. Last night I got home around ten fifteen, ten twenty.'

Now he just looked confused. 'If you know, why do you ask me?'

'Well, frankly, I need confirmation. It's a silly argument I'm having with someone. But it's important to me. So please try to focus on *last* night.'

'I say whatever you want me to say.'

'It's not like that. I don't want you to lie for me. I want you to remember what I know to be the fact.'

Somehow he'd gotten obstinate and angry. 'I do remember. I know when you got home. It wasn't ten twenty. It was two hours later.'

Nothing was going to alter that testimony. Try cases for years, one gets to know something – not much, but something – about witnesses. This guy would stick to his story. And because of it, I was about to lose everything I valued.

EIGHTEEN

I didn't call Betsy; she called me.

'And?' she asked.

'Look,' I said. 'Can I see you?'

'What's wrong? The doorman won't confirm the time?'

I couldn't talk for a moment.

'Rick?'

'I just . . . can't imagine why he's doing this. He's insisting it was two hours later.'

Her pause, longer still.

'Maybe it was,' she said.

'Jesus. Would I have told you about this guy if I'd had the slightest doubt about his confirming the time? Would I have told you just now about his saying two hours later if I thought he was telling the truth? Let me see you, please. Tonight. I'll buy you dinner. Any place you like. Daniel's?'

She said, 'I can't let you buy me dinner, much less at Daniel's.'

'How 'bout Le Cirque, then?'

'Oh, that's brilliant. I'm *here* tonight. Salad at my desk.'

'I'll bring it. What do you like? And if I'm a suspect, it'll give you an excellent opportunity to pump me.'

'Rick, we're talking now. What do you want to tell me?'

'I went straight home last night. I have no idea whatever why my doorman is misremembering, or worse. Someone may be pressuring him.'

'Noted.'

'That's a lead.'

'Gotcha.'

'Meaning?'

'Meaning I'll check it out,' she said. 'We finished?'

'No. I want to see Doris.'

Another pause.

'She's still in the hospital,' Betsy said.

'Exactly. I don't happen to know which one.'

Silence.

'Look, call her,' I said. 'Tell her I want to see her. I could obviously call every hospital in the city and eventually find her. But I want her to allow me to visit her. And I want you to know about it.'

'You think she'll say it wasn't you?'

'Of course. That's the point.'

'I wouldn't be so sure. For one thing, unless she's made a remarkable recovery in twelve hours, she'll be disoriented.'

'Call her. Please. Find out. She's a strong person. My guess is she'll welcome the company. And when you finally realize the absurdity of this charge, maybe you *will* let me take you to dinner.'

'I'll have someone call her, Rick. After I've called her doctor.'

'You're a saint.'

At least that made her laugh.

Betsy must have acted immediately, since she got back to me within a half hour.

'Well, you have your dinner companion, after all. But it'll cost you. Take-out from Bernardin. She said she's already sick of hospital food. You'll find her in the Greenberg Pavilion of New York Hospital, room fourteen twenty-three. There's visiting for another . . . about fifty minutes. So you better get moving.'

'What did she say when you told her I was a suspect?'

'I didn't talk to her, but I understand she said, "Ridiculous."'

I felt almost giddy relief. 'Thank God. At last, some reality on the subject. And, I take it, she's over the worst?'

'I don't know about that, but I gather she's much improved over early this morning.'

'Betsy, again, I'm really grateful. Everlastingly grateful.'

'By my watch, if you don't—'

'I know, I know. I'm going, I'm going.'

Le Bernardin is not a take-out restaurant. On the other hand, the circumstances were extraordinary. And the maitre-d', like the eminence of any such establishment, had sufficient range to take circumstances into account. He produced, on short notice, an artfully wrapped package. It was handed to me as I stepped through the door. My radio car encountered no cross-town traffic. Ten minutes later, we pulled into the semi-circular driveway of the hospital with a feast likely to have exceeded anything ever served in that building.

'I thought the cold dishes the best bet,' I explained to Doris, while laying out two ample bowls of crab gazpacho, three shelled lobsters, and a medley of caramel treats.

She had a private room with a view of the East River, though I doubt she had spent much time at the window or any place out of bed. Her face was covered with bandages. And I knew she was slender, but propped up on the pillow in a hospital dressing gown, she looked like a grounded wraith.

In the courtroom, Doris personified energy. A force of nature and smart as hell. She'd be an awesome judge. I visualized the woman beneath all the tape and gauze: brown hair, wide brow, pert nose. You took one look at her, you wanted to kill the bastard who had smashed her face.

'The young man who called me, rookie cop, what's his name?'

'No idea,' I said.

'I don't know either. Anyway. He said the most ridiculous thing. He said—'

'I know.'

'But that's absolutely absurd, Rick. How the hell did your tit ever get in this wringer?'

'It's a bad movie. Like a bad Hitchcock.' And I told her.

'Fucking hell,' she said when I'd finished with all the dreary details. 'If you'll pardon my native tongue.'

'It's a language I'm fluent in. Especially now.'

'So. Anyway.' Her voice was inflected, but Doris, known for expressive gestures, lay inert on her pillow. 'You're out of it now. I can easily put this nonsense to rest.'

'Thank God. No. Thank *you*.'

'Well, I don't know who the fuck was in my apartment last night, but it sure as hell wasn't you.'

Then, out of nowhere, she started shaking.

'Doris?' I went to her bed. Now she seemed to be sobbing, although with her face bandaged it was hard to tell. 'Doris, can I do something? Get the nurse?'

'That fucking son-of-a-bitch. I'm going to kill him! I'm going to find out who it was, and I'm going to kill him.' The declaration seemed to calm her. 'I've got to pee.' Painfully, she swerved her body around so her stick legs hung over the side of the bed.

'You want me out of here?' I asked, standing, now feeling very much in the way. 'It's already past their deadline for visitors.'

'No. I want you here. Don't move. I'll only be a minute.'

'Let me help you, then.'

'You want to put me on the john?'

'Not quite what I had in mind.'

'Just be a good boy and sit down, OK?'

'Going to,' I said, and did.

Like all hospital gowns, hers, in back, insufficiently guarded her privacy. Of which she seemed, shuffling into her private bathroom, oblivious. Her stream was also quite audible through the door. We were good friends. We had tried cases against each other and had also been on the same side. We had never, however, been intimate. I suspected she was suffering still from the shock of that incident more deeply than I had realized when I'd first come into the room.

Doris got herself back into bed. When I rose to give assistance, she put up her hand. 'Nothing against you, ole buddy, but, somehow, right now, I just don't like being touched.'

'I understand.'

'Yeah? Really?'

I could hear her thinking, *You been raped too, then?* 'Doris, I'm so sorry.'

'Forget it. I'm just real angry, Rick. I meant what I said before. I'd happily kill the son-of-a-bitch.'

'Me, too.'

'He's a real sick bastard, this guy. He knows just how to scare you. Just how to fuck with your mind. Straps you down. Tight. *Know what that feels like? Jesus!*'

My scalp retracted; I could imagine it well enough.

I hesitantly asked, 'You got any clue?'

'As to who he might be? Shit. I have no idea whatever. You'd think I would. This prick picked me out. He was in my fucking apartment.'

'He preys on successful women. It's not necessarily someone you know. He might have gotten your name out of the newspapers.'

She started laughing with some bitterness, or crying. Again, with the bandages, it was difficult to determine which. 'You know what's ironic?' she said.

'Ironic?'

'Yeah, well. In my rape fantasies, the perpetrator is usually a beautiful woman. You know that?'

'I thought it possible.'

'Well, now you know.'

NINETEEN

Another wait. Doris would talk to Frank, Frank to Roger, my life would re-start.

I wasn't cut out for inactivity. Without the pressure of the next trial and sixteen other cases in the queue, I felt rootless. Spacey, too. I had trouble getting to sleep, and had bad dreams when I did. I seemed to have lost the core of myself. Or maybe I didn't want to try to find it, now that I had all the time in the world to look.

Also, with no income, I had something else to worry about while I waited. My salary as Chief Assistant had barely covered the rent on my current place, Ali's maintenance, school tuitions and minor expenses. I still had the expenses but no income and, having been at the job for so short a time, no severance. Since paying off college loans and the apartment on East Seventy-second, I'd saved very little. So, for the first time in a while, I had money problems. Maybe I could have used a change of scenery for a spell, but I wasn't about to head off to some resort.

What I did mainly was watch old movies. I love movies, old and new, foreign, domestic, studio films, independents. It was one of the things Ali and I had binged out on together. Everyone had a screenplay in his desk; I had several. When I stopped being a lawyer, I thought, maybe that's what I'd do, write movie scripts. But during this period, with all this leisure time, I couldn't write anything. And though I watched movies, I didn't enjoy them. Nothing worked. I couldn't stand myself.

After almost a week of this, I started bouncing off the walls. I'd called Betsy; I'd called Frank. Neither one had responded. For two days. It was pointless calling Hazzard again until I had straightened things out with the DA's Office. And it was risky calling other firms until I'd spoken with Hazzard. So I was marking time. At the mercy of other people returning my calls. Or not. This, definitely, I did not love.

With mixed motives, I called Hayden at his office.

'You know Emma's out of rehab.'

He said he knew.

'And you know what she's doing?' I said.

There was a longish pause.

Then Hayden said, 'No reason for you to know this, Rick, but I'm a student of psychology.'

'That right?'

'I majored in it at college,' he said, 'and since then have kept up. Auditing graduate courses and the like. Lots of reading.'

I waited for him to make his point.

'You've helped me, and I'm grateful for it,' he said. 'But now, with Emma – if I could get her committed, I would. The problem is, while I think – using the vernacular – she's out of her goddamn mind, she's not insane. Certainly not legally. So we're just going to have to let her hit bottom. *I'm* going to have to.'

His concern, not mine, he was telling me. 'Probably right, Bob.' Though we both knew, the bottom for Emma was more likely to be her last breath than the beginning of rehab.

'I've tried everything else,' he said. 'Experts, institutions, five different types of treatment.'

'AA, NA?'

'Done it. Lots of times. Taken her to twenty, thirty meetings – driven her there myself.'

'I'm sorry, Bob.'

'You're a good man, Rick. I really like you. And I'll never forget what you did.'

I got Betsy on about the sixth try.

'You're avoiding me,' I said.

'That obvious, hunh?'

'Not funny. Why?'

'I'm no longer on the case. Yanked off two days ago.'

A stunner. 'This have something to do with me?'

'Not something. Everything.'

'What? Your arranging for me to see Doris? They didn't like that?'

'*They,* in this case, happens to be my superior officer, Captain Chacon. And yes, he didn't like it. I think it's fair to say, he didn't like it a lot.'

'There was nothing improper about it,' I said. 'Otherwise, I wouldn't have asked.'

'Well, there's such a thing, I learn, as the appearance of non-objectivity.'

'You're not a goddamn judge, for Christ's sake. You're not even a prosecutor. You're a cop. Cops don't have to be objective.'

'Tell it to Chacon. I'm sure he's going to want to talk to you.'

'What the hell for? Hasn't Doris cleared this nonsense up yet?'

'You really ought to talk to Chacon.'

I tried Frank instead. Again. With Betsy, who answered her own phone, you could sometimes get lucky and catch her. Frank was insulated by three secretaries. If he didn't want to talk to you, he didn't talk to you. I now fell into the category of someone to whom Frank did not want to talk.

I dialed the main switchboard at One Police Plaza, asked for Captain Chacon, got a recording and left a message. A half hour later, as I was still wondering how to waste the rest of the morning, the doorman announced from downstairs that there was a gentleman in the lobby who would like to talk to me on the intercom. I said, 'Put him on.'

'Ricky? This is Vincente Chacon. I heard you'd called. I don't want to barge in on you, but . . . it's a fine morning; thought you might like a walk in the park.'

It got me riled, and maybe it shouldn't have. I leave a message for a call-back, and the guy lands on my doorstep? Right away calling me Ricky? You get it everywhere, this instant buddying up. Cold callers, you'd think they'd know better. Bank tellers, who used to be super-polite. People phoning out of the blue, tradesmen, everyone. Now here was this guy I'd never met, this cop investigating me for raping women, and not only was he showing up at my home uninvited, trying to trick me into prison for crimes I didn't commit, he was acting as if we were friends. Maybe I was old-fashioned. Maybe the police force no longer taught the importance of paying respect. Or maybe he thought I was a molester of women, entitled to nothing but contempt.

And maybe *that's* what riled me.

'Give me a couple of minutes,' I said, taking the bitterness out of my voice.

'I'll wait. Take your time.'

The man waiting for me outside, dressed in a brown suit with vest, his closed eyelids lifted to the sun, was older than me, and exceptionally homely. He had a melon face with almost no forehead, pock-marked yellowish skin, longish nappy hair, and, when he heard me coming, a smile equipped with seemingly twice the normal allotment of teeth. About my height, he must have been fifty pounds heavier, which strained the buttons of his vest. Though suited up for an office, he looked comfortable basking in the rays. I had on only a polo shirt and khakis but felt the heat immediately. He suggested we cross the avenue into the park.

'I got your message while in the neighborhood,' he explained, after we'd walked a bit in silence. He greeted several joggers trudging past and a lady dog-walker, as if he actually knew them. 'The automatic trace told me you were still at home. I thought I'd take a chance and drop by, since I wanted to talk to you too.'

The man had beautiful speech, like a trained actor's. From it, you would never have pictured him; indeed, it transformed his appearance.

We'd gone several hundred yards down a sloping path, and I said, 'Let's take that bench.'

He glanced at it, then nodded and took the unshaded side. We were quiet for a moment, Chacon enjoying the setting. 'I know you're a lawyer, Rick, but I should tell you . . . nevertheless . . . you may wish to retain one.'

At least that got me to laugh. 'Are you giving me a *Miranda* warning?'

'Of course not. We Mirandize only suspects in custody. You know that. On the other hand, you are a suspect, so anything you say may be held against you.'

'You know, this thing is really fucking up my life.'

'I'm sure it is,' he clucked, not unsympathetically.

'I'm having a goddamn hard time taking it seriously.'

'I suggest you do, I really do.'

'What the hell's happened to Doris Strickland's testimony?

Two days ago she assured me she'd tell you guys that whoever attacked her, it wasn't me.'

'Really? She told you that?'

'Be pretty stupid of me to make it up.'

'Well, I've got to say, Rick, that's not what Ms. Strickland is telling us.'

Or, obviously, he wouldn't be here. I sensed the unreality recommencing. 'Damnit!' Suddenly dizzy, I put my head between my knees.

Chacon started rubbing my neck. 'Easy there, fella.'

'Sorry,' I said, straightening up. 'It's making me sick, now.'

'The thing is,' he said, 'while we don't have enough to charge you, too much evidence points right at you for us to say you're not a suspect. I sympathize, Rick, I really do. This limbo status must be hell for a guy like you.'

'There's a kind of guy who might enjoy it?'

'Well, you know,' he said with some bite, 'there are all types.'

'Can you tell me exactly what Doris said?'

'Sure. No problem. She said she can't be certain. The mask, the gloves, the altered voice, etcetera. On thinking it over, however, she just can't rule you out, no matter how improbable it might seem.'

'She say why?'

'Yeah,' he said. 'The walk. Same thing the others picked out. Seems you got this gait, a little lop-sided. I noticed it, too, as we came down here. Your right shoulder's a little lower than your left.'

'That's why you wanted to take a stroll,' I said.

''Fraid so. I'm a little sneaky that way.'

'Comes from carrying a heavy briefcase, the one-sidedness does. College, law school, years of going to meetings, and to court.'

'Bet it does,' he said almost solicitously.

'My guess is, must be, oh, at least half a million guys in this city with the same condition.'

'You know, that's probably a good guess.'

'Nevertheless, you think it's evidence pointing at me.'

He breathed out heavily. 'What am I to do? What would you do? It's all these little things. I agree with you. On the surface it seems ridiculous. Guy like you, good-looking guy, successful. About to become New York County District Attorney. At your age, sky's the limit. If you had any such tendencies – shit! – be a lot less trouble for you to pay some hooker a few hundred bucks to role-play the scene.'

'Look—'

'I know. You've got no such tendencies.'

'That's right.'

'Sure, Rick?'

'Damnit, yes! I'm a normal heterosexual guy, not—'

'Then you've got such tendencies.'

'That's what you *think*? Every guy, including yourself, has the tendency to abuse women?'

'Absolutely. Question is: are there enough checks built in to stop us from doing it? It's an old problem. The reptilian brain. The id. The super-ego. Fortunately, more than ninety-nine per cent of the male population has been conditioned against such uncivilized behavior. But every now and then someone slips through the filter. Could be anyone. Any walk of life. Could be normal in every other way.'

'Like me.'

'Like you.'

'That's twisted.'

'Well, with you there's the gym suit and the ski mask and the fact that you know all these women. You've been picked out of a line-up by three victims, and the fourth, who knows you real well, says she can't rule you out. You walk just like the perp who did her.'

'It's not me,' I said quietly.

'And, of course, you'd have to say that.'

'It's true.'

'I want it to be true. I want this guy to be some real ugly dude, hateful in every way, no redeeming virtues. But I know that's not going to be the case. He's too smart, too smooth. And that's another thing. If you were *unchecked*, to use that word again, you'd act just like this guy. You've seen the video. He's an upper-class charmer. Smart, literate, clever.'

'It's not me.'

'As I say. I want to believe that. But Rick, you know, if it is you—'

'*It's not me!*'

'I know. But let me say. When people have this sort of problem, there are ways of dealing with it. Confession—'

'Oh, shit. Not getting through. Listen to me! It really, really is not me.'

He sat back. 'That's what Betsy thinks.'

'That right?' I said, immoderately pleased to hear it.

'Yeah. That's what she thinks. Trouble is. Betsy, you know, she's great on procedure. Process. But instincts? That's something else. I'm not real sure I trust her instincts.'

'Which is why you took her off the case?'

'No.' He gazed skyward, seeking more sun. 'I took her off the case 'cause she likes you too much.'

I laughed out loud. 'I think you missed that one, Vincente.'

'Oh?'

'She thinks I'm a self-seeking pol.'

'You know this because that's what she called you? To your face?'

'Exactly.'

'Well, you see. That proves my point,' he said. 'You are a self-seeking pol. Right? If she didn't like you, this woman would have been like starch. Polite. Correct. She would never have told you the truth about yourself.'

'So you deduce she likes me because she insulted me.'

'No. I don't have to deduce anything. I know she likes you because she admitted it.'

I swiveled about to draw his attention. 'Why are you telling me this?' I asked.

'Hmm,' he said, looking me in the eye. 'Good question. I'm not sure of the answer. Maybe . . .' He stared at me harder. 'Just to see how it will play out?'

TWENTY

Saturday afternoon. Rye, New York. Three-story, sixteen room white clapboard house. One-acre backyard with flower gardens and hundred-year-old trees. There's a party in progress, with a barbecue, in the middle of waspy white suburbia. Something wrong with this picture?

The host, Carter Denison, had been living in the house for ten years. The neighbors had not shunned him. No one had thrown rocks through his windows or burned crosses on his lawn. Indeed, many neighbors attended the party, and the country clubs of the area had fallen all over each other to get him to join. He was a prize catch. An 'acceptable Nigra' – the term used by one Cheeveresque clubman proposing him for admission.

Carter's own style of dealing with such people was wry condescension. He joined the club that had the best golf course, for himself, and the best pool, for his kids, who were only a little older than mine. That he might have been a token admission in the eyes of certain club members didn't faze Carter in the slightest. It was not simply that he thought of such types as buffoonish stock characters. He regarded himself, with considerable justification, as being vastly superior to most everyone else.

The occasion for the party was the eleventh birthday of Carter's daughter, Julie. So I picked up Ali and the kids in my twelve-year-old Jaguar. We drove to Rye like a real family. Carter and his wife Nona greeted us as if we were a real family. It made me feel like a fraud.

Nona was about fifteen years younger than Carter and had to be nearly the most stunningly beautiful woman in the world. She could have passed, as they say, for white. She could have passed for being a film star or super-model, even after having two kids. But Nona always played against her looks. Which is why, I suppose, she'd become a lawyer. That and brains. She was easily Carter's match and mine, and I delighted in her company.

Robin, her ten-year-old son, delighted in the company of Molly, despite the almost two year age disparity which at their stage in life is enormous. So they were friends, and he grabbed her as soon as we arrived. Along with Julie, the two of them took protective custody as well of Sam. Ali watched them as we talked briefly with other guests, pols and nodding acquaintances. She then fell in with Carter at the grill – her attention given over completely to him – while Nona and I stood to the side, sipping rum and tonics, fixed on each other's eyes.

'So how's it going, big guy?' Her smile was complicit.

Continuing the look made me smile too. She was at least my height and possibly taller.

She kissed me. Just friendly. 'Answer the question.'

'You want the party answer?'

'Nope.'

'Well, then, let's see. You talk to Carter about this? The craziness going on in my life?'

'Yep.'

'So you know,' I said.

'I do. It is, without question, *the* most ridiculous thing I've ever heard.'

'Thank you. And nothing's changed. Well, that's not true. It's gotten worse. You read about this new incident, last week?'

'You know who it was? The victim?'

'Yes,' I said. 'You know her too.'

'Don't tell me.'

'I'm not going to.'

'If it leaks out, I don't want *that* on my head.'

'Exactly.'

'But you could talk to her, Rick.'

'I already have.'

'And? What? I don't believe it. She's not taking you out of this?'

'Right.'

'What is it with the bitch?'

'Don't really know. I went to see her at the hospital. She agreed, no way it was me. Next day, she punted.'

'Shit.'

'Yeah.'

We both drank. Nona had on a black silk linen shift that defined the word slinky. It also allowed her breasts maximum freedom and air without actual exposure. No one could have been indifferent to this sight of her, and she had no reason to complain of inattention from me. In one past incident, involving my ill-timed entrance into a beach club cabana, I'd glimpsed Nona *au naturel*. She had thought it hilarious, making a face that reduced our embarrassment to sub-suicidal. But I knew how spectacular the beauty was of which this gown gave only a provocative suggestion.

Nona, I'd learned, came from a sect of near-white folks who were as parochial and passionate in their opposition to cross-breeding as the strictest Hasidim. Carter was light-skinned but not nearly white enough for Nona's people. When she married him, she was disowned. It didn't seem to bother her that much. But possibly she was just good at hiding it. With Nona, you got very close fast, and then hit a wall. Not completely impenetrable, but there.

'Rick, baby,' she said. 'Maybe you need a lawyer. Maybe that time's come.'

'You're hired,' I said.

'No, no. Not me. I'm too involved.'

'Are you?' I asked hopefully.

She wrinkled her small nose 'Yes.'

'Who you thinking, then? Joe Stein?'

'You could do worse,' she said seriously.

'I've thought of it. Mainly because he's your partner.'

'I'm not selling, Rick, but I actually like the man, or I wouldn't be there.'

'I understand. Maybe later. Somehow, I keep thinking, I can make this go away. It really *is* absurd.'

'What does Ali think?'

I gave her a look that wasn't entirely sweet.

'Oops!' she said. 'I thought maybe, your coming here together today . . .'

'Transportation arrangement.'

'That's it?'

'That's it.'

'I'm sorry, baby.'

'Me too,' I said.

'That white girl's out of her fucking mind!'

'You have my authorization so to advise her.'

'Don't think I haven't.'

'I know you have. And I thank you for it.'

'Any time, baby. Because I speak the truth.'

Some new guests were arriving; a middle-aged couple displaying the grin–grimace of greeting.

''Scuse me, darling,' said Nona. 'Chores.'

I looked about, recognizing that new guy who had come in as Tom O'Hearnan, Counsel to the Governor. Elsewhere, on the sweep of lawn, or clustered near the bar, were US Attorneys, Federal judges, a law school dean who was angling for office, and the editor of the editorial page of the *Times*. It was the kind of party as to which Ali once quipped, 'The eye contact is entirely among the males.' I always wondered about this trait of Carter's, using his daughter's birthday as an excuse for a round-up of bigwigs and pols. It was, of course, conceivable he simply enjoyed entertaining such people. Not likely, but conceivable.

I watched him in the center of a heated conversation with four other men and one lady judge who liked being one of the boys. Since I couldn't make out the words, their explosions of sound and exertions of energy seemed all the more exaggerated – like a bunch of NFL linemen celebrating a sack. Would these people even recognize themselves, I wondered? Especially Carter whom *I* scarcely recognized. His conviviality bordered on violence.

I stood alone in the sunshine, open lawn ten feet around me. Nona and I must have been giving off some powerful rays of 'don't interrupt.' A lot of these people had arrived while we'd been talking. Or maybe, I thought, it was me. Perhaps the rumor machinery had already turned me into a rapist. Perhaps the next event at this party was that everyone would pick up a stone.

As it turned out, Frank Seaton came over brandishing a stogie. 'This kind of party, I really enjoy it,' he said pleasantly, a bit comical in his conception of suburban garb, red slacks and navy polo.

'Me?' I said. 'I seem to be able to take anything.'

An off remark, and his face showed it. 'I know you've been calling me, Rick. I feel like a shit not calling you back. But, y'know, there's a print-out of all my calls, even from my cell phone. And it'd look ridiculous my making a call from a phone booth.' He laughed as if it were funny, and as if his distancing himself from me should be understandable. 'Also, every time I think I may have something good to report, absurdity strikes again. Like with Doris.'

'How about something real simple? Like I've known this guy for sixteen years. Like I'd stake my own career and reputation on my judgment that he could not possibly be guilty of these crimes?'

Frank shook his head with sufficient vigor that his cheeks flapped. 'No one knows yet you're a suspect,' he whispered.

'Roger Hazzard knows.'

He looked shocked. 'I can't imagine how.'

'Call him and ask. He might tell you. And while you're talking to him, deliver the speech I just suggested. I'd kind of like my life back.'

'Let me think about it.'

'You got a problem?'

'Everything's now a problem with this case,' he said gravely. 'The press is hounding the Office and me. You'll see a story tomorrow. They've made the link to the New Jersey incident. So they've got four cases, no names, but all prominent women. It's driving them fucking crazy. Like wild dogs. In a goddamn feeding frenzy with no food.'

We talked for another few minutes before Tom O'Hearnan lured him away. I wondered as I watched them go, how long it would take Frank to serve me to the inhabitants of the pound. I ended up thinking, not that long.

Driving home that night on the Hutch, with the kids seat-belted and sleeping in back, Ali said, 'How could you even talk to that guy? Why didn't you just cut him, after what that son-of-a-bitch has done to you?'

'One of those *Men are from Mars* things. We're better at dissembling. Besides, I've been trying to get the guy on the phone for days.'

'And, what? He'll call Roger?'

'He'll think on it.'

'*Think* on it! The bastard's supposed to be your friend.'

When we pulled in front of the Seventy-second Street building, both kids were still fast asleep. Ali said, 'Want to come up?' and my senses started racing.

'What for?' I asked, the question and blunt tone generated involuntarily by too many months of resentment.

She squeezed her eyes together for a moment. 'Shit! *Stupid!* You know, I'm feeling mellow with all that gin. I could just go with it, like pretend. Then really self-lacerate. And what I'm doing – I'm being a goddamn tease. What I hate the most. I'm sorry, darling. I'm really sorry. I'm all fucked up right now.' She started getting out of the car.

She had something to regret; so had I. More. 'No point waking the kids,' I said. 'I'll help you carry them upstairs and leave.'

She gave me a look that was almost like love.

TWENTY-ONE

Sunday it rained. I walked out in it, bought the *Post* and the *News*. It was as Frank had predicted. Front page stories – 'Serial Rapist,' 'Sadistic Sicko,' 'Midtown Maniac' – whipped up from a paucity of facts. As yet, however, there was no connection to me.

I went out to the art museums. Took in a movie. Walked through the crowds, dodging umbrellas. Loneliness can be palpable, especially in crowds. It directs you inward. And accusations make you feel guilty. Bad combination. It made me consider, would I actually be capable of raping a woman? *Think!* The most extreme circumstances of provocation and freedom from punishment. I didn't believe so. And it was more than having what Chacon called the 'checks.' I could visualize actual rape, the ugliness of it. It wasn't something I could do. And I certainly wasn't angry at women in general. In general, I preferred their company to men's.

Afternoon wept into evening. I sat at a sushi bar on Amsterdam Avenue, mesmerized by the dexterity of the chefs and the raindrops patterning the window. The sake mellowed my loneliness. The sashimi did little to diminish the buzz. I walked home in the rain, which did clear my head a bit. Cruising into my apartment, I felt more than ever as if I were transiently boarding in some expensive hotel suite. I left the lights off and, from the large front window, watched the rain fall into the park as I deliberated about calling Betsy.

I'd been thinking about it all day. Spurred by Chacon, what he had said about her supposed liking of me. He'd probably invented it. By his own admission, the man fancied himself a manipulator. But I'd never know how Betsy felt unless I called her. Sometimes you get lucky that way. In the final analysis, I think, it's usually the woman who picks the man. A man can be attracted to twenty women before one says OK. And, if she's as gorgeous as Betsy, chances are she's just cut dead twenty guys better looking than you. Then, of course, you're really lucky.

She picked up on the first ring. I said, 'Hi, it's me, Rick. You don't like dinners, so how 'bout meeting for a drink?' She told me where I'd find her in ten minutes, and hung up. Not even a 'How are you?'

Her choice was a tavern on Ninth Avenue, around the corner from her building. Wood-paneled, wood bar, beer mugs hooked to wooden racks affixed to a tin ceiling. There was a juke box playing some old Nat King Cole dreamy ballad, and everything was bathed in blue light. You were meant to think: old, seeped in history, character. It looked like a film set. She was already perched at the bar, in slacks and a sweater, with a drink that looked like scotch on the rocks.

'Whatta you having?' I asked, taking the next stool.

She downed the remains. 'Chivas.'

'Two,' I said to the barkeep, whom I mentally placed as a wrestler, possibly still on the tour.

We took our drinks to a booth, also wooden.

'Come here often?' I asked, as we settled in across from each other.

She gave the cliché a smile. 'A fair bit,' she said, staring at me over the rim of her glass.

'Is this place a hundred years old, or was it built to look that way two months ago?'

'I wouldn't know.'

'All this paneling. Initials carved in the wood. I wonder if you can buy it like that.'

'I wouldn't know.' Still she peered at me over the rim.

'I was surprised you were home,' I said.

'Yes? If I'm not working, I'm home. Quite a lot.' She relaxed a little, took a deep swallow of scotch.

'How so?'

'Usual reasons.'

'There's no guy, then?'

'No guy,' she said.

'Good.'

'Glad you're pleased.'

'Sorry.' I winced. 'That's inexcusably selfish.'

'We're all selfish.'

'I know. But one does try to moderate the tendency.'

She gave kind of a low throaty laugh. 'Does one!'

'I do. Try, at least. Not successfully. Why I called has nothing to do with the case.'

Her smile now was teasing me. 'Good.'

'I was home alone. Watching the rain. Thought: Wonder if Betsy's at home—'

'Watching the rain?'

'Yes.'

'Was.'

'So,' I said. 'That's why I called.'

'Excellent timing,' she said.

There was a small bowl of peanuts on our table, and I scooped up a few. Betsy watched. I had the impression she'd brushed her hair but had left the house in what she'd been wearing. Blondes should always wear that shade of blue sweater: dark, with some green in it, with black slacks. Helps to have those long limbs, though. Helps to have that face.

I said, 'First time for me . . . usually a disaster. It's the performance-anxiety thing.'

'You're talking about sex?' she said with a mock nonchalance, as if finding the subject further down on a printed agenda.

'Yeah. A real shambles for me. But I do get better. I need to be given some patience.'

She smiled and took several peanuts. 'With me,' she said, flipping them into her mouth, 'it's the disappointment factor. I'm not that unusual with my clothes off. All the normal parts in the normal places. Very ordinary.'

'Well,' I said. 'My expectations aren't extravagant.'

She laughed. 'Oh, good.'

'I guess we've warned each other now. Of the worst.'

'Seems so.' She finished her drink.

'Shall we?'

She looked at mine.

'I'm not much of a drinker,' I said.

'Maybe it would help your anxiety.'

I laughed and took a modest swig. Never liked the stuff. I eased the glass toward her.

'Sure?'

'Absolutely,' I said.

'This won't get me drunk,' she said and downed the rest of my drink. 'It's just something I can do.'

'I'm in awe of you. Beautiful *and* talented.'

'Come,' she said with a smile. 'I want to fuck you. I've been thinking about it. Can't quite explain why.'

It wasn't a disaster after all. Of course Betsy saw to that. One would have had to have been comatose not to have responded to Betsy in a mood to make love.

She did, as she'd said, have the normal parts in the normal places – but, oh my! What parts! What places!

It's no great insight to perceive that couture is more about promise than concealment. Or that, with most of us, drop the cloth, dash the promise. With Betsy, the opposite was true. And she knew it. She reveled in it. She loved admiration. She invited it. Standing on a small oval rug, for example, reaching up to her bookshelves, stretching her spine, you could see her mind working: Look at me! Am I not perfect? Have you ever seen a figure of such exquisite slenderness, such perfect proportions? Or curling in bed. Scissoring her legs. Her beauty stopped the heart.

And what she did without restraint or inhibition took me completely out of myself. Obliterated self-consciousness. I never thought about performing. I never thought at all.

Later, she brought me a glass of water. Covered by the blanket, I watched her bring it to the bed. And drank.

'You're uncharacteristically silent,' she said.

'Yes?' I shook my head and smiled. 'Nothing to say fits the enormity of the occasion.'

She gave this a smirk and lifted the blanket a bit. 'Enormity, you say?'

'That's terrible,' I said, with a laugh.

'You raised it,'

'Much worse!'

'You'd like to be serious,' she said, leaning back.

'You don't do serious?'

She shrugged.

'Keep it light, you think?'

'Don't you?' she said.

'Me?' I said. 'One exception, which now appears to be over.'

'Your wife?'

'Former . . . wife.'

'Ah,' she said.

'And you?'

'Hmm. We're now talking about ourselves?'

'We are,' I said.

'I haven't had such a relationship, as it happens. Serious relationship.'

'Never?'

She shook her head.

'You do give off an aura of independence.'

'That's me,' she said off-handedly.

'Family?'

'None to speak of.'

'And no present guys,' I said.

'Just hasn't come my way. I enjoy sex, as you probably just noticed. But . . .'

'Love 'em and leave 'em?'

'Put you off?'

'Not at all,' I said.

She laughed.

We fell into silence.

'Nice Sunday,' she said.

'Nice Sunday.'

'This is not meant to be a challenge,' she said, 'but you want to sleep here? The alarm goes off at five thirty.'

'I'll take off.'

She looked at me askance. 'I'm not pushing you out the door, Rick. I mentioned the time only because most guys don't like to get up that early.'

'It's my normal hour.'

'Is it? Then stay. We'll just sleep. No demands on your . . .' She removed the cover entirely, took a closer look at me and laughed. 'I misread the situation.'

I took a deep breath. 'Amazing, isn't it?'

'I don't know about that, but it is rather conspicuous.'

'Hardly *my* M.O. It's you.'

'I should hope so!' she said, getting close again. 'Seeing that I'm the only other person in this room.'

The Sixth Victim

Jane Hentchoff's Westport house comprised the spoils of her third divorce. It occupied the last of three lots on a street dead-ending at an inlet to Long Island Sound. If she stayed there on a Monday night, especially in the fall, the street was usually deserted. It scared the hell out of her, but she often stayed anyway. She told her office, 'I'm working from Westport.' Then cowered in her bed at night listening to the house creak and the buoys jangle, while she read the evening emails.

She thought of this fear as a weakness. 'So I'm here alone, so what?' she would tell her friends. 'There's nothing here worth stealing. And no burglar wants me. I'm past my prime, six feet tall, and have a jaw that juts out like a box at the opera.' And everyone would laugh. Most loudly Jane, until the sun went down, when she was in bed alone, and the house started creaking.

Everything got better, actually, when she turned off the light – those minutes before drifting to sleep, listening to the wind, the current lapping against the sea wall. And with a high wind that Monday, she expected to hear the house creak and moan.

Not, however, a sharp groaning sag in the floor joists in the upstairs hall. A sound made unmistakably by a footstep. The step of a man. The man with a gun looming in her bedroom doorway.

Who seated himself calmly on her bed.

She began sobbing. He grabbed her hair and said, twisting it, 'Crying won't help anything, you understand that?'

She gulped air, as if having spasms, and he rose to turn on a lamp.

'What's amazing,' he said, resettling himself on the bed, 'is how women at your elevated level – women in *control*, boss-women, women of arrogance – turn into frightened little children. Their will breaks very quickly. Just show them a gun, or a sharp knife. They'll do anything, say anything. Are you like that, Jane?'

'Yes.'

'I thought so.'

'Why me?' she shrieked.

'You can scream all you like,' he said. 'With the wind outside . . .'

'*Why me?*'

'Get out of bed, Jane.'

He pulled back slightly to give her room to get up. She didn't move. He showed her the handgun, holding it out in his palm as if he were a jeweler displaying a brooch. She started whimpering again, lurching out of the bed in short jerky movements. While he watched, she stood barefoot in her pyjamas on the deep pile rug, her mouth silently pleading.

'Now, I'm going to need you to take your pyjamas off.'

She started crying again.

'Jane, I've told you. It won't do any good.'

'I'm forty-seven.'

'This is not about sex, Jane. You're being punished.'

'*Punished?*'

'I said, take it off, Jane.' He aimed the pistol at her belly, and she hastily unbuttoned her top.

'What for? What have I ever done to you?'

'You personally?' he said, wagging the gun at her. 'Nothing. All right, very good. Now the bottoms. I'm going to have to hurt you, but if you do what I say – excellent. Now turn around and bend over. If you do what I say, I *will* let you live.'

TWENTY-TWO

The week started badly. By Wednesday I thought it could not get much worse. I missed calls I wanted, from Betsy. Had plenty of calls I didn't want, from pitchmen, live and recorded. Had lunches with friends in other firms who hadn't heard I'd left a job I'd barely begun. Couldn't understand why I had; couldn't understand why, if I had, I wasn't going back to my old firm.

There were no openings in their firms. Nor interest in me. Certainly not for what I'd been used to doing, and earning. At that moment, I couldn't assure anyone I'd stay out of prison, much less rainmake for an entourage. Had I just stepped down as District Attorney, after one or two terms of even reasonably favorable press, I wouldn't have had to give assurances of anything. Offers would have teemed from the heavens. Everyone would have just assumed I'd generate business. Well, it obviously wasn't happening that way. On the road to glory and riches, I'd taken a skid on my ass.

So now I started panicking about money. With the next round of bills, I'd be broke. I'd known this, been worrying about it, but hadn't quite reached the panic stage. I'd been assuming things would move faster. Or that some job offer would materialize. The reaction of friends was a wake up. Not just the lack of openings; the queasy look on their faces about the ambiguity of my situation.

The surprising development was that no one seemed to have the facts. Nobody, I'm sure, believed the line that Seaton's flacks had put out, that I'd simply left to pursue other interests. But no rumors seemed to be floating around either. No news items had appeared, or even the page six kind of innuendo. Whoever had leaked to Roger Hazzard was not likely to have drawn the line at the press. Could it be that the libel lawyers were putting a lid on it? They wouldn't, I knew, if there were any basis at all on which to ride the story.

Then I got careless.

What set me up was the story in Wednesday's press. Another rape, another powerful woman. I learned later that day who it was: Jane Hentchoff, PR guru, head of her own firm. Known as Calamity Jane because of her specialty, which was damage control. And, of course, I knew her, had stayed in her house in Westport, had twice been in her apartment for dinner, was familiar with her routine.

I acknowledged as much to Chacon, who called that afternoon. He asked me whether I knew a woman by that name, and it was evident she'd been the victim. He asked me to come downtown to his office. I said I'd be glad to. He suggested, maybe, I'd want to have a lawyer join me. I said, 'Look, Vincente, I keep telling you. To associate me with these crimes is some sort of bad twisted joke. I do not need a lawyer.'

At One Police Plaza, on the fourteenth floor, which housed Chacon's department, Betsy was standing at her glass cubicle, apparently waiting for me to emerge from the elevator. Others were engaged, doing their jobs, or preparing to leave for the day. She gave me a funny look, as if she'd wanted to say something but couldn't. As if she felt under wraps. And as if she wasn't quite sure anymore whether to trust me. Then her eyes lowered, making clear that the last thing she wanted was for me to approach her. It should have been a warning. I should have had a lawyer. Relying solely on your own innocence is stupid. Being a lawyer myself, I should have known that.

Chacon's office had a window and interior glass walls; only his, unlike Betsy's, went to the ceiling and had blinds he could close. They were shut when I went in. He didn't rise from his desk but beckoned me to take the chair facing it. A pretty dark-haired wife and three kids were what I made out from the photographs.

'So. Rick.' Warm smile. We were still on a first name basis, it appeared. Only fair. I'd been calling him Vincente. 'You have something, maybe, you want to tell me?'

A laugh burst from me. 'You've read *Crime and Punishment*, right?'

'Of course.'

'I am not Raskolnikov,' I said.

'And I,' he said, 'am not nearly as clever as the inspector in that book, whose name . . .?' He looked upward. 'I have it! Porfiry Petrovich, eh? But I do have more to go on.'

'Really?'

'Yes. Sorry. I do.'

'Which you will share with me, in the fullness of time?'

'Something new, Rick. Your doorman, Luis, whose language I speak. He tells me you left your building Monday night at approximately nine fifteen and did not return by the time he'd gone home, which was shortly past midnight. Can you account for your actions?'

I said as calmly as I could, against the rage that was rising, 'Luis is mistaken. And this – unaccountably – is the second time. I did not go out Monday night. I was home alone. I watched a movie.'

'I see.'

'I assume you've also talked to the guy on the Tuesday morning shift – who was it? Hector. Who should have told you he did not see me come in, but did see me go out that morning at about six thirty in my running shorts.'

Chacon let out an exasperated breath. 'There's a back entrance to the building. Apartment owners have keys.'

'Then why didn't I use it when I supposedly left the building Monday night?'

'Good question,' he said, rising to catch a beam of sun at the window. 'What's the answer? Maybe you want to tell me. Maybe, when you went out, you had a different destination? This woman was an afterthought? Some sudden urge you couldn't control?'

What I couldn't control any longer was my anger. 'Another five minutes of this, I'm going to lose my fucking mind. You are now officially harassing me!'

I got a big shrug with facial movement to match, a very Latino gesture. Which, in other circumstances, would have made me like this man. 'Luis has no motive to lie,' he offered.

'Really?' I said. 'Well, I'm beginning to wonder about that. What I know is that Luis *has* lied, or has been mysteriously mistaken. Twice. I've no idea why. I'm sure as hell going to find out.'

He looked a trifle nervous, but it might have been an act. Chacon was more subtle than I'd first given him credit for. 'I'm sure it's unnecessary to caution you,' he said.

'Quite.'

The slant of sun was extinguished. Chacon sat down. 'I'm afraid we're going to have to ask you to participate in another line-up.'

'Oh, shit.'

'I didn't think you'd care for the idea,' he said.

'Forget it. I'm not doing it.'

'We have enough to charge you already, Rick. I'm trying to avoid that.'

'Vincente, first rule. Don't try to bullshit a bullshitter. You have nothing. Even if I'd gone out Monday night – which I didn't – whatta you think? Two million other guys in Manhattan did too? So that's what you got, at best, a one in two million shot. To go with a ski mask, also owned by thousands of others. To go with the lies of a doorman whom I barely know but, for some reason I'll soon get to the bottom of, is trying to frame me. And you got this flaky line-up procedure you guys use, which is notorious.'

'We can force you to participate. As I think you know.'

'You've finally done it, Vincente. Made me spend money on this. I'm hiring a lawyer.'

'Good idea, Rick. There's even a better one.'

My laugh was bitter. 'Confess to crimes I haven't committed?'

'Y'know,' he said. 'I'm reading this case study. Just picked it up. Some man, a prominent doctor, it seems—' He interrupted himself with a laugh. 'Real Jack the Ripper story with a touch of Jekyll and Hyde. Except this doctor didn't know what he was doing, killing prostitutes. He had a colleague testify at trial about his delusions. And how confession under psychoanalysis had transformed him. It was the colleague, an early Freudian, who wrote the study. But the point is—'

'I know the point.'

'Yes? You've read this study?'

'Vincente,' I said getting up. 'Are you charging me?'

He remained seated, reflecting. 'I figured, first let the man get a lawyer. The lawyer will advise him to cooperate. Then, we'll see.'

'That's what I thought. You're not charging me. So, I'll find my way out.'

From behind the desk, he gave me a look meant to be sympathetic.

I said, 'If you're not guilty, you don't confess. False confession doesn't make you feel good. Makes you feel bad. Only crazy people confess to things they haven't done. I'm not crazy. Am I communicating?'

I got a small dismissive wave.

On the way to the elevators, I looked at Betsy's cubicle. It was empty. I glanced around the floor. Cops still working. She was nowhere to be seen.

On exiting the building, my life changed again. Not for the better. One flashbulb, then another. A single photographer, young guy with a beard. He took off like an antelope. I thought of running after him and smashing the camera; then realized, with a stab, I wasn't any longer fast enough to catch him. I really hadn't thought Chacon would have stooped this low.

TWENTY-THREE

I called Nona from my cab, heading toward the FDR Drive. She got Joe Stein on the phone. They agreed to see me as soon as I could get there.

I knew Joe at college. We were both on the track team. I'd always liked him, though we'd never been close friends. Different track events usually attract different temperaments. I was a sprinter, in a manner of speaking. What the coach referred to as a 'pork chop'; someone who got to eat at the training table but rarely won a race. Joe ran the long distances, two and three miles. He didn't distinguish himself at that either. But, in the fall, he ran cross-country. At that he ranked best in the East, and was elected captain of the cross-country team.

He hadn't changed much. Short narrow frame, bullet head, snub nose, elfin ears. My age, but he looked ten years younger. In shirtsleeves, butt against the front of his desk, rocking as he talked, he might have popped in from a workout. Nona, who knew most of the story from Carter, had already briefed him. I filled in more details, including the meeting I'd just had with Chacon.

'It's an old trick,' Joe said, 'sign of desperation. They have videotape on this guy, and they still can't bring him in. The press is beginning to hound 'em. So they put the pressure on you; if you're the guy, maybe you'll crack. Confess, run, do something stupid. If not, maybe the real guy'll get careless, thinking they're nailing you. Fucking feeble. They know it. That's why I say it shows they have nothing, they're running scared.'

'So what's my play?' I asked. 'I'd be calling Jane Hentchoff right now, if she weren't the victim.'

'Right. That's the first move. Damage control. Sully's better, though. Anyway.'

'Patrick Joseph Sullivan?'

'You know him?'

I shook my head.

'Sully and me,' he said, 'we've been through, what? Four, five wars together. He'll do it. He loves this sort of thing. Guy getting fucked over by the authorities.'

'So let's call him.'

'I'll feed him,' Joe said.

'You don't want me to talk to him?'

'Not yet.'

There might have been good reasons. You either trust someone or you don't. 'All right,' I said. Then thought some more. 'What about the line-up?'

'Forget it,' he said. 'There won't be one.'

I gave him a questioning look, and turned to Nona who seemed as clueless as I.

'It's Chacon's way,' said Joe. 'Not a bad guy, but he likes to push people's buttons. Tell you one thing, do another. Besides, it'd be pointless. They've already fucked up their identification proof for your case. He just wants to add to the pressure. Make you think he's tightening the noose.'

'And there ain't no noose, baby,' said Nona, fist pumping the air. 'We're going to show that. You've come to the right place.'

I smiled at her. 'What about Luis?'

'Let me talk to him,' said Joe.

'You want me to say nothing? Even if he's there tonight?'

'Yeah. You OK with that?'

We were still having a kind of standing meeting, with Joe leaning back against the edge of his desk, me braced against the conference table, and Nona at ease between us. I had no question but that she was on my side and believed me. Joe was one of the few – maybe the only – criminal defense lawyers doing high-profile cases who was not himself high profile. Or, by reputation, high maintenance. I thought, I'm probably in the best place I can be.

'All right,' I said. 'I'll get out of here and let you guys do your job.'

I had never thought about it before – I'd never had reason to – but I did going down in the elevator: how hard it was for a trial lawyer like me to give himself over to another practitioner, even one as good as Joe Stein.

At home, I called Ali, having debated it on the ride uptown.

'Look,' I said, 'tomorrow's press'll have a story on me.'

She could tell what kind from my tone. 'Oh, shit,' she said.

'I'm afraid I got teed up for a photographer.'

'Molly,' she said, with a gasp.

'That's why I'm calling. It was either ruining your sleep tonight, or giving you a bad shock in the morning. Or, even worse, missing you before the kids went to school.'

'Rick, this must be unbearably awful for you.'

'I'm not happy. I've retained Joe Stein. He's getting P. J. Sullivan to maybe take the edge off. Warn Molly and even Sam, someone's telling lies about their dad, not to believe them. You'll do that?'

'Of course.'

'Good girl.'

'Darling, I *wish* I could do more.' Her voice hung over that statement as if she might add to it.

Only my imagination.

'Night, Ali,' I said. 'It's OK.'

Don't *wish*, I thought, hanging up. Just do.

TWENTY-FOUR

T en o'clock that night. Betsy on the phone, and it was her
quarter – literally, since she was calling from a booth. I
assumed she shared Frank Seaton's phobia of cell phones.
'I'm in the bar,' was all she said. I said, 'I'll be there in ten
minutes.' It took, maybe, twelve.

Seated straight up on a barstool, she glanced at her watch.
'What took you so long?'

'Had to flag down a cab. Seems our night doorman didn't
show up.'

'Luis?'

'You remember him?' I said, taking the next stool and
registering the oddness of her outfit: oversized aquamarine
cashmere top, black work out tights and several ropes of
splashy costume jewelry necklaces. I might have thought,
dance class, but for the necklaces, but then thought of ball-
players with their chains.

'Of course,' she said.

'Seems also Chacon's been talking to him.'

'So I gather,' she said.

'You know where Luis is?'

'No.'

'What was that look you gave me this afternoon when I got
out of the elevator?'

'Mixed emotions look.'

'Anything in the mix spring from suspicion?'

'If it did, you think I'd have called you tonight?'

I said. 'You know about the photographer?'

'*Now* I know about the photographer. *Then* I didn't.'

'Or you would have warned me.' I made it sound like a
statement, but it was a question nonetheless.

She hesitated. 'Probably. Because I think that's dirty.'

'Good word. This kind of dirt? How long you think it takes to rub off?'

'When we catch the guy—'

'*When*? You mean *if*, right? How many guys – how many hundreds of guys don't you catch? I seem to recall your saying something like that.'

She studied her half-empty glass. 'The repeaters we catch. The more they do it, the more mistakes they make, the more pressure we get. It helps, not surprisingly. People, resources. Goosing up the priorities. Helps a lot.'

I looked around the bar, the vacant seats, the blue lights, the ancient phone booth. 'You get the papers in the morning?'

'Ah,' she said. 'You want the funnies read.'

'I don't expect them to be that amusing.'

'No.' Her eyes clouded for a second. 'Chacon can be a real prick.'

'Well, we'll see in the morning.' I started to get up.

'No drink?'

'Among the options available to us right now, booze ranks a very poor second.'

'Rick . . .' Her laugh was a bit sharp. 'I wasn't going to call you tonight.'

'Glad you did.'

'Yes?'

'Yes,' I said, and thought about saying more. Like how getting her call almost salvaged the day.

'You're a sweet guy.'

I never know how to respond to a statement like that.

She smiled. 'You said you wanted to be my friend. I think you actually meant it. That you'd have my back.' Then, softly, 'You give off those vibes, Rick. You probably don't even know it.'

'This is why you almost didn't call me?'

'How much more do you want to be?' she said.

'You're warning me again.'

'Yes.'

'Not necessary.'

'You know what I've learned in my job?' she said. 'Or maybe

re-learned, because it's so fucking obvious? Abused people abuse people. No exceptions.'

If maybe now I understood her, I still didn't know what to say.

She put her hand to my cheek. 'Just remember. I've told you. I'm a very uphill person.'

Second time, same woman, is always more interesting, uphill or down. What she likes, and doesn't, is better defined. Betsy's pride was her spectacular body. So she had the right acolyte in me. But first we played.

Her games. The way she grabbed my wrists on the bed, I expected ropes, silk ties, even handcuffs. None needed. She didn't want my hands in play for a while? Great. I kept them over my head. Then she wanted to push me down on my back, lean over me, dangling that necklace in my face. Fine. Her cashmere sweater flew up her arms, her sports bra trailing it. I would have followed her anywhere, but she liked this position, heels of her hands digging into my shoulders, her ass squeezing my belly.

'You do massage?' she said.

'Sure.'

She rolled off, flopped down, on her belly. 'Lower back.'

I went under her shoulder blades.

'Lower,' she said.

Small of her back.

'*Lower!*'

'There's the pants thing,' I said.

'Band's elastic,' she said.

'And that cotton thing?' I said, tugging down on the pants.

'Comes off too.'

It turned serious, eventually. With the wrestling. Betsy liked wrestling, because she was good at it. And I was being so careful not to hurt her. I needn't have worried. She was trained at it, and it excited her to win. With me, the pressure of bodies was enough. Her breath in the hollow of my neck was enough. But she gave me no reason to doubt her warning. For her, arousal and release were serious matters. Everything else was play. Post-coitus, she wrapped herself in my arms like a baby.

And that's how we slept. Until the alarm went off – as promised – at five thirty. I got a big morning-mouth kiss. She sashayed around with nothing on, while putting up the beginnings of a breakfast. We showered together, soaped up real good, kissed, fooled around. I felt, one minute, this could last; then, the next, I'm being used somehow. Despite her warning, which applied to both possibilities. And then I thought, I'm over-thinking this. Take joy in the present, I reasoned, and joyous expectation of whatever we might do next.

Except read the newspapers, which arrived at six twenty.

As agreed, Betsy opened them. 'Not that bad,' was her first reaction. Then, 'You have a flack on this?'

'Sullivan.'

'You owe him,' she said.

As for the *Times,* my photo appeared on the second page of the Metro. The story came out as a confusion of 'conflicting reports.' On the one hand, I'm a suspect, according to a 'high-level source.' On the other hand, there's this hint I might be assisting the investigation. Why I'd left the post as Chief Assistant in the first place was a question left hanging, and that spin wasn't great. Stories in the other papers looked like clones of the *Times,* or vice versa. It could have been worse. Without Sullivan, it doubtless would have been. But there was a tar smear all over me. I couldn't get clients now, much less a job.

Strange, one's reaction to calamity. Takes a while to hit. People work more for respect than for money. I'd just lost whatever respect I'd had and spent almost fifteen years trying to build. Then I understood why I wasn't feeling more. The shock was so huge I couldn't feel the devastation. I couldn't feel anything.

When I put the last paper down, Betsy said, 'Six months from now—'

'Don't,' I said.

'You're right,' she said. 'This really sucks.'

We sat at a plain birch table in the kitchen/dining area of her apartment. I was thinking out loud. 'The creeps who do this, rape women, the serial rapists? Is there some common profile, beyond the obvious?'

'What's obvious?'

'Hatred of women. Which I suppose comes from how they feel about their mothers. So is there?'

Her look was suspicious. 'Why?'

'Why do you think? I'm talking to an expert. I want to know.'

'They're usually under fifty. Shitty self-esteem. They enjoy their own press. Get off on it, actually.'

'That's it?'

Long look. 'Most of them suffer erectile dysfunction.'

Shouldn't have surprised me, but it did.

She said, 'Under normal circumstances, Rick, they can't get it up.'

I let it go, her asperity. 'Any psychiatrist you know of who specializes in sexual rage? Anything like that?'

'OK, Rick, what the hell's in your mind?'

'You know of any such shrink?'

'I don't. Answer my question, please.'

'Can you find out for me?'

'The animals who do this don't go to psychiatrists. Especially the kind of shrink you're talking about.'

'This guy, Betsy, is different. With all due respect. His selection of victims is pretty goddamn sophisticated.'

'I realize that. But every one of these women had a story about her in the press.'

'Even so,' I said. 'Picking names out of newspapers – not your average subway stalker. The kind of guy who would do that might be looking for help.'

'Doubtful.'

'It's a good enough lead for me.'

'So what are you doing now?' she said. 'Joining the investigation?'

'I've got lots of time. Can you think of anything better I might do with it?'

'Forget it,' she said. 'You're not trained. You'd get in the way. Sorry, but that's the fact. And you could damn well get yourself hurt.'

'Are there any self-help groups? Twelve-step things?'

She didn't answer.

'So,' I said. 'What's it called?'

'Sexaholics,' she said.

'Where do they meet?'

'I'm not going to be a party to this,' she said.

'I'm not asking you to come to meetings. Although . . .'

I caught her arm heading at me.

'Darling,' she said. 'I'm serious. I am. Stay away from the investigation. If the Department can't get this guy, you're not going to be able to. I know you're a good lawyer, but you don't have the resources, you don't have the skills, the experience—'

'How about the motivation?'

'Yes. You have that.'

'And your help? Which is all the additional resource I need.'

'You'd get me fired.'

'I'd try not to,' I said.

'How comforting.'

'Best I can honestly do. You in?'

Deep breath. All kinds of body language. 'I'll think about it.'

'Let me know. I'm starting this morning.'

She must have thought about it fast. What I got from her was a warning, reckless of her to have given.

I'd returned to my apartment, called the building management company to learn they still hadn't heard from Luis, and was half way out the door when the phone rang.

Betsy. At the high end of her range of agitation. 'I'm on a pay phone. They're getting a warrant for your arrest. Hentchoff's told Chacon you're the perp. *She* called him. I'm not even supposed to know about it. Chacon doesn't know I know, which is how I could tell you. I learned by accident. Call your lawyer, now.'

'Hentchoff. Jesus Christ!'

'Rick, you hearing me?'

'Jane Hentchoff, I can't believe this. I haven't seen the woman in months.'

'Rick, I said call your lawyer!'

'I'm taking off.'

'You're *what*? You know better.' She waited a beat. 'Rick?'

I said nothing.

'Rick?' She waited another beat before yelling. 'You're not fucking serious!'

'It's gotten too bizarre.'

'Flight is the absolutely worst thing you can do!'

'Betsy, I'll never forget that you made this call. Never. Really. But I've got no fucking choice.'

TWENTY-FIVE

I had about four hundred dollars stashed in my apartment. I threw the money, my keys, some clothes and my cell phone into a gym bag and made my way to the Chase branch on Broadway. No lines this early; cashing a three thousand dollar check, which pretty much drained my account, took only minutes. I knew what fleeing would look like. The alternative, however, was waiting around to be arrested, being put through the system, being stopped from tracking the guy whose atrocities were being pinned on me. And if I stayed, fought the charge, got an acquittal – then what? Live the rest of my life as the guy who beat the rape rap?

It was not until I hopped on a train in the PATH tubes that I felt the full measure of what was happening. Never in my life had I imagined I'd be a fugitive. There were actually people out there bent on hunting me down, authorized to do it, determined to lock me up. By now, the press had probably been alerted. Visualizing the effects was almost as injurious as the damage these people wanted to do to me. This wasn't who I was. Yet in the dark reflection of the train window I saw the look of the man I'd become. Virtually everyone I knew would now think of me as a vicious criminal. For a moment I felt like one.

But only for a moment. In the next I got angrier than I'd ever been. Almost put my fist through that window in rage. It was no accident I was being hunted. I'd known this for days but had tried to rationalize it as paranoia. Someone was impersonating me – mimicking my walk, gestures, whatever. It was easy enough to understand why someone who liked raping women would want to cast blame on somebody else. But picking me was not likely to have been random.

On the outskirts of Newark, built on wet ground, there was a four-story cinder-block motel offering a view out front of a dump yard: mountainously stacked trailer truck containers and silos of used auto tires. From the rear of this structure the view was more filmic: rows of electrical wire towers studding miles of New Jersey swamps. I chose a room in the front. It was not a decision based on the scenery. I wanted to spot any cop car that pulled into the driveway for something other than the monthly bribe. I had to assume someone was being bribed to allow this establishment to operate. It was the sort of place where the terminally bored desk clerk, encased in a bullet-proof plastic bubble, takes cash through a slot from the johns signing in as Dick Tracy or Mickey Mouse.

The fourth floor room was dark and smelled of road fumes, smoked cigarettes and Chinese take-out. I'd paid for AC and TV. Both, surprisingly, worked. Before leaving Broad Street in Newark I'd bought some cheap clothes at an Army-Navy and a popular men's hair dye product. The bathroom was barely large enough to turn around in but was tiled and had a functioning sink. I stripped down, read the instructions on the package and did what I had to do to turn my sandy hair dark brown. While waiting for the dye to work, I tuned in CNN, sat on a coarse plaid bedspread and waited for my reputation to turn to shit.

It didn't take long. I was staring at my altered appearance in the bathroom mirror when I first heard my name on the tube. Then I heard it repeatedly. Then, flipping channels, found it was everywhere. Old photos of myself leaped on to the screen. Pictures of my family – where the hell did they get those? Details of my divorce. Even a video clip of an oral argument I'd once made to a federal court in Washington and another of a Court TV interview. The media liked this story, and it burgeoned through the day. Not surprising; it had everything. Guy touted to be the next DA, now a fugitive rapist. Big shot, shot down. Secret life. Sadistic sex. For TV news, it was the gift that kept on giving.

I knew what this story would do to Molly and Sam. Nothing cut me as deeply.

I had to put my head between my legs so I wouldn't pass out, then reason with myself. I'd bolted as a matter of pride, the idea being I could find this guy better and faster than those trained and paid to do it. So get on with it, I thought. Get the fuck on with it. I picked up the phone book and called a cab.

TWENTY-SIX

I knew more than her name, I'd had access to the computer file. It was an odd name, Diane Nethersong. I knew her phone number and address. I knew she was still on leave of absence from Goldman Sachs. When I got back into Newark, I dialed her home from a pay phone. She was the reason I'd come to New Jersey. After the first three rings hope dwindled. By the fifth it vanished. On the sixth, someone picked up.

'Miss Nethersong?'

Long silence. 'Tell me who's calling,' said a woman's voice.

'My name's Eric Corinth.'

'Yes?'

'Until very recently, I've been Chief Assistant District Attorney in Manhattan.'

'I know who you are.'

I hesitated. 'Then you know what I'm being accused of.'

'It wasn't you,' she said.

I'd have felt more jubilation if Doris, at first, hadn't said the same thing.

'I've been watching the news,' she said. 'I know they've got the wrong man.'

'Would you talk to me? Meet me somewhere?'

She hesitated. 'I can see why you'd want to.'

'Would you, then?'

An even longer pause. 'I'm sorry,' she said. And hung up.

She owned a brownstone in a gentrified section of Hoboken. I buzzed, then waited at the front door. Braced myself for being jumped by five cops brandishing handguns. Out of desperation, I'd assumed the risk.

The door opened, and my relief was damn near overwhelming. Not a policeman in sight. Rather, a wiry young woman with a lovely, small, poised, mostly serious face, hair frizzled in a thick wheat-colored maze around her temples. And dark blue eyes. It's not a feature I normally notice, eye color. But her stance, scared and vulnerable in her gray sweatshirt and green satin gym shorts, with the grayness of sky and shirt somehow deepening that blue, made the image indelible.

I realized it almost immediately. This beautiful young woman was my physical ideal. So now everything's surreal, I thought, including the irony. My life's going to hell in a handbasket, and I'm suddenly meeting great-looking women. It hadn't occurred to me yet that the connection wasn't accidental.

I held on to the door, and she wasn't quite strong enough to push it closed.

'A minute, please,' I said. 'Two at most. Outside'd be great. On the stoop. Anywhere. Please, just talk to me.'

She looked up and down the block. There were people in evidence, although they were walking elsewhere. She eased out tentatively and rested – alighted, one might say – on the top step as if she might fly away if I moved. I sat down slowly across from her.

'Thank you,' I said.

She didn't relax.

'I've two young children,' I said.

She glanced at the street again. Rows of parked cars; no one in sight.

'You may be the only person in the world right now who could help me avoid hurting them or—'

'I'll tell them,' she said, rising. 'The cops. I will. But I'm sorry. I'm going inside now. Alone.'

Door slammed, hope lost. Within seconds I blacked out.

TWENTY-SEVEN

I t was night. I was freezing. The wind whipped my face, the part of it not pressed to the mud. It felt like mud. It was too dark to know for sure what it was.

Someone was tugging my arm. 'Eric?'

'Rick,' I said, automatically, and then rolled over. I saw Diane Nethersong in a sweatshirt and jeans, her hair blowing every which way.

'Why are you in my backyard?' she asked.

I hadn't the slightest idea where I was, and my look must have said so.

'You're covered in blood,' she said. 'Your face, your hands.'

I could see now; backyard it was.

'You're still on the news,' she said. 'They've found your stuff at the motel.'

I sat up, and began to wake up.

'You're shivering,' she said.

I nodded, shivering more.

Then she stunned me.

'You'd better come in for a minute,' she said. Her lips were tight, as if she had forced herself to say those words.

Perched on the toilet lid in her upstairs bathroom, I'm thinking: *What the hell am I doing here?* Diane, standing, wielding a washcloth, swabbed the blood and mud off my face. 'Scrapes,' she said. 'Nothing deep.'

I'm noticing things about her. Small wrists, slender neck, wisps of light hair on a slender right arm as her sweatshirt sleeve rides up it.

I looked up to her eyes. 'What happened? To change your mind about . . .?' My fingertips waved between me and her upstairs hallway.

'Why did I let you in?'

'Yeah.'

She shrugged. 'You passed out on my stoop. I went upstairs to call nine one one. When I looked out the window again, you'd disappeared.'

'I have this condition . . .'

'You black out.'

Her knowing this confused me.

'It was on the news,' she said, spreading Bacitracin over the raw spots on my face. 'That you do that. They seem to know a great deal about you. But to get into my backyard? You had to get to the corner and climb two brick walls. They're not that high, but, for someone who'd passed out . . .'

I gave a low laugh. 'Until recently, I would have sworn, when this hits me – when I black out – I stay put. Absolutely inert. Wherever I land.'

She put the tube back in the medicine cabinet and, with those deep blue eyes, gave me a long, slow look of appraisal. 'You can have a sandwich,' she said.

Another shocker.

I thanked her, following her downstairs, no less bewildered. On the way to the kitchen I had a better look at the house. There was a theme, Americana: early American furniture, quilts on the walls, a lovely eighteenth century portrait that, by my standards, could hang in a museum. What was she – thirty-one, thirty-two? Impressive. On a hall table, there was a model of an old proscenium stage. It was elaborately wrought with fly lines and pulleys and a real curtain.

What was I doing here?

'So, you were asking . . .' she said, working ham and cheese slices on to a roll. I sat on a high stool at a kitchen island. Her hands were shaky, passing me the plate. It was warm in the kitchen, and she hoisted the sweatshirt over her head. The tank top she wore under it rose and fell with the move, briefly exposing a flat tummy with abs. She started to say something, then stopped. I continued to have the impression she was pushing herself, forcing herself to speak to me.

'You don't have to—' I began.

She cut in, impatiently dropping the sweatshirt on the island counter. 'The real question is, why did I take your phone call in the first place? I haven't been answering the damn thing.

I've been screening. Somehow the machine got screwed up. And somehow . . .'

I took a big bite of the sandwich.

'Intuition?' I said, in a muffled voice. Famished as I was, the ham, cheese and mustard each sent a different, sharp, exhilarating sensation to my brain.

'You know,' she said, 'I don't believe in that.'

'Who would?' I said, going for another bite.

'I'm a real hard head. B School. *The* B School.'

'Harvard.'

'That's what I said. Then Goldman. Eight years. I deal in numbers. Economic realities.'

'Only way to go,' I said with a smile.

'So, why'd I pick up that phone?'

'I don't know,' I said. 'But there's an even more important question. At least to me. Sorry.'

'Why I'm so sure you're not the guy?' She pressed her lips together. 'Here I'm going to disappoint you.'

'You don't know why. Also a mystery.'

'Right.'

'What you don't believe in, maybe? Intuition?'

She shrugged and crossed her arms.

'I don't believe in it either,' I said. 'There had to be something for you to operate on. Something in my voice, maybe?'

'Couldn't be the voice,' she said.

'He had one of those . . . electronic—'

'Things, right.' She shivered, grabbed the sweatshirt and wrapped her arms around it hard.

'And now that you see me?' I said. 'In person?'

'No way you're him.'

She climbed on to a stool the other side of the island, the sweatshirt now bunched in her lap. She crossed her legs, put on a show of being comfortable. I kept thinking, how can this be happening? The woman everyone else is accusing me of attacking is feeding me sandwiches.

'The guy who thinks otherwise,' I said, 'is a cop named Chacon.'

'He's called me,' she said. 'He wanted to come here.'

'You refused to see him?'

'I told him, not now. Not yet. Maybe in a few weeks.'

'Yet,' I said, slowly, 'you were willing to dredge me up out of your garden.'

'Yes.' She paused. 'The fact is, I regretted sending you away.'

'Did you?' She'd surprised me again. 'Why?'

My look inquired further; hers said, not yet. I asked whether she had noticed anything about the attacker's walk, whether he had that slightly one-sided tilt I'd apparently developed. She hadn't noticed. I asked whether she'd seen his hands.

Her face tensed. 'He had gloves on,' she said.

I knew his routine. I'd seen the video.

She said, with a sudden sharpness, 'Before he did to me what he wished to do . . . with his bare hands . . . he taped my eyes.' As he'd done with the other women.

'Look,' I said, 'I'm really sorry—'

She broke in. 'We're both victims.'

'Yes.' I thought, how many women in her situation would empathize with a guy in mine? I didn't know any.

She said, 'It's what I realized when I sent you away.'

'Thank you. For that. And for rescuing me from your garden.' Which sounded terribly inadequate. 'If I could find the words—'

'You don't have to. The fact is . . . it wasn't easy for me to go out there. It isn't now.'

'I understand. And I'll leave in a minute, with everlasting gratitude.'

'Finish your sandwich.'

'Thank you,' I said again. 'One more thing I should mention. He picked us both. So, quite possibly, we both know him. In fact, I may have met him after you did. Because in every other instance, he made sure the woman would remember the way he walked. So she would identify *me*.'

I told her about the other victims: Cassenov, Lambeth, Delfine, Strickland and Hentchoff. She knew none of them.

'Where are you going now?' she asked.

'I'll find another motel, some flophouse I can walk to.'

'First kind of place they'll look,' she said. 'Why don't you buy a car and drive West? Get lost somewhere in America?'

'I don't want to get lost. I want my life back. I want to find out who this guy is, and I don't trust the cops to do that. For the obvious reason that they think they already have.'

She thought about that, her face showing strain, as she waged an internal argument. Finally, she tossed the sweatshirt back on to the island top. 'OK,' she said. 'Then you can stay here.'

'What?' I thought I hadn't heard her right.

'Yeah, it makes sense,' she said, reasoning further with herself.

'Diane—'

'From a number of standpoints,' she said. 'Yours, certainly. It's a perfect hiding place, for one thing. They'd never dream you'd be here. And if you want to get back into the city, they'll have everything covered: buses, trains, bridges, tunnels. You'll need someone to drive you. In the back seat of a car, like a package under a blanket, or on the floor would be better.'

I looked at her in wonder. 'Why?' I said still not believing my ears.

'Because you're the one guy in the world right now who's as angry at this prick as I am. Because I need to have somebody else in this house. Because I can't eat and don't sleep at night; I get maybe five hours in the middle of the day. Except today, when I spent hours watching clips of you, and now I think I know you. Because I don't want you caught. Because I also don't trust the police to find him. Because I want you looking for him. Because I feel I can trust you. Kind of. Almost.'

'Why?'

'That thing,' she said. 'That thing I don't believe in.'

TWENTY-EIGHT

Diane – 'Call me Di, rhymes with princess' – gave me a bedroom on the top floor. Spare, dark wood floor, and starkly colonial: rag rugs, single chest, wooden rocking chair, four- poster bed – infinitely better than a flophouse. By the time I awoke, she was gone. A note in the kitchen said, 'Gym. Be back soon. Help yourself to breakfast.' With almost everybody else in the country wanting to tear me apart, this simple note damn near undid me. I stood there in her kitchen

Alan Hruska

in my bare feet and rumpled clothes, feeling her kindness pierce my resentment. Only lasted a moment – but I resolved some day, somehow, to repay this young woman I scarcely knew.

I ate some of her bran flakes, peering at her view of the Hudson from the bay window in the kitchen at the back of her house. Still fall, but the river looked wintry. Ink-black currents. The world was chilly again. At least mine.

I had calls to make. Joe Stein, Betsy. Ali, to whom I really wanted to talk. I wondered whether they'd tapped her phone. And, if they had, would that mean they'd be able to trace my call? Not knowing this rankled, since it was the sort of detail I'd had the opportunity to learn. In any event, after taking a shower and leaving a note for Diane, I wandered out on to the streets of Hoboken, watching out for cops and hunting for a pay phone.

I found one about ten blocks away, at the edge of town near a bus stop. Must have caught Ali as she'd arrived for work.

'Will you accept a collect call from . . .' My voice interjected, 'Blessed Studwell?'

In happier days, such a pseudonym might have gotten a laugh. Ali just accepted the charges.

'Are you all right?' she shot out.

'Yes, darling. I'm OK. I'm doing what I believe I have to do.'

'What's going on, baby?' She was crying.

'I'm not entirely sure, but it's obvious someone who knows me is trying to frame me. And doing a good job of it. But I have some leads. I don't expect this to take forever.'

'*This?* What are you doing? You're trying to catch the guy on your own?'

'I'm the only one looking for the bastard, darling. Everyone else is looking for me.'

'A policeman came to see me.'

'Chacon?'

'Yes.'

'Don't trust him,' I said.

'I won't. But he did say there were aspects of the case that troubled him deeply. That they were keeping their minds open.'

'I'd love to believe it.'

'But you don't.'

'Not a word. How are the kids?'

Big breath. 'OK,' she said.

'Really?'

'Yes.'

'What aren't you telling me?'

'Nothing,' she said. 'Nothing to worry about. Molly fainted again, but she's fine. I took her to the doctor. He says not to get alarmed, it may never happen again, and he'll keep an eye. Sam is fine. At that age they don't really understand what you've been accused of. I told them some nasty snitch had blamed you for doing something you didn't do and you'd straighten it out soon. It's me who's getting the weird reactions. People are treating me like a celebrity.'

I might have laughed at this, if I hadn't been troubled by the news about Molly. 'What a world!'

'Yeah. You wouldn't believe the attention. But baby, are you sure you wouldn't be better off—'

'Giving myself up? Yes.'

'It's dangerous, what you're doing.'

'You think being in prison isn't?'

'You could have gotten out on bail.'

'Maybe. Not so easy arranging bail for violent crimes. And even if I had, it could have taken days, which are critical, plus a huge, crippling loan for the bail money, which I would've ended up forfeiting, leaving the jurisdiction.'

'Oh, Jesus!' She was crying again.

'I've got to go, darling. I'll be fine. Just take care of yourself and the kids. Tell them I love them. And . . .' I hesitated. 'I love you.'

She hesitated longer than I did. 'Me too.'

I hate that locution. It's an ambiguous cop-out. But she'd already hung up.

Diane was back by the time I returned. At the bay window table in the kitchen, with a cup of coffee and the Friday *Times*. Looking fresh-faced and beautiful in an ivory sweater and periwinkle linen shorts. When I helped myself from the coffee-maker, she pushed two packages toward me on the table. Jeans, denim shirt, black tee shirt, socks, boxer shorts.

'Universal outfit,' she said. 'I guessed at the size.'

I glanced at the labels and then, appreciatively, at her.

'And the style of underwear, of course,' she added.

'You're infallible.'

We both drank some coffee.

I said, 'You're being very good to me.'

She gave this a dismissive gesture. 'You see the news this morning?'

'I heard a bit on the radio, why?'

'They're still all over you,' she said.

'I know.'

'Repeats of yesterday mainly. Same clip, cops looking at your gym bag. What a seedy room! So they know you're in New Jersey. Or were. I figured you'd need a change of clothes.'

I looked at her with speechless gratitude.

'Payback for last night's sleep,' she said. 'First time I put six hours together since . . .' She grimaced.

'I'm grateful you feel . . . well, that you can trust me.'

'I don't, you see. Not entirely. That's also kind of the point. I'm making myself do this. Brainwashing myself. You're my ticket to re-entry. I'm frightened of everyone right now. I haven't gone out. I haven't talked to people. Until this morning. The probability that this guy is messing with your mind, like he did with mine, and fucking up your life, somehow makes things easier with you.' She stopped for a moment. 'I'm not sure this is making any sense.'

'Yes, it does.'

'You're like the patch,' she said.

'Against phobia?'

'Right.'

We had a silent moment.

'I noticed the model on your hall table . . .'

'The stage,' she said. 'It's at Bennington. Bennington College.'

'You went there?'

'I even graduated. You needn't look so surprised.'

'No, I—'

'It's written all over your face.' She laughed. 'I'm an actor.'

'Are you?'

'You're thinking, business school, Goldman Sachs, doesn't compute.'

'I'm thinking, actually, what you said last night about intuition.'

'So you know something about this?' she said.

'Well, something. Stella Adler, Sandy Meisner, Lee Strasberg . . . the *method*. It's all about intuition.'

'In England they laugh at that stuff. They think acting is pure technique.'

'And you?' I asked.

'Big subject.'

'But you're no longer . . .'

'Acting?'

'As a career.'

'Bigger subject.'

'Which you'd rather not talk about.'

She shrugged. Because she was doing it to me in the kitchen, I could see how transporting she'd be on the stage. She had this unusual affect: apparent vulnerability and inner strength.

'Another time,' I suggested.

'We'll see,' she said.

TWENTY-NINE

We drove into Manhattan in Diane's Mercedes, parked in the indoor lot at Worldwide Plaza, and strolled down Eighth Avenue. An adult bookshop at Forty-third sold an adult-content newspaper. Sexaholics Anonymous ran an ad in it with a schedule. Meetings were held most nights, including this one at nine o'clock, at the Ninety-Second Street Y. Di and I looked up from perusing the classifieds. Three morose-looking males were perusing us.

We grabbed a cab. I said, riding toward the meeting, 'You don't have to do this. We could meet later.'

'You've got to be kidding,' she said. 'You think I'm here just to chauffeur you around?'

Entering a meeting that had already started, we slipped into two back-row chairs. The room, in the basement, was presumably also used for small theater productions. A man with gray ringlets and granny glasses sat on a stage addressing an audience of about eighteen men and women, mostly middle-aged. The speaker's tone was light, self-deprecating. He was a pedophile. He knew his Nabokov and Balthus. His descriptions of his problem were, in fact, Nabokovian, replete with references to 'dewy lips,' 'split peaches' of bottoms, and so forth. Basically, he liked little girls and had been imprisoned for it twice. He'd lost his family, lost his fortune, done thousands of hours of therapy and rehab to little or no avail. What helped were these meetings.

The audience, including Di and me, thanked him in unison. The leader of the meeting, a handsome woman about my age, called on people to share. A woman in the front row admitted to having an obsessive desire for teenaged boys. Two younger women were lesbians, and they liked 'mature, elegant' ladies. Several of the men were gay, one confessing a passion for 'rough trade.' The final speaker was a woman with a large nose and dyed auburn hair who said that her problem was simply she wanted sex with anyone who walked, man, woman, any age, and she wasn't that particular about certain species of animals.

Risible material, if it weren't so sad. The people 'sharing' had broken lives. All had lost their families, friends, possessions and, at some point, their dignity. It was the latter, mainly, they were trying to reclaim.

When the session ended, a number of the members lingered around the coffee urns set up in the back. The first speaker, sidling up to Diane, drew us into the circle.

'Welcome to the meeting,' he said.

'Thank you,' I said.

'Haven't seen you guys before. Been to other meetings?'

'No, this is our first.'

'You came together?'

'Yes, we did.'

'Takes a while,' he said. 'To share. We understand. No pressure. When you're ready will be time enough.'

'Thank you again,' I said.

I could see the attraction. Spill your guts to a room full of sympathetic listeners. Must even be a huge impulse to make it up, just for the attention. I wondered whether there were groups for people like that.

But I didn't like taking Diane there. She was out of place. Or maybe it was because she'd been abused by someone who *should* have been there.

Driving home, I said, 'We could go to an awful lot of those meetings.'

'And not learn anything, you're saying?'

'That's what I'm saying.'

'We never have to stay that long,' she said. 'Two, three minutes would do it. Basically, we're looking for someone you know.'

'Yeah, but the lead might be something else.'

'Then we'll have to be patient.'

'I could tour the strip shows,' I said. 'The S&M joints.'

'That *is* over my line,' she said, turning into the Lincoln Tunnel. 'But don't let that stop you.'

To anyone as claustrophobic as I am, the tunnel dripped with menace. Condensed humidity on pipes looked like leaks. Tile cracks bulged as if from the pressure. And driving within those walls – tunneling through dirt – seemed a comment on the futility of what we were doing. Which reminded me, when we surfaced, of the other thing I thought we should do.

When we got past the tolls, I climbed off the floor and sat staring out the back window until Diane craned her neck.

'You all right?' she asked.

'Yeah, I've been thinking.'

'About?'

'What we need is a hacker. Someone who can hack us into hospital files, shrinks' files.'

'You think this guy's raping people, then going to a shrink to tell him about it?'

'I didn't say it was likely. But he's not necessarily standard-profile. If he's someone we both know, probably coming across as an OK guy, he's sufficiently together to function in a seemingly civilized way.'

'Meaning he goes to a shrink?'

'He might,' I said. 'He might be as miserable as the people we saw tonight, and getting treatment.'

'The odds against this—'

'Everything we try'll be a long shot. And this should be easy to do. There can't be that many specialists. Every one of them should be online. And if there are nerds who can hack into NATO files, how much of a challenge can this be?'

'All right,' she said. 'I'll find you a nerd.' Her tone was depressed.

'Waste of time, you think?'

'No, it's fine. It has as much chance of working as anything else.'

'Very little,' I said.

'Right. But fine. That doesn't mean we shouldn't try it. As you said, we should probably try everything.'

'You sound discouraged,' I said.

She shrugged.

'We've just started,' I said.

'We're smart people,' she said. 'We should have better ideas.'

'And?'

'I'm thinking.'

'And?'

'Let's just shut up until we get . . . to my house.'

She had almost said, 'Until we get home.'

THIRTY

In Diane's kitchen we drew beers from the fridge as I listened to two messages on my cell phone. The first, Joe Stein, urging me to come in. The second, from Betsy, with another good reason not to.

She'd run checks on about fifty people she knew I knew, or figured I did. People I'd mentioned: other lawyers, clients, friends. Only one had a record for a sex crime. Juvenile. Supposedly erased, but somehow Betsy had gotten it. In high school, he and two other boys had forced a fourteen-year-old girl into the boys' locker room and taken turns. I heard the name, and thought something had to be wrong with the report. The guy I knew could never have done this. It was Carter Denison. And if he'd actually been convicted, even as a juvenile, his being appointed to the Federal bench was a miracle.

I told Diane who Betsy was and repeated her message about Carter. If we were going to be partners in tracking this guy down, I had to – as they said at the meeting – share. It didn't seem to help.

'I know him,' she said, blood draining from her face. 'Met him about six months ago at a fund raiser.'

'And?' Betsy's news was now making me angry.

But it threw Diane into a state of confusion. 'I just don't know.'

I remembered Carter at his party, masquerading, face tight.

'In a sense,' she said, 'this makes things harder.'

I waited.

She said, 'You're not going to confront him. Or publicly accuse him. Your friend Betsy already has the information. She's not ready to pursue the guy. She's probably not even ready to shove these facts at Chacon.'

I took a swig from the beer bottle. 'So what's your thought? You've been chewing on something for more than an hour.'

'You won't like it,' she said.

'I already don't like it. Tell me anyway.'

She took a seat at the booth in the bay window, and I joined her, sitting opposite. She said, 'Basic research – the sickos who do this tend to be egomaniacal. They think, in a better world, they'd be getting praise for what they're doing, not punishment. The thing that drives them absolutely berserk is a copy-cat. Someone trying to get the credit they feel they deserve.'

'A copy-cat,' I repeated.

'Right.'

'I think I know where this is going.'

'I told you you wouldn't like it.'

'So you're going to do what?' I said, voice rising. 'Tell the cops the same creep has come again? Make a false report?'

'How high could the penalty be?'

'Not insignificant,' I said. 'But even past that. Play it out. What do you think it achieves?'

'We smoke him out. I make it very convincing. The press eats it up. Even if they don't have my name, they're told it's the same woman, same guy, second time.'

'And then what?'

'Who knows? But he can't like it. So we're shaking the tree. There are all kinds of possibilities.'

'Such as?'

'Could be anything,' she said. 'Most likely, he comes after you. Figuring you're the guy copying his style. Thinking, maybe, you're trying to pin it on him.'

I closed my eyes and thought about Carter.

'So you up for that?' she asked.

I went to bed with the question in my mind. Not the answer; the question. And not to sleep, but to bed. Sleep seemed extremely doubtful.

I thought Betsy was right, you never really knew people, their full range for good or evil. Still, when I tried to imagine Carter in that locker room, what came to mind was his sense of humor and decency, his common sense. It just didn't fit with a rape conviction.

I visualized the incident he was supposedly involved in. Three guys torturing a girl – because rape is torture. Even if Carter had only been in the room, how could he have just stood by and done nothing to help her? Not the guy I thought I knew.

I saw the girl's face, the hurt, shame, anger and terror. Then Carter's face transformed. Glazed ugly savagery – under a ski mask.

Another thing came to mind. He'd advised me to do the line-up.

For Di, Carter was little more than a name. Now a suspect. But she was willing to consider almost anyone as a possibility, except maybe me. Which was wonderful and hard to explain.

We'd had this little scene, before retiring. She said on the stairs, in a slightly strained voice, 'We'll just say good night, then.' If she hadn't turned red, I might have thought nothing of it.

I said slowly, stopping, still a bit unsure, 'In the present circumstances . . .'

'Exactly,' she said. 'In the present circumstances. All that talk at that meeting and everything.' She tossed her hair back. 'It's good. Shows some healing going on. And here we are, thrown together. Same roof. Friday night. You're not totally gruesome.'

'Thank you,' I said.

'Sure thing. Give a compliment, I say, when one is due. And I know it would just be friendly, part of the patch idea.'

She had me going, I did not know where. 'It's OK,' I said. 'I like you too.'

She nodded. 'Noted. Thank you.'

'Right,' I said. 'We keep our focus.'

'Cool,' she said. ''Night.'

''Night.'

So in addition to lying awake over Carter, I had to think about that.

Saturday morning, over scrambled eggs, with the sun off the river rimming her juice glass, Diane announced I looked like shit. 'You didn't sleep well?'

'Three hours. Maybe.'

'All that talk about sleeping together, probably.'

'Probably,' I said, trying for deadpan.

With her in pyjamas and a bathrobe, it was almost as if we had. And I sat there wishing we had. I was certainly attracted to her. I'd screwed up my life with Ali, took on lots of confusion with Betsy, but with Diane I had no confusion, at least insofar as my own feelings were concerned. She was a sweet, bruised, beautiful young woman with a sharp tongue and a soft heart. Already, I'd trust her with my life. In fact, I was doing just that. And I'd felt this clarity about her after what? Less than two days? Actually, I think, the first two minutes.

'I slept like a baby,' she said. 'Put my head down and slept. Eight hours. Y'know the last time I got eight solid hours of sleep? Never. That's when.'

She caught me staring. 'What?' she said with a small laugh.

'I could see you on the stage. Your face is remarkably expressive.'

'That's kind,' she said.

'You still do it, don't you? I know there are lots of good amateur groups in the city.'

'Amateur?' The corners of her mouth pulled down.

'I've insulted you?'

'I did two plays last summer at the Provincetown Playhouse.'

'Did you! Which plays?'

'*Miss Julie*—'

'Strindberg. Impressive.'

'And *The Homecoming*. Pinter.'

'Provincetown. You're a pro. So why—'

'Don't I drop everything else and do it full time?'

'You've been asked that question too often,' I said.

'It's all right.'

'But you'd rather not get into it.'

'Not right now.'

After a strained pause, I said, 'You know, I was recently divorced.'

'Yes. The news had reached me. And a couple million other people.'

I gave a tense laugh. 'She's going out with her boss, Bob Hayden.'

'Oh, yes?' she said. 'I know him too. Met him, at least. On an underwriting about a year ago.'

'You know everyone I know?'

'Doubt it. But I know Carter and him.' She looked at me pointedly. 'And I'm sure we could find a few more.'

I said, 'About that plan of yours.'

'Forget it,' she said. 'Bad idea.'

Her vehemence surprised me.

'It would probably get you killed,' she said. 'But it made me realize, when I thought of the risk to you. It's so obvious. The guy is not merely someone who knows you. He probably hates you. Not dislike – hate. Who is that, Rick?'

I spread my hands. I honestly didn't know.

'Someone you beat up in court maybe? Someone in your law firm who's got reason to be jealous, or worse? Because maybe you insulted him? Or stole his clients?'

I thought of Hazzard again with his obvious, absurd resentment, but I didn't believe he was capable of anything this extreme. No other names came to mind. 'I'm clueless.'

'We don't get this guy soon, the cops'll get you. I mean it!'

'So let's get on with it,' I said. 'What we've started doing. The hacker. Everything.'

'Right. Plus one other idea I had that's not totally ridiculous.'

'I'm going to like this one?'

'Yeah. I'm thinking you will. Probably too much.'

The doorbell!

We looked at each other, paralyzed for a moment.

'Get upstairs!' she said.

'Whoever it is—'

'Don't worry. No one's getting in here.'

I did the stairs three at a time. Went to a window on the second floor. Peeked out. Chacon. Leaning against the door, talking through it. I pulled away. All he had to do was look up, out of curiosity or just to catch some rays, and I'd be dogmeat. But she'd cracked the door open. I could hear down the stairwell.

'I'm Vincente Chacon.'

'Yes?'

'We talked on the phone.'

'I remember.'

'I'm really sorry, but I happened to be in the neighborhood—'

'It's a bad time.'

'There's someone here?'

'I'm sorry, Lieutenant—'

'Captain. May I come in for a moment?'

'Actually, no. I told you on the phone. I don't want—'

'Yes, you're right, I shouldn't have just barged in like this, but you may be in danger. Our suspect, Eric Corinth, fled immediately to New Jersey, to a motel not far from here.'

'And you're suggesting he may be coming here?'

'If I could just—'

'Aren't you out of your jurisdiction?'

'Yes. That's right. I am.'

'Good day, Captain.'

The sound of a door closing reverberated up the stairs.

I gave it a minute, then peeked again. He was gone, and I heard Diane on the stairway.

'Guess who,' she said, still a bit shaken.

'I saw.'

'Wanted to talk, he said. Full of apologies.'

'What does he know?'

'I think . . . nothing.'

THIRTY-ONE

Di dropped me off on Tenth Avenue. 'Here's where they walk.'

'Being streetwalkers.'

'Yes.'

'You know this?' I said.

'I've been told,' she said, craning up at me through the open car window. 'You talk to them. One of them may know something. Guy like this, who likes to abuse women . . .'

My eyes closed – at the futility and danger of prowling the streets. But I said, 'Gotcha. Everything we're doing is a long shot.'

'And risky,' she said, and sped off.

I waited for a while, but she, or her informant, was wrong about Tenth Avenue. My own source, Emma, knew better. Hookers trolled Eleventh. So I wandered out there to find one.

Not a problem, even at lunchtime. Or maybe especially at lunchtime. There seemed to be plenty of drivers who knew this spot, cruising both sides of the avenue. I let several working girls go by – something about them, too hard, too extreme in their dress. Besides, I knew where I was, knew whom I was looking for, patrolling her turf. If any of these women knew anything, it was likely to be Emma herself.

Strange, I thought, how I didn't want to tell Diane about Emma.

I ducked into a bakery on Forty-seventh, bought a raspberry muffin and ate it on the corner, watching the traffic go by. From the sounds that trucks make, you'd think they were in agony. With people, the distress is in their faces, their shoulders, the attitude of their hands. Without conscious thought, I started moving.

A thought intervened. A new one. Betsy. She would know if there had been any developments in the investigation. It was Saturday, she might be home. Less risky than a phone call. And not a place they'd be looking for me.

Heading down her block, I glimpsed a young woman in a gray turtleneck descending a stoop, then striding in my direction. Not Betsy. Younger, shorter, carrying a book bag, skirt flouncing. A student, I would have said. She stopped, which stopped me. Stunned me. Her appearance had fooled me completely.

'Emma?'

She flinched and blew past me, toward Tenth.

'Emma!' I caught up and kept pace.

'Whatta you doing here?' Her voice, sullen, bounced as she walked.

'Looking for you, actually.'

'What for?'

'You may be able to help me.'

She picked up her pace.

'What are you so pissed off about?' I said.

'You wouldn't understand.'

'Try me,' I said.

She started muttering. 'Fucking sister, fucking hard-ass bitch.'

I grabbed her arm, managing to stop her. 'Your sister lives in that building? The one you came out of?' I thought I might black out.

'You OK?'

I got the words out. 'Is Betsy Spaeth your sister?'

'Step-sister,' she said.

'Jesus Christ. She's Bob Hayden's step-daughter?'

'I thought you knew that. You know Bob.'

'No, I didn't know that!' I was yelling. 'I work with Betsy. Or did.'

'Lucky you.'

She was walking once more, and I took off after her.

'Emma, for Christ's sake, listen to me! I need to talk to you. I need your help.'

'*Ew*, yeah,' she said.

'Did you say you had an apartment around here?'

She came to a quick halt.

'You want to come to my apartment?'

'Yes.'

'What for?'

'For what I said: to talk.'

'We can talk here.'

'I'd rather not . . . stand here.'

She gave a dark laugh. 'Right.'

'It's not what you think.'

'Right,' she said once more, as if humoring me.

'Emma!'

She cocked her head at me and took a few steps. 'Well, come on then . . .' Faint smile. 'If you're coming.'

She led the way. Three blocks north, near Eleventh. We trooped up the cabbage-smelling stairs of a tenement to a room on the fourth floor. She opened the door, and two fur balls flew out.

'You do have cats,' I said, removing one from my ankle.

She gave me a look of pure scorn.

The room was a pit. Sink, stove, bed; window admitting the minimum of light. To darken things further, a mud-colored carpet covered the floor; black and gold tapestries deadened the walls. The place stank from cats and God knows what else. But it had a TV and an air conditioner which she flipped on and smacked. It made a whirring noise and moved the air around.

'How can you live here?' I said.

'You're supposed to say, "nice place."' She was scooping some liver-smelling paste into a dish, which the cats started attacking before she could get it to the floor.

'You think this is a nice place?'

'Whatever,' she said. 'Suits me.'

I suggested we go to a coffee shop, and she shot me another angry glare.

'I gotta pee,' she said, slipping into the bathroom.

I took a seat on the one chair, upholstered but armless, glanced around, saw more mess on the surfaces, grime in the corners. She came out in a moment, while the toilet was still flushing.

'So,' she said, straddling my lap, beginning to work on the buttons of my denim shirt. 'Lets see what we have here, hunh?'

'Whoa,' I said gently. 'What I need is to talk to you.'

'Absolutely,' she said, hauling herself up. 'We'll talk.' With two deft movements, she dropped her skirt around her ankles and whooshed her turtleneck over her head. Standing there: a lanky kid in a white cotton bra and flower-patterned bikini panties. 'Yes?' she said. Part of an act, stagey and sad.

'You're lovely.' Actually, I thought she was a miracle. 'Now put your clothes back on, OK?'

She twirled around, lowered her briefs a bit under her tush and twirled back again. 'How you like them apples?' Her mood had swung suddenly to playful.

'You've put on a little weight.'

'Yes?' She got close again. 'Still want to talk?'

Lifting her as I rose from the chair, I dumped her on the bed to a chorus of mattress springs.

'I see the needle marks have faded,' I said, half-sitting on the edge of the sink.

She snatched her clothes from the floor. 'I do that. Detox. Couple of times a year. I do it for the pain. And shit,' she said with disgust, 'why are you even pretending to care?'

'What makes you think I'm pretending?'

She shrugged and began dressing herself.

'I didn't know your grandmother,' I started, 'but Bob mentioned you'd lived with her, and I gather –'

'You don't know shit.'

'– she was a great woman.'

'You mean my step-grandma? From hell?'

'OK,' I said. 'We won't go there.' I fished out a hundred dollar bill.

Her eyes, rising over the top of the turtleneck, fixed on the money.

'There's a guy raping women,' I said. 'A serial rapist. He's trying to pin it on me.'

'That's a new one.' She got up, pushed me away from the sink and ran the water for a moment before cupping her hand under it for a drink. 'So what's this got to do with me?'

'Sick, *sick* guy,' I said, retaking the chair. 'His thing is to humiliate. Physically, mentally. I thought, maybe, there might've been rumors of someone like that preying on the street girls.'

She returned to the bed, glanced at me with some interest but still not pleased.

'You apparently don't watch the news or read newspapers – but I'm being blamed for these crimes.'

'Pretty stupid,' she said.

'Thank you. But the police of two states are hunting my ass, so if you're really pissed off at me, now's your chance. Pick up the phone, cops'll be here in under ten minutes.'

She crossed her arms over her head. 'Coppers. Great. What I need.'

We stared at each other for a moment.

'Fine,' I said, getting up. 'You know nothing. I'll get out of here and stop annoying you.'

From beneath the tent of her arms, she spoke. 'You ever hear of the WWPA?'

I looked blank.

'Working Women's Protective Association? Sometimes known as the Whoring Women's Protective. For short.' She uncovered her face and smiled.

'Can't say I have.'

'They've got a phone number. Here,' she said, looking in her bag. She found it, and wrote the number on a matchbook she plucked from the top of the stove. 'There's a woman who runs it. If any guy like that's been on the prowl, she'd know about it. Or her staff would. Former working girls. A good bunch of ladies. Problem is, now that I think of it . . .'

'She's not going to want to talk to me.'

'Yeah, that's the problem. At least not on the phone. Maybe if she met you . . .'

I took another hundred dollar bill from my pocket and dropped both of them on the bed. 'Would you set that up?' I grabbed her pen and wrote my cell phone number on her matchbook.

She stared at the money.

'What's wrong?' I said.

She shook her head at it.

'I've used your time,' I said. 'And I want more of it.'

She rolled up both bills and stuck them in my shirt pocket.

'Why?' I said.

'You don't get it, do you?'

'Get what?' I said.

'If I can help you, I'm gonna help you. I don't want to be paid for it.'

'Thank you.'

She shook her head at me.

'What?' I said.

'You.' She laughed. 'For someone with my issues. Like made-to-order perfect.'

'This is a joke, right? You're making fun of me.'

'No,' she said, suddenly serious. 'You give off this . . . fucking aura, man!'

'What *aura*?'

'You make me feel somehow you're going to protect me.'

THIRTY-TWO

I fell asleep on her bed. Cats, stench – I was too tired to care. And I was touched she'd allowed me to stay there.

Emma took off for Hunter College. 'Open enrollment,' she said. 'Only way I'd get in anywhere.' Before leaving, she called the WWPA woman, left a message and scribbled out two addresses. One, an S&M club in the meat packing district – 'Authentic,' she said, 'not for tourists, and the kind of place the kind of guy you're looking for might go to.' The second, a church uptown which housed a meeting for sexaholics.

'Richies,' she said. 'Saturday nights, eight thirty.'

How did she know these things?

'How do you think?' she said, going out the door with a whimsically patronizing look.

I awoke around five fifteen with a splitting headache. I hadn't

eaten anything but half a muffin in eight hours. I got out of
bed, went outside, wandered east to Betsy's block. Reckless. It
was getting dark already, but not cold. An Italian restaurant on
Ninth Avenue had a table in its front bay window which I took.
More reckless still. I wanted to look out on the avenue. Which
meant others, looking in, could see me. From an elderly
perplexed waiter, I ordered red wine, a bowl of soup and some
pasta.

Then I called Betsy on the house phone and told her where I
was. I wanted to know why she hadn't told me about her relationship to Bob Hayden. But she hung up before I could ask.

The wine arrived while I was on the phone. The waiter came
back apologetically, said the kitchen didn't really open until
six. He brought a basket of bread sticks.

When I was on the second glass, I saw Betsy materialize
from the passing crowd. I went outside to meet her.

'Are you out of your fucking mind?' she said under her
breath, looking around furtively.

'Come inside. I've got a table.'

'A table!' she said, following me. 'You're going to get me
fired. No, arrested, to say nothing of what's going to happen
to you.'

'You could always turn me in,' I said.

'You know I'm not going to do that.'

'Thanks. What do you want for dinner? And this wine's not
too bad. We could get a bottle.'

'I'm not going to have dinner with you. You think I'd have
dinner with you?'

'What is it about dinner? There's some symbol involved here
I'm not getting?'

'Half the cops in this city are roaming the streets with your
picture in their pockets, and you want to sit in the window of
this restaurant and have a leisurely meal?'

'We could sit in the back.'

It was as if she saw me for the first time. She laughed. The
waiter reappeared. Bald, stooped shoulders, unemployable by
any yuppie establishment, which this decidedly wasn't.

'What're you having?' she asked me.

I told her.

'Same,' she said to the waiter who wrote and left. 'OK? We're having dinner. Happy?'

'Happy? Well.'

'Rick, what the hell are you doing? Can you tell me? You're a goddamn lawyer. Why aren't you fighting this in court?'

'Too late for that now.'

'No doubt,' she said, in mounting tones of rebuke. '*Now*.'

I took a long swallow of wine.

'You know this,' she said, 'yet you fled anyway. I called you so you could get a lawyer in time to keep yourself out of the pen, the walk, the system. Not so you would incriminate yourself.'

'I realize that.'

'So why the hell didn't you do what I asked?'

'Because it was pointless. Suppose I won? Then what? Become the guy who couldn't be proven guilty of raping six women? But who knows? Maybe he did?'

Her wine came. She drank some. She wasn't happy.

I asked, 'What are you going to do about the information you turned up on Carter?'

She sat back, unhappier still. 'Nothing. What did you think?'

'You could pay him a visit. See how he reacts.'

'I'm not even on the case.'

'Tip Chacon?'

'I know it, he knows it,' she said.

'You learned it because you knew we were friends. Chacon doesn't know that.'

Our soup came and, to me, tasted like haute cuisine.

I said, 'What if Carter weren't a Federal judge?'

'What are you saying? You really think he's the guy?'

'Let me tell you. I can't imagine anyone I know doing these things. But the guy doing them is someone I know.'

She put her spoon down. 'So I'll go see him.'

'No. Forget it. Don't. I don't think he did it. He couldn't possibly have.'

'Make up your fucking mind, Rick.'

'I haven't got a mind. I lost it two days ago.'

Then I remembered the main reason I'd called her.

'Why didn't you tell me Bob Hayden was your father?'

'What?' Her spoon suspended over the bowl.

I stared at her.

'Why the hell should I've told you who my father was? Have you told me who your father was?'

'My father's dead.'

'So's mine,' she said.

'I *know* your father.'

'Step-father.'

'And I know your sister.'

Her eyes closed. 'Emma.'

'I just saw her.'

'Shit,' she said, peering out the window over my shoulder.

'What's wrong?'

'Just get up,' she said, fatigue and panic in her voice. 'No words, go to the men's room, *now!*'

THIRTY-THREE

I did what she said. No looking back. Men's room was down the stairs in a dank basement corridor. I went straight in, took a stall, locked it and sat with my legs folded under me on top of the toilet. Then waited.

And waited.

Five minutes went by. I got up, rubbed my legs. I wondered whether it might be safe to dial my voicemail. I heard a pounding on the stairs and sprang back into a lotus position atop the john.

The men's room door banged open. One guy took the urinal, the other tried to open the stall door. I watched it rattle. 'Fucker must be outta order.'

'You see that cunt sittin' alone in the window seat?'

'Blonde babe?'

'You know who she is?'

'How the fuck should I know who she is?'

'Well, I do.'

'Yeah? Who is she, then?'

'Lieutenant Spaeth, that's who. Sex crimes. I worked with her on a case.'

'Doin' what? Directing traffic?'

'Fuck no. Responsible work. Interviewing people. Neighborhood people.'

'Say, how the fuck long it take you to piss, anyway?'

'Shit, man. Have a little fucking patience, will ya? I'm having a little trouble here, OK?'

The stall door shook again from a blow. I could see the hook plate hanging from the door jamb, my life dangling on the loose screw barely holding the hook in place. I fixated on it in a panic.

'So'd you fuck her?' Evil smirky laugh.

'Yeah, right. In my fucking dreams. Broad like that. See . . .' Flushing sound. 'It's all yours. See, that's what's fucked up with this world. We're all supposed to be people. But a broad like that and you and me, it's like two different species. A broad like that doesn't go with people like you and me.'

'What're you? A fucking philosopher all of a sudden?'

'Well, whatta you think? You think I'm wrong? I'll bet this guy, y'know this guy they're lookin' for, the one who's raped all those ritzy women? I'll bet he's one of us. I'll bet he just said to himself one day, I've had enough of this shit, man, bein' put down. Y'know, I can almost understand it, gettin' back his own.'

'So whatta you say we go up there, grab her on some phony charge, take her off somewhere and do her? How 'bout that?'

'Oh, great.'

Another flushing sound. 'Doesn't appeal to you?'

'Like thirty years in Attica.'

'That's what's stopping you?'

'Yeah, that's what's stopping me.'

'That's it?'

'Pretty much.'

Their conversation faded out when they took off down the hall.

I could hear Chacon in my ear, 'See? What did I tell you? The checks!' But what these guys grasped, I thought, and maybe Chacon didn't, is that they were, in effect, a different species. Maybe early Cro-Magnon? Evolved humans didn't think like that.

I gave it another minute, then emerged from the stall. I had a choice. There was a window, already open, above the toilet. I thought I could probably climb up and squeeze through it, rather than risk the stairs. I hated leaving Betsy, especially with the check. She'll understand, though, I thought. And I'll make it up to her. Two minutes more, I was already into the alley, heading toward Tenth Avenue.

On the cell phone. Not at all conspicuous. Half this crowd was walking and talking. There were two messages for me. From Diane: 'Where are you? And why aren't you calling?' Emma's was more involved. The gist was, if I'd get myself to the lobby of the Edison Hotel at eight thirty that night, a woman from the WWPA would recognize me from Emma's description and make contact. Not smart using the mobile for a message like that, but there it was. Necessity.

The thing about Tenth Avenue, particularly at this hour, was not to stand still. Stand still, and you're loitering. Probably with a purpose. And you're very likely to be approached by someone who thinks he or she can serve that purpose. Or collect rent for your entertaining it on his corner. Or throw you in a lock-up, to fill a quota, because this he or she is sporting a badge.

So I speed-dialed Diane on the move. 'All's well?' I asked, neutrally, in my best upper-class English accent.

'Quite well, thank you,' she said, mimicking the voice. 'And with you?'

'Topping,' I said.

'So glad.'

'What would you say to about nine thirty tonight? Place I last saw you?'

'Splendid. Oh, and darling. I found that skilled technician we'd been looking for.'

'Excellent.' I assumed she meant the hacker.

'Well, cheerio.'

'Cheerio.'

We wouldn't have fooled anyone, had they been listening. Indeed, had they been listening, it could only have been because they already knew whom they were listening to, in which case they'd be picking me up at the Edison later that night. Still,

Diane and I had to talk, so we might as well have amused ourselves.

I walked north, then east. At Columbus Circle, I dropped into the Eighth Avenue subway. No one followed me, as best I could tell. I joined the masses on the platform, blending invisibly with the subterranean life of Manhattan.

THIRTY-FOUR

I n the Edison Hotel lobby, the few sofas and chairs were occupied, groups were milling about, talking, people were checking in. No cops in sight.

I made two tours on the carpet. A shapely middle-aged bleached blonde in a beige and orange checked suit rose from a sofa in the middle of the room. 'You Emma's friend?'

We got a booth in the coffee shop. The pre-theater crowd had just cleared out. Her name, she told me, was Cheryl. She didn't ask mine; she'd been given it.

'I doubt I can help you,' she said, as a determined waitress chugged up with a pad.

Still starving, I ordered a burger while Cheryl studied the menu. 'Maybe the fruit platter,' she said. Then excused herself to go to the Ladies'.

I was staring at the scene without seeing it, eyes drifting to the window on the street, when two uniformed cops, male and female, barged into the restaurant. They talked briefly to the manger at the cash register, flashed a small photo, put it back, all the while their eyes scanning the room until they focused on mine. The one with the photo pulled it out once again and consulted it.

Then they walked toward me.

Two big-butted hippos with sticks and a swagger, guns and stuff jiggling all over them. I thought, Now it starts. Life in prison.

I could see their faces marked with disdain, white guy, black woman. They loomed over me.

The male cop said, 'What's your name, sir?'

'*Como?*'

He really hated dealing with dumb immigrants. Looked at that photo again, then down at me. Fuzzy head shot: generic clean-shaven guy in a suit and a tie. Guy in the booth: growth of beard; darker, shaggier hair; haggard face. My mother couldn't have made the identification. 'No problem, sir.'

'Oh, *si, gracias*,' I said.

They left. I was dizzy. Cheryl returned.

'What's wrong?' she said.

'Nothing. All good.'

I didn't look it, I'm sure.

'You feeling OK?'

'Absolutely.'

The food arrived. Service here made McDonald's look sluggish. And, as starved as I still was, I thought I could actually eat.

I reached for the ketchup, watched Cheryl pick at her salad. Full face with a button nose. Probably once a hot ticket. I began devouring a burger with fries.

'As it happens,' she said, 'there *is* some bastard out there right now who's causing a problem. Not that that's so unusual.'

'He's violent?' I said, chomping into the sandwich.

'Threatens violence. He's scared quite a few of these girls.'

'Has he actually attacked any of them?'

'I'm not sure. Two say he has.'

'You know who I am, so you know what I'm charged with, and whom I'm chasing.'

'That's right.'

I forked some fries. 'Your women have actually seen the face of the man you're talking about? He hasn't been disguised?'

'They've seen him. And they're all describing the same guy. There's no doubt about it.'

I must have lit up. She could see my excitement, tried to help, tried to access the memory of what she'd been told. 'Beak nose,' she said. 'Medium height, thin-ish. Expensive tailoring. And – this is the odd part – though he looks like a society mug, he's got a Brooklyn accent. An odd Brooklyn accent, but definitely not posh.'

'You're English,' I said. 'A Brit.'

She looked at me enquiringly. 'Ah. "Society mug." A thing my father used to say.' She laughed. 'I came here when I was seven.'

Two more cops sauntered in from the street. I froze. They began looking around. I brought my coffee cup to my mouth, covering half my face, tried to concentrate on not choking. Two sips, real steady. They left.

Cheryl, in silence, had watched the whole thing.

I restarted my breathing. 'Why do you trust me?' I asked.

She gave me a careful appraisal. 'Emma trusts you. I trust Emma. And –' she pulled her hair back '– I can see why Emma trusts you.'

'Thank you.'

'But I'm afraid I haven't given you much.'

'You might have, actually,' I said.

'Really?'

'Yeah, there's a guy I know, fits your description.' I laughed. 'Perfectly, in fact. Especially the accent.'

'Brooklyn accent?' she said with surprise. 'This narrows it down for you?'

'It's the physical description plus what you said. An *odd* Brooklyn accent.'

She thought for a moment. 'I suppose it could be the Bronx or from some parts of Queens. They're very similar.'

'Or Old New York,' I said. 'Peter Stuyvesant's time. Back to the Dutch. It's where the Brooklyn accent originally came from.'

'You're kidding. People like that, still living here?'

'As your dad would say, "society mugs". Descendants of the first settlers. Very proud. Aristocratic. And exceedingly posh. Most think of themselves as the only society worth keeping.'

'You know such people?' she asked.

'Some of them. Including one who happens to be the head honcho of my former law firm.'

She still couldn't get over it. 'I lost my accent in two years. These people still have theirs? After what? Four hundred?'

'Why do you think?'

'Makes them feel special?'

'Not just special,' I said. 'Better than anyone else.'

Diane, parked on Tenth for a half hour, wasn't pleased. Even less so, when I told her, as I settled into the back seat, what I'd been doing. She put her own spin on the facts.

'So that's it?' she said, thrusting the car into traffic. 'Whoring around all day?'

'That's not what I said.'

'Right.'

'And if I had? Whose idea was this?'

'I said talk to 'em. I didn't tell you to fuck 'em.'

'Well, I didn't. As it happens.'

'Boy!' she said scathingly.

'Don't believe me.'

'Of course I don't believe you.'

'The reason being?'

I got a tight-lipped refusal to say.

We headed into the Lincoln Tunnel. We were having a fight. A very odd sort of fight. We sounded like squabbling lovers, after having known each other for three days. *What was bugging her?*

Leaning over the back of her seat, I told her what Cheryl had said about the man with the Brooklyn accent. 'So,' I said, 'I've got maybe a lead we didn't have before. There's someone I know who looks like that, talks like that, dresses like that, and knows me well enough to convince others he's me.'

'Yes, and? Name?'

'Let me get some more facts.'

'What?' she said, riled again. 'You don't trust me all of a sudden?'

'Of course I trust you. It's not that.'

'Oh, great. Bullshit coming.'

'It's nobody you know,' I said.

'If it's the guy we're looking for—'

'Please. Let me get more facts. This is really a very *very* far-out possibility.'

Why didn't I want to name Roger? I hardly knew. Years of training: you don't out your partners. He no longer was, but still I hesitated. It felt wrong. At any rate, we endured stony silence for the length of the tunnel.

I asked about the hacker.

'Tomorrow afternoon.'

'And?'

She took her time. 'Guy I heard about at Goldman. Quintessential geek, misfit. Got laid off. Unlike you,' she added, 'who just got laid.'

We drove the rest of the way in silence. I was unwilling to comment on her statement; she refused to say anything until I did. The car pulled into her garage. We started upstairs. With one arm over the banister she said, 'I guess you'll sleep well tonight.'

'Di, cut it out.'

She laughed without humor. 'Someone ought to be getting laid around here.'

I looked at her in disbelief.

'You're right,' she said. 'I don't mean it. Going through the motions. It's the kind of off thing I used to say. And get away with. When I was funny.'

'I understand,' I said.

'No, you don't.'

'OK.'

'*You don't!*'

'*OK.*'

'Shit! Goodnight.'

I took it. I was the outlet. It was part of the rent.

THIRTY-FIVE

Leon Agonich, the hacker, lived in Washington Heights, near Columbia Presbyterian Hospital, a stone's throw from the Bronx. On the drive there Diane and I barely talked. I missed my kids, which put me in a foul self-pitying state of mind. Diane had been moody all day.

I naturally got the blame for whatever went wrong, being the person closest to both Diane and the subject of her annoyance. When she pulled in front of Leon's building, she jumped out and let loose a torrent of vexation, concluding with, 'Fuck! Where the fuck am I supposed to park this car?'

She stood astride the street in a bright red fleece vest, her small serious face freckled in the sun, her lips puckered with discontent.

I noted there was a parking spot less than twenty feet away.

'Oh, great choice! Stay in the car and get raped in this wonderful neighborhood, or go upstairs with you and say goodbye to my hubcaps. And who knows what else? Probably the whole fucking engine.'

'Actually . . .' I said.

Her hard stare dared me to reason her out of her anger.

'I think people in this neighborhood respect cars. Especially a Mercedes.'

Her look intensified.

'OK,' I said. 'Anything gets stolen is on me. We go right to the dealer, replace it, I pay.'

'Brilliant,' she said. 'Put a bill for my car on your card. Why don't we just schedule a joint press conference?' She gawked at me in derision. 'Let's get out of here.'

In some bygone era, Leon's building had been constructed to house families of means. Its downstairs lobby, appointed in marble, featured high ceilings and wide halls. Only four apartments to a floor. All had views of the Hudson River, and Leon's were spectacular. Everything else there was now run-down. Including, as it turned out, Leon.

He greeted us in a black sweatshirt, his rolls of fat looking like a pile of Michelin truck tires. Tufts of black beard and the thickness of lenses concealed much of his physiognomy. What could be seen was lumpish and moistly, unhealthily white. Yet his greeting rang out at the door. 'Hey! Most wanted in ten states! Way to go, Ricky boy!' We had never met before.

I stepped inside with Diane. 'I'm putting you at risk,' I said to him. 'You understand that?'

'Hey, man. My whole life's a risk. Come in, come in.'

We would have been in his living room if he'd had one. It was now a large windowed space filled with equipment. There were stools, and we sat on them. Leon's flesh sagged and cascaded atop a frayed upholstered bench in front of his main terminal.

'You're a fucking celebrity, man, y'know! There's something

on you every five minutes. There must be five thousand cops out there looking for you, prowling the streets. Not ten minutes ago, there was a bulletin on CNN. You devil, you.'

I glanced at Diane, saw her flinch. 'I hope you understand,' I said to Leon, 'I'm not the guy who's doing those things.' He waved it off. Of course he knew, the gesture said.

I unfolded two sheets of paper, handed them to him. 'These lists – these are most of the shrinks in Manhattan known for treating aberrant sexual behavior. My afternoon's work.'

Leon glanced at the sheets, twirled about on his bench with surprising agility. He spoke as his fingers flashed at the keys. 'Little ahead of you here, Rick. Had a few minutes before you arrived.' The image resolving itself on his screen extended to at least twice the length of the lists I'd handed him. 'I've been into a number of these systems already,' he said. 'Doesn't seem to be a problem. The shrinks I checked had their complete files accessible online. No sense of security.' He laughed. 'But then, why would they?' Confirming from our gaping mouths that we were appropriately dazzled, he declared, 'So. Where'd you like to begin?'

I picked doctors affiliated with New York Hospital and Columbia Presbyterian. Each organized his or her files differently. Figuring out how took Leon a matter of seconds. What amazed me was the number of hits. In the seven doctors' records, out of nearly two hundred patients, I recognized eight of them.

We read their case histories. Diane and I, who weren't intimate, sat there skimming detailed sexual confessions in the presence of someone we'd known for all of ten minutes. Awkward, especially for me, since I was the one who could put a face to each file. Or at least the social mask.

In essence, these were agonized people spilling their angst in circumstances they thought safe from prying. I didn't feel great about being the one peeking. And I didn't think I was learning much.

Neither did Leon. 'So whatta we really looking for? Gotta be a guy, right? And an enemy. Someone who hates your guts. Any of these qualify?'

Not that I knew.

I ordered some take-out, and we moved on to other hospitals.

Remarkably similar sorts of cases with the same incidence of hits. By midnight I'd compiled a list of nine men. Too many. Too many for any purpose. How could there be so many sexually messed-up patients just among the people I knew? And none of them, so far as I knew, was an enemy. Di and Leon were now bored, the project having long since lost any titillating effect. Diane wanted to leave. She was worried about her car and, in her words, 'terminally fatigued.' We had already run through all the major hospital-affiliated specialists, but there were still some individual practitioners to check. 'Five more,' I suggested. They shrugged. We started alphabetically. On the fifth doctor's patient list, Carter Denison's name came up.

I said, 'Let me look at this by myself.'

The psychiatrist involved had an office in Harlem in his home. Once a week Carter trekked up there from the Federal courthouse downtown to confess the agonies of restraint. 'I think about it,' Carter told this man. 'I dream about it. And what's worse, I feel no guilt about it. It's not every woman I see. It may not be more than one out of thirty or forty. But that one! My mind goes to work, I really can't stop it. I may be talking to her about the fucking weather, but I've got this picture in my head of holding her down, thinking she's enjoying it, vain prick that I am.'

He found a woman, a court clerk, who apparently shared his predilections. She went with him to a hotel in Chinatown two, three times a month. 'S&M-lite,' he called it. He still thought about gang-raping the fourteen-year-old girl, and two others he'd gotten away with. He told the psychiatrist he had the impulse in check, but, given the lie Carter was otherwise living, he could just as easily have been lying about that.

I hated having this information about Carter, but the fact remained, there was absolutely no reason for Carter to dislike me, let alone hate me enough to try to incriminate me. When I started this search I'd expected someone else to turn up. The guy who fit Cheryl's description. Him I might have suspected of resentment.

I paid Leon three hundred dollars. I promised him another three thousand if the information led to nailing my impersonator.

A contingent deal, but fair, I thought, in the circumstances. And if I got my life back, I'd be able to pay him. Seeing us out the door, Leon said, 'Next time bring me something hard to do.'

Downstairs, under a streetlamp, Diane and I looked at her Mercedes, hubcaps intact, and then at each other. 'Fucking know-all,' she said with a dry laugh.

'Want me to drive?' I asked.

'Nobody,' she said, 'I mean *nobody* drives my car but me.'

'Yes ma'am,' I said, opening the back door.

'No, front seat. Until the tunnel. I'm getting a stiff neck trying to talk to you.'

On the West Side Drive I said, 'I know it's late, but would you mind making a quick stop at that S&M club I told you about?'

'Boy!' she said.

I didn't react, and she didn't pursue it. She knew, and I knew she knew. I wasn't going there for fun.

From West Street, the building looked abandoned. As soon as you pushed through the outer door everything changed. Cover charge, payable to a model wannabe, was fifteen bucks. A lot for a glimpse. The actual club spilled out into the basement. A dazzlingly lit lucite staircase spiraled into an expanse of stainless steel and mirrored glass. This place had the backing of serious money. No chains, rubber or leather in evidence. At the glistening bar and tables, patrons, mainly male, sat suited in black or gray, more Armani or Prada than Savile Row.

I recognized no one. An effete, probably the manager, informed me I'd just missed the early show. In that case, I said, I'd come back some other night.

Diane feigned surprise at my returning so quickly. 'What happened? Someone come at you with a whip?' Her car left the lot as the door closed.

She flipped on the radio. CBS News. First thing we heard was my name. With an 'alleged' in front of the word rapist. 'Fugitive' was unmodified. On WINS we had to wade through the sports. Two minutes later, the same report. Except more frenzied. And scary. This guy (me) sounded like a monster from hell.

'You're getting all the publicity,' she said.

'Want some?'

'No thanks.'

The tunnel. Even on the floor in the back seat, it made me sweat.

As usual, I surfaced after the toll booth. 'I love our routines,' I said, climbing into the front at a stop light, trying to sound calm.

'Yeah,' she said. But her heart wasn't in it.

At home, she said, at the foot of the staircase, 'Totally wiped out. Going right up.'

'Me too.'

Ascending, she stopped abruptly. 'At some point,' she said, 'we're really going to have to sort this thing out.'

I didn't ask.

'Right,' she said, leaning back against me. 'That thing. Good night.'

'Good night.'

THIRTY-SIX

It took me an hour at least to get to sleep. Replaying that scene on the stairway, for one thing, then pretty much every scene since the nightmare began. I thought, we're looking for a guy with a grudge against me. So what's his next move? Who's his next victim?

Drifting off past midnight, I woke like a shot at three in the morning. *What the hell! His next victim? How could I have been so stupid? Obviously, Ali! If someone hates me, she's the target. And fits the profile. Success, boss-lady, press coverage.*

I roamed downstairs. Began thinking, this is crazy! If she were so obvious a target, why hadn't he struck before this? Which gave me relief for two minutes. Then it hit me again. My fear wasn't crazy. It was this guy who was crazy. And for that twisted mind, this was exactly the right moment: the height of the operatic media delirium about me.

I called Ali at four a.m., but got her machine as I'd expected. She always turned the phone off at night. Waking Diane seemed out of the question. A few hours earlier, she was too tired even to try to disguise it. And as for the car – I heard her voice: only she drove that automobile.

By four forty-five, or thereabouts, I crashed on the living room sofa where Diane found me at seven in the morning. 'Good night's sleep, hunh?' she said. I jumped up, threw on some clothes and sprinted out the door, saying only, 'Tell you later.' At the pay booth I'd used that first morning, I caught Ali just before she left with Molly and Sam.

'Baby, you're OK? The kids?'

'Of course,' she said. 'Why wouldn't we be?'

Of course I couldn't tell her, and shouldn't have called at all.

Finally, she said, 'Are *you* all right?'

'Well, no sleep. Wanted to make sure you're all safe.'

'Safe?'

'Yeah. Look. I've got to go. Be well.'

'Rick, what's going on? You think that guy's coming for me? There's a cop stationed in the lobby of this building every day, just waiting for you. And I chain the door every night.'

I hung up. Stupid, I swore at myself. Stupid to have called.

Diane was still having coffee when I got back. I sat down and explained myself.

'You're still in love with her, aren't you? Your wife?'

'Ex,' I said.

'Ex, whatever.'

'It's dwindling.'

'Dwindling, bullshit. I see a man in pain.'

'Lack of sleep.'

'Sleep deprivation doesn't look like that. Love deprivation looks like that.'

I made a helpless face, and she waved her hand at me with impatience. 'So what're you going to do?' she said. 'Go there every night?'

'It'll be tonight. Or tomorrow. If it's going to happen.'

'You know this,' she said, as if it were preposterous.

'I do.'

She thought for a moment, got it. 'You've been charting him,' she said. 'Like a stock.'

'Since he's started, he hasn't gone longer than a week.'

'And this would really get back at you.'

'If I allowed it to happen . . .'

'She could call the police.'

'There's a cop there already. Waiting downstairs. Not there for her, though.'

'For you.'

'Right.'

She thought some more. 'You'll want a lift into Manhattan, I suppose.'

'This is the way we might catch him.'

'Or the cops might catch you.'

'Or the cops, me,' I acknowledged.

'And me. Harboring's bad enough. Chauffeuring's got to be double the sentence.'

'You're right. I should get out of here.'

'I'm not suggesting that.'

We thought about it.

'You could let me off ten blocks from the building,' I said.

'Twenty,' she said.

I laughed.

'I must be out of my fucking mind,' she said. 'You know, I'm not an altruistic person. I'm a self-interested person. This is uncharacteristic of me.'

'Wouldn't help, then, if I said thank you?'

'No. Makes it worse. Rubs it in.'

THIRTY-SEVEN

Diane dropped me at eleven that night in the middle of Yorkville, Eighty-second and Lex. I walked to Seventy-first near Park. There was an empty brownstone for sale hind Ali's building. Its street-level door, to the right of the 't stoop, led to the basement. I picked up a brick, punched in a small pane of glass, reached in, found the lock and opened it. I knew about this building. It belonged to the estate of one of the retired partners of my former firm. The sign outside warned of surveillance by a security company. In fact, that service had been discontinued for a year. Nothing left inside was worth stealing.

A faint memory of the place helped me feel my way in the dark inside the old subterranean kitchen where the original owner had probably installed a cook, three scullery maids and a butler. All of whom, I'm sure, were billeted in the unventilated attic.

In a few minutes I'd trudged into the backyard garden. Not much of a wall between it and the paved courtyard to Ali's building. It was a bright night – lots of stars, big moon, no clouds. I might have hoped for more cover. Yet any cops would have been visible, had they been there, when I jumped to peek over the wall. The courtyard looked empty. I jumped and peeked again. Seemed like no one was bothering to guard the rear. Which meant they didn't really expect me to be this reckless. Nor did they expect anyone else.

Climbing over the wall presented no problem, given a rusty lawn chair to prop in front of it, vines growing all over it and the fact that its height was not much more than my own. It had been built for privacy, not security from marauders. And while getting into the back of Ali's building should not have been easy, it always was. I'd served two terms as president of this co-op – bad job, everyone's whipping boy, but it gave me the keys to the building and I still had them on my key chain. I doubted I'd need the back door key, however, and I was right. The service staff never bothered to lock it. Too much trouble, and what was the point? Break-ins? Unheard of in eighty years. And it was the staff's main exit and entrance for the procurement and consumption of coffee.

It also led to the back stairwell of the building. Because of cost-cutting, only two staffers were on at this hour, and their post was the front door. The cop, if one was still there, probably kept them company. Someone to talk to. And they could prevent anyone entering that way from getting upstairs, since they controlled the front elevators. Access to the back stairway was barred by an iron grill gate, when locked. Of course it wasn't locked – never was until the change of shift at midnight.

I thought, moving up the back stairs, when this is over, I'd get the current co-op president on the phone. I'd say – what was his name? – Phil. I'd say, Phil, what the hell's going on? How could you let the security in the building get so damn lax? And I might even say, wasn't that way on my watch. Which would be bullshit. Of course it was. Who the hell thinks about security but someone like me, who wants to break in?

Well, there I was. Seventh floor. Breathing hard at the back door. Our moment of truth, Ali's and mine. I had the key, but she'd said she would put the chain on. I didn't believe it. She often chained the front door, though it was effectively guarded by the doorman's control of the front elevator, but never the back. It was the entrance Maria, the maid, used each morning after Ali left for work. Ali had long since stopped trying to remember every day to take the chain off, so she just stopped putting it on. I had an idea where the building staff kept a chain cutter in the basement, but the thought of going down there, rummaging around, the noise of using it – forget it. So I'd gone straight upstairs. And the key turned in the lock, the door opened – success. Good old Ali. Totally dependable. Said she would put the chain on. Didn't.

I opened and closed the door without a sound.

I stood there, in the back hall, next to the maid's room, in the dark silent apartment. Everyone was asleep. I put the chain on, took three steps into the apartment and, adjacent to the laundry room, stopped again. Listened. No sound. Then I heard a creak, but that was normal. Then someone moving overhead. Our upstairs neighbor. Otherwise, silence.

I crossed the main hall. A floorboard creaked, I stopped for a moment, listened again, and continued.

Molly's room in the children's wing: light from somewhere fell on her, just a silver shaft, but I could see her plainly, breathing steadily, no bad dreams. A fierce surge of protectiveness welled up in my chest, filling me with tenderness. Burning tears filled my eyes. Then I felt a backlash of anger. That anyone could threaten my children! I could kill such a person. Without hesitation. Without thought. Even Carter. And certainly the society mug.

I moved on to the next room.

Sam, too, was sleeping deeply, one cheek mashed into the pillow, hair matted down over his eyes, nose running slightly. I attended to him with a Kleenex, at which he stirred but did not wake. I stood there admiring him for another moment. A gorgeous boy, the image of his mother.

Moving stealthily once more, avoiding the floorboards I knew would creak, I retreated to the back hall and then the maid's room. Boxes littered the maid's bed. We hadn't had a live-in for years, and now used the room for storage. Quietly, I moved the boxes into the back hall and, at long last, took off my shoes and lay down on the bed. Tried to sleep. Of course, I couldn't. I studied the ceiling, studied the walls. Tried all the tricks. Emptied my mind. I must have lain there, what? Two hours? Until, finally, I dozed off, thinking the whole thing, my panic, coming here, ridiculous.

The Seventh Victim

It started as a dream. I was even dreaming the pain but it woke me. Pain wracked my shoulders. I had no freedom of movement in my arms or legs. I couldn't see, I was hooded. I couldn't open my mouth, it was taped. Sounds were choked off in the back of my throat. I had the sensation of being dragged by someone a lot stronger than I was. Propped up, my head pushed hard into something, a cushion, a mattress? Then, an excruciating pain, like a shoulder separation. What? What? What? Blinding pain, something hit me. Blackness, I was out.

Not for long, I think. When I came to, I could see, take everything in, if only dimly. Ski-capped figure on the corner of the bed. Ali bent strangely, her head facing me, tape over her eyes. Pillows, cushions hoisting her in the middle. Her mouth was slack, her hair plastered down her face, like Sam's. Only Ali, I now saw, was naked. Her behind stuck up in the air like a comic lewd figure in a bawdy play, her legs splayed apart.

Wrenched rudely by the arms, I tried again to scream at the

bastard. He was dragging me to the foot of the bed. He wanted me to see. This perverted maniac wanted me to watch what he'd be doing to my wife.

He spoke in her ear. He didn't have to do anything. She'd do it all. I could conceive of the threats that would make her display herself like this, split herself, open herself wide. One ungloved hand oiled her, probed her with a doctor's incurious thrust. Her mouth was dead, expressionless. Shock? Sheer terror?

Pinioned to the floor, I struggled with rage. With one knee on my throat, he pulled my trousers down. Then he hauled me up, draped me over her, shoved me next to her on the bed. I heard him, face to mine, shout at her, as if the words were coming from me, until she moved sightlessly, hoisted over me, flopping in my face. Then yanked down. That's what he wants, I kept thinking. I heard him croak commands as if from my mouth, felt her mouth, the inside, her tongue, soft. No way could I stop what happened next.

THIRTY-EIGHT

I blacked out and apparently slept. Pre-dawn, I bolted awake. Ali lay beside me, unconscious, the tape still over her eyes. My legs remained taped, not my hands or arms. Both of us were naked.

Lying face down, I could turn over and start removing the tape from my ankles. Ali finally stirred. Started whimpering in fright until she realized or remembered her eyes were taped. She clawed at the tape, got it off. Looked at me, her eyes blinking fast, remembering more. Legs free, I rubbed my face, began scratching all the unbearable itches.

'Goddamnit,' I said.

Ali rolled out of bed. She'd always been thin; now she looked thinner. These were not the circumstances in which I wished to renew intimacy with her body. By the time I got into the bathroom, she already stood head down in the shower. I did not join her but waited my turn. Coming out, she didn't cover herself. Gestured for me to let her pass. I soaked even longer than she had.

When I emerged, Ali, wearing a bathrobe, sat at the kitchen table, coffee cup in front of her. It was just past six thirty a.m. and not yet fully light. The kids wouldn't wake up for another half hour. I took some coffee and sat opposite.

What the hell could I possibly say?

So I said, 'Are you OK?'

And she started laughing. Bad sign. I thought, She's in shock. But when I went to her, she waved me away. She said, 'You know, I'm not feeling any of the things you're supposed to feel. I'm angry, but I've been angrier. At work, sometimes, when someone's tried to screw me over, I've been angrier. I'm tired. But I've been more tired. I should feel humiliated. I suppose that was the point of it. I'm not really hurt physically, so I suppose the idea was to humiliate me. But, hey,' she said, and it was almost a screech, 'I've been hit by a maniac. It's happened. It's over. The kids are fine. I've checked. They're sleeping as if it were any other night. And that's going to be my state of mind. You understand? I'm not going to let any creep have an effect on my life. *OK?* I don't even want to talk about it.'

Throughout this speech I thought, delayed reaction? Suppressed hysteria? And I? Dangling on the edge. Oddly, the need to calm Ali worked for me. I said, 'I think you ought to see someone this morning. Maybe check into a hospital.'

'*No hospital!*'

I took a few moments, a few sips of coffee, then began explaining why I was there. I didn't get very far.

'You want this, Rick, you want to talk about it?'

'I—'

'You were here . . .'

'This guy – he's getting at me. I don't know why, but he is. I felt you were at risk.'

'And so you picked last night to come here?' She sounded incredulous.

I said, 'He got in here very quietly. I don't know how he did that.' She wouldn't meet my eye. 'Don't you think you should call the police?'

'No.' She said it flatly, in a tone brooking no disagreement.

'You're just going to let it go entirely?'

'I have nothing to tell them that others haven't already told them.'

'Well, you could tell them it's not me. That would be helpful.'

'Oh, really? You think they'd believe that? From me?'

She was acting too strangely for me to be able to talk to her. I got up, looking for the bread where it used to be kept. Still was. I put some in the toaster and sat down again at the table. 'I've learned something about our friend Carter,' I said. 'Something quite unpleasant.'

She just stared at me

I related what I knew about Carter's juvenile arrest and his confessions to his shrink.

'It's not Carter,' she said.

Her vehemence surprised me. 'How can you be so sure?'

'Just believe me.'

'OK,' I said doubtfully.

'It's not what you're thinking. It's smell,' she said.

'Carter smells?' I asked.

'The opposite. No smell. None whatever.'

'Whereas . . . last night?'

'Unmistakable.'

'You sure?' I said, remembering nothing unusual.

'Quite sure.'

We sat in silence.

'There are grounds to suspect someone else,' I said.

Icy stare.

'Roger Hazzard.'

'Are you demented?' she said.

Out of the corner of my eye I spied him, listening to every word. My son Sam, in the doorway looking up at me. 'You and Mommy are talking very loud.'

'Oh, my God, darling,' said Ali, going to him. 'Did we wake you?'

'Yes, you did.' It was a grievance.

I said, 'I'm sorry, Sammy. Would you like to go back to sleep?'

'No,' he said. 'Could I have breakfast now?'

Ali looked at me with an expression that said, you ought to go. Mine conveyed the opposite: see how nice it would be if we could be a family again – which, in the circumstances, wasn't the smartest message I might have sent. She shook her head and glanced toward the door. I kneeled to give Sammy a kiss.

He wrenched away. 'Where have you been?' he said, in a voice filled with resentment.

'Oh, Sammy! I missed you so much. I had to be away. Someday soon I'll explain it.'

'Come sit down, sweetheart,' said Ali.

'I want Daddy to give me breakfast,' he said, being contrary, I thought, because he was confused.

I looked at Ali again. Tears brimmed in her eyes, but her look ordered me elsewhere, and I went.

THIRTY-NINE

I called Diane who called Leon, and we arranged to meet at his apartment. I took a subway. I figured, they can't cover every station, every car, every minute. And they couldn't. I got to Washington Heights, undetected, in half an hour. But in the station I got the chills. Literally shivered on the train and while walking to Leon's apartment. I held myself and tried to stop the tremors. Couldn't; but the sun did. For a time, it blanched out images of the night.

Leon said he wanted to pick up some breakfast, and I gave him money enough for three. 'Lots of hot coffee,' I told him. 'Strong.' In the meantime, Diane arrived. 'Where'd you park?' I asked. Shouldn't have. Got me a stare that would have crystallized antifreeze. It had been a morning of them.

'I'll probably never see that car again,' she said.

We took a glance at Leon's screen. He had already found the liquor license of the S&M club I'd identified. The name of the club was Agony Un-Ltd. And it wasn't incorporated. The company that owned it was, with the bland name of Southside

Importers, Inc. Since I hadn't stuck around for the floor show, I could only imagine what they imported.

Standing there with Diane, waiting for Leon, my head started floating. It was a weird, *weird* sensation of unreality. Last night was real; this wasn't. Last night I watched my wife being sexually violated. Not only couldn't I stop it from happening; I was made to participate. My face turned ugly with revulsion.

Diane was looking at me as if not sure who I was. 'So what happened last night?'

I had almost forgotten she was in the room. 'Last night,' I repeated. 'You might say the strategy worked.'

'*He was there?*' she fairly yelled, suddenly excited. 'He was actually there?'

'Yes. He was there.'

'*And?*'

'And. I was sleeping when he arrived. So I couldn't greet him properly.'

Her look became wary. 'He totally got away.'

'That,' I said slowly, 'would have been preferable.'

She blinked. 'You have no idea who he is?'

'Sorry,' I said.

'Well, I'm not completely indifferent to your misfortune, man. What happened?'

I said, with all the control I could muster, 'I really don't want to go into details.'

'What fucking details? There're only a limited number of things can be done. And he does 'em.'

It was Diane now who was on the brink of hysteria. Again, the need to calm someone else helped me. I said as gently as I could, 'Leave it, OK?'

'Right,' she said. 'Leave it. What a bizarre fucking conversation this is!'

Leon returned with coffee and doughnuts. He had his own insights to share. 'Guy like this,' he said. 'It's only a matter of time before he starts killing his victims.'

I thought, He might be right. How often could a psychotic like this threaten ultimate violence without committing it? Without needing to? So there we were trying to track down a serial rapist and potential murderer, while munching on doughnuts and sipping coffee. And probably this guy, this maniacal abuser of women, was doing something equally banal, while considering his next outrage.

Leon worked his magic. Southside Importers, Inc. Certificates of incorporation led to articles of incorporation, which led to the names of the individual incorporators. Usually dummy names, but, I thought, Let's see. With a particular target in mind, I gave Leon the name of my old law firm. He penetrated the firm's vaunted security system in less than three minutes and was into the client list within four. In another moment, he had the incorporators of those clients. But none were also incorporators of Southside, the S&M club owner.

Back to the Southside incorporator names. Had any of these people also been incorporators of other corporations licensed to do business in the state? Leon's fingers flew once more over the keyboard. The screen changed, fingers flew, the process repeated itself several times. Now there was a list. Six companies that one or more of these people had incorporated in addition to Southside, each of which had additional incorporators. Back into the firm's system. Now there was a match. A client called Melchiore Multimedia. Partner in charge: Roger Hazzard. I could hear Roger's voice, in that distinctive Old Dutch New York accent, explaining to the firm that he'd brought in this new client which was a company managed by people of sufficiently high character and integrity to warrant the firm's taking it on.

Diane said, 'Hey, I know that guy. We did a deal once, at Goldman's, in which he represented the issuer.'

Leon looked up from the screen. 'Bingo?' he said, studiously blasé.

'Bingo,' I said, and it was.

FORTY

I called Roger from Leon's apartment and was put right through. I said, 'Roger, before one of your secretaries tries to get the cops to trace this, let me tell you what I know,

OK? About Melchiore Multimedia, Southside Importers, Agony
Un-Ltd. and all the prostitutes on Eleventh Avenue you've been
beating the shit out of.'

Hardly a beat. 'Would you hold for a sec, Rick?'

I could see him in the outer room of his suite frantically
signaling his secretaries not to beam in the cops after all.

'What do you want, old boy?' he said, returning after a few
moments. Jauntiness fails with a mouth full of tremors.

'I think we might have things to talk about. What do *you*
think, Rog?'

'Yes, all right. When? I've got an opening – let's see. Next
Thursday? That good for you?'

I barked out a laugh. 'One hour. Bronx Zoo. Snake house.
That's good for me. I'm sure your driver can find it.'

'Jesus, Rick. Couldn't we make it someplace more convenient? I've got a schedule.'

'Whatta you know? I don't. And I like the metaphor. Oh,
and Roger? If you set me up – what I know, everyone knows.
Capisce?'

'I hear you.'

'*Ciao*, baby.' Not normally my tone, which probably really
freaked him.

I liked more than the metaphorical appropriateness of the place.
I liked the fact it was public, lots of people, kids, even on a
school day, and lots of space. Diane drove me up and stayed
in the lot. But on the way there I had a chance to fill her in on
my relationship with Hazzard, including his unfounded conviction I'd been sleeping with his first wife. When I told her who
that was, she exploded.

'This, in your view, is an *unlikely* suspect?'

'That's what I thought, Di.'

'Jesus!'

I knew my way to the snake house. Sammy liked snakes. I
never knew why, but he did. And I was deliberately late in
appearing, giving Roger time to stew. So as I walked into this
edifice, there he was, next to a glass case of reptiles, inattentive
to their slithering; instead, fixed on the entrance, waiting for
me. In his tailored suit with its pinched waist and flared double

vents. With his groomed blow-dried hair and aristocratically beaked nose. Looking foolish and frightened. In the snake house. I loved it. I could have strangled him, literally.

'Let's go,' I said, beckoning him on to the path. 'Just walk.'

We did in silence. Maybe four hundred yards. I wanted to see whether anyone, even at a distance, walked with us. Odd couple, Roger and I; he all suited up, and I in my jeans, with a growth of beard and mustache.

I knew all the species of animals here that were allowed to run freely within the large landscaped grounds. As we walked, I watched the school kids and tourists lining the fences, trying to feed them, or just admiring life forms one doesn't see grazing in Yokohama or Berlin. Fine day for it. Leaves now a riot of color. High clouds, sun warmer than usual for late fall.

'Let's sit here,' I said, indicating a bench, far from the animals, and therefore from the crowds.

Roger began. 'I don't know who you've been talking to, but the fact is—'

'I've made a big mistake?' I said with a laugh.

That took a little wind out. 'Right,' he said nonetheless.

'Don't think so,' I said, and told him what I knew and how I knew it, implying I knew considerably more.

When I finished, Roger looked away. 'So you think, what?' he said. 'That I'm the man doing the things the authorities are persuaded you're doing?'

'Where were you last night?' I asked.

'Last night?' His surprise seemed genuine. 'Last night I went to that club you're talking about, why?'

'You score?'

'No. One doesn't, you know, that often. It's a very hit or miss sort of thing.' He thought I might share the humor.

I didn't. 'So you did what? Pick up some hooker?'

'I went home. Directly home.'

'Abby can vouch for this?'

'Abby's in Paris.'

'How convenient.'

'Rick, what's this about? I heard nothing on the news this morning. Nothing happened last night.'

I studied his face. Maybe some experts can tell, by mere

observation, whether a man is acting or for real. I can't. Not unless he's a complete airhead. I can tell sometimes when he's digging his heels in, but not, if he's good at it, whether he's covering up. And Roger was hardly an airhead. A weak self-seeking butt-suck, but not stupid. Also, I really had nothing on him. He was a sadist who terrorized prostitutes; that didn't mean he was the serial rapist the cops believed to be me.

'What do you want, Rick? Are you blackmailing me?'

My laugh was so caustic it turned a passer-by's head. 'Roger, I'm a hair's breadth away from turning you in. You knew every one
of these women, and were married to one. You're a certifiable sadist. You're a far more likely suspect than I am. I give you up, and I'm a free man. With my life back, such as it is. Can you think of a single reason why I shouldn't do that? Trade my misery for yours?'

He no longer had the look of a man who might negotiate his way out of this; he looked scared. 'Because I didn't do it?'

'Well, you see, that doesn't seem to make any difference. I didn't do it either. But in your case, I'm not convinced.'

'You make good on this threat,' he said, now welled-up in self- pity, 'and you ruin me. Even when I'm cleared of the rape charges, my life is over. Professional life, married life. My children.' Tears actually came to his eyes. 'Rick, don't. When you're free of this, I'll be your biggest supporter. And see, that's the difference. You *will* be clean once they catch the guy. You mark *me* with this – by bringing up those other women – the mud will stick.'

'You, however, deserve to go to prison. Whether or not you've raped these women.'

'What I do with them – these prostitutes . . .' He gave a deprecating laugh. 'That's role-play. I don't claim it to be a socially desirable activity, but I pay them extremely well. They know what they're doing. What they're getting into.'

'That you're going to bash their faces in?'

He clucked. 'I don't think I've ever actually done that. Maybe a bruise. You can get carried away a bit. That's the idea of it. But then I increase the tip enormously.' He shook his head as if in self-rebuke. 'It's a disease, my friend. I'm under no illusion this is healthy stuff. I've been to all manner of shrinks, although not for years. They don't do me the slightest good. Although, I must say, it's almost a relief talking to *you* about it.'

I gave this a beleaguered sort of sigh he took for impatience.

'Please, Rick. Don't destroy me. I didn't do this. I'm role-playing with these women so I don't do anything disastrous.'

'I'll think about it,' I said, and got up. He also started to rise, but I pushed him back down.

'Cell phone?' I asked.

He handed it over.

'You stay here. Ten minutes.' I turned away from his pleading face and walked off.

From a distance, I glanced back. Roger was still where I'd left him, sitting erect in his fussy way, now sporting a bemused expression.

When I returned to the car, Diane was dozing. She stirred when I tapped on the window. Still rubbing the sleep from her eyes, she opened the door. 'Sorry. No Z's last night.'

'Want me to drive?'

I got that 'nobody, but nobody drives my car' look again and, laughing, went around to the passenger's seat. Then, we both just sat there with the windows open.

'So?' she finally asked.

'He's not the guy.'

'You're sure?'

'Yes. No. Well, I'm not sure enough he is, and I seriously doubt it.'

'Why?'

'He stinks. Reeks of cologne or after-shave or whatever exotic scent it is he douses himself with. I'd forgotten that. But the son-of-a-bitch is marinated in it. I doubt he could wash it off if he wanted to.'

She thought about that, no doubt in relation to her own experience. 'And the guy last night didn't stink?'

'No. Frankly, his body odor was not what I was focusing on last night, but *that* smell I'd have noticed. I noticed it on Roger in the open air. I'd sure as hell have picked that up in a closed room.'

'So you're letting him off.'

'What else?'

'So he can go on beating up women.'

'Oh, Christ! Di, what do you want?' I was suddenly unbearably tired myself. 'This city – at least five million people doing terrible things. No doubt to people they love. What would you like – to go after them all? New career – social avengers! Holier than thou!'

'You're over-reacting,' she said.

I took a breath, she was right. 'Sorry.'

'We already have the stuff on Roger. And he's hurting people.'

'Then *you* turn him in. Go right to the press. Page Six. They'd love it. Their kind of story.'

'Shit,' she said.

'I agree.'

'We're not making progress,' she said.

'We're hitting dead ends, that's all. Want to stop?'

'No,' she said.

'Then let's get on with it.'

She gave a dark look to the windshield and started her car.

FORTY-ONE

A bear-like man, hair springing from every surface, leaned heavily into the chancel rail. 'My name is Gus,' he said, 'and I'm a sexaholic.'

'Hi, Gus!' sang out all of us in the chapel, about twenty troubled souls, Diane and me included.

'I've been coming to these meetings now for more than a year,' said Gus. 'And y'know what? I'm sick of the plot line. Early promise, that's great. Fabulous success, terrific. Then, *wham*! Total ruination. As if the thing that got us there – that drove us to succeed – is the same damn thing that now makes us fuck up, no pun intended. Believe me, no pun intended.'

Gus, of course, was talking mainly about himself. Head of his own advertising agency by age thirty-six; wonderful wife, three special children. Then, a bigamy charge, suspended sentence; second bigamy charge, one year in prison. Loss of business. Loss of family. Barred by court order from seeing his children. Married at one stage to four different women, while having sexual relations with five others, not including chance fornications at swinger parties and sex clubs.

'And you've heard this,' he said. 'Automatic pilot? Out of control? I'd shift into a gear – and it *was* like changing gears – where the guy doing these things was not someone I knew. I mean this! To each woman, I was a different guy. And it was like I was outside myself watching that guy operate.'

Where he left me wondering was how any woman could have been so attracted to this hulk in the first place, much less nine women at once. Diane, however, seemed suspended in awe. Made me jealous as hell. I looked around the pews. Women enrapt. So what the hell did I know?

The next speaker, for quite a few moments, had me wondering what he was doing in the room. Tall, blond, thick-necked, waspy, garbed in a Brooks Brothers suit of banker's gray – and, as he then admitted, he *was* a banker. 'My name's Tucker,' he told us. Once a prep school All-American lacrosse player, he remained active in the sport. But, the thing was, he liked to hurt people. On the playing field was fine from his standpoint, but the bedroom was better. Women made better victims. Much sharper gratification. And often, unlike the situation in men's sports, penalties could be avoided for even serious, deliberately inflicted injuries. Like rape. Date rape. Gang rape. Any sort of forcing that involved the infliction of pain.

'There's a mechanism in me that doesn't work,' said Tucker. 'Some brake-like thing that doesn't activate. I feel it stirring – but then, some sexual, hysterical over-ride takes over. Ten minutes later, I look at what I've done, I say, "Oh, my God. How in the world could I have done that to her?" I'm back into myself. I hate myself. But it doesn't stop me from doing it again.'

Tucker concluded routinely. Since going to meetings, he'd been getting his life into some sort of order. Working on his program, his faith in his higher power. There was hope yet in salvation, and so on. Just for today.

The assemblage shared. All but Diane and I. Sitting together, we were conspicuous, but these people were used to having curiosity-seekers at their meetings. Their view was, no one came, even to fulfill a prurient curiosity, unless he or she had another, hidden reason. Indeed, to their way of thinking, everyone was sexually dysfunctional one way or another. Stay long enough, you'd find out why.

We stayed for coffee. There were no cops in this room, or I'd have been picked up already. And I had cause to talk to Tucker. So I eased over, Diane in my wake. I introduced us both. First names only, that was the style. Thanked him for sharing. Feeling like the imposter I was, I said, 'We may have a mutual friend. Betsy Spaeth?'

Not entirely out of left field. He did say lacrosse. He did mention the name of his prep school. And he did say gang rape.

If you're going to catch anybody, you have to be lucky. At some point in the investigation, you need a break; something has to fall in your lap. For me it was Tucker. When I asked him whether he knew Betsy, and the shame lit up his face, I felt I'd hit pay dirt. It happens. His question to me was, 'Are you a cop?'

'No,' I said. 'But I do have some questions. And your answers might help save a life.'

We stayed in the chapel after everyone else drifted out. When some ecclesiastic came to close it, we talked in the hall. You gave Tucker a listener, he'd talk all night long. And we were extremely sympathetic to him. Especially Diane.

Diane's being there was crucial. A smart, lovely young woman listening with deep empathy, taking Tucker's side.

Because there was a side here, of sorts. According to Tucker, at prep school, Betsy was the consummate cocktease. She was breathtakingly beautiful, knew it, and got off on ensuring that the randy adolescents she dated didn't, after giving them plenty of reason to believe they would. That fact, Tucker repeatedly emphasized, did not excuse what they did. 'It simply was a fact,' he said. 'At one time or another, she had doubled over every boy in that room, if you get my meaning.'

I got it. Diane looked puzzled.

Tucker turned red. 'Blue balls?'

'Ah,' said Diane.

'It started out as a gag,' he said. 'We were just going to teach her a lesson. Threaten to strip her, but not actually do it. But she got so pissed off. Started screaming insults, sexual taunts. It kind of developed. And then no one could stop. I think – I'm not sure of this, and it will sound like a rationalization – but, I think, not even Betsy.'

Interesting, if true, but not particularly relevant. I said, just to keep the information flowing, 'Yet she pressed charges.'

'She did,' he said, and paused as if he might stop there.

We both urged him to continue.

He gave a deep sigh, which, for a big jock like Tucker, came off as slightly ridiculous. 'After the incident, one of the guys panicked and told his parents. His mom then panicked and told other moms. The result? Ten sets of hysterical parents. The mothers came flying up to the school. Their version of the facts? Betsy was a slut who had lured us into acting out. And the women on the faculty – most of them – actually agreed with the moms. So Betsy had no choice, really. Once the whole thing got out in the open, she went to the police. They believed her, as they should have. But some of the parents hired this sharp defense attorney from New York who somehow turned everything upside down, like it was Betsy who was the defendant. Bad things came out about her. The local prosecutor, an idiot, didn't protect her. Betsy was furious, and it didn't help when we were all let off so lightly. I've seen Betsy since. Last year, in fact. I've made my peace with her, kind of. But I'm not certain she was ever that angry at *us*.'

'What bad things?' I asked.

He looked at me.

'You said "bad things came out about her."'

'Right. Bizarre, actually. They found two witnesses, two creepy guys. You know, there are sex clubs, S&M dives, all over the city.'

'So I gather.'

'At seventeen, she was, according to these witnesses, a sensation in some of these clubs.'

'As what?' said Diane, incredulous.

'A dominatrix,' said Tucker. 'Can you believe it? Seventeen!'

FORTY-TWO

The mind does race. And, in so doing, can get out ahead of itself. Mine was way out there. An idea too improbable to have ever before entered my head was now taking it over. On the drive home, I sprang it on Diane. We almost went off the road.

With Diane screaming, 'You're saying I was raped *by a woman*?'

'I'm just saying – we've been thinking it had to be a man. But that's not necessarily the case. All that's needed is a sick mind and a strong body. Betsy certainly has the body. And given what Tucker's just told us . . .?'

'I know, but still. This is some far-fetched theory.'

'We have to consider everything.'

'Yes, I know,' she said, 'but *Jesus*!'

'Were you . . .?'

'*What?*'

'Never mind.'

'Penetrated?' she said. 'Is that the word you want?'

I said nothing.

'Why? You think a woman can't penetrate? You ever hear of a strap-on?'

'I'm sorry,' I said.

'Forget it. But, believe me, it wasn't a woman.'

We drove in silence.

Finally she said, 'Even apart from the fact that I know this is totally implausible, how would she even . . .? I mean, why me? How does she pick me out? I've never met the woman.'

'Has your picture ever been in the papers?'

She threw me a sidelong glance. 'What do you think? I'm a nobody?'

'Seriously.'

'Of course, seriously. Financial press, usually. Once in the *Wall Street Journal.* Reviews in *Variety* last summer and the Massachusetts dailies.'

We drove for another few moments before I asked, 'Would you necessarily have known?'

'Whatta you mean?'

'Man or woman?'

'Yes.' She seemed to fight with it. 'Of course.'

'Because?'

'OK,' she said emphatically with the most extraordinary look on her face. 'I think we've gone about as far with this as we're going to go. Unless you have something to contribute.'

'Maybe later,' I said.

'What's going to happen later?'

I shrugged.

'What do you *think* is going to happen later?' she said.

'I don't know,' I said.

'What do you *want* to happen later?'

She was looking hard at the road.

'Rick?'

'What *you* want,' I said.

'And?' she said. 'You think – *what*? Whatta you suppose—'

'Why don't we . . .'

'Hold this conversation . . .'

'Yeah.'

The car swerved wildly, and she swore. What I heard, in mid-imprecation: 'To say nothing – *absolutely nothing* – about being dangerous. While I'm driving, for crissake!'

In her bedroom, Diane said, 'I'm not sure I can do this.'

'Me neither,' I said.

'Why not?' she asked sharply.

'It feels . . .'

'On demand?'

'No, not that, but . . .'

'It's true,' she said. 'I'm using you. I need to do this, and you're . . .'

'Here?'

She grimaced.

'Not a problem,' I said.

'I mean in normal circumstances,' she said, 'this wouldn't happen . . . for months. *If!*'

'If ever?'

'Not that you're—'

'Totally gruesome.'

'Right,' she said. 'Not totally.'

'I'm tremendously attracted to you.'

'Are you?' she said weakly.

'Yes. I am. And for the record . . . I asked you.'

'Because I pushed you. I'm pushy, I'm pushing you now, I'm—'

'Di, it's absolutely fine. It's wonderful.'

We needn't have worried. After the anxieties, everything felt right.

Diane surprised me. For being so shy for a big talker, and for being exquisite. In her running clothes, she might have been taken for scrawny. Not so in the altogether where, for me, she epitomized everything beautiful in the female form. When I said something to that effect, she put her hand on my mouth. Unlike Betsy, who reveled in exhibiting herself, Diane persisted in turning off the lights and covering up.

For Diane, the turn-on was verbal. Suited me. I expected my usual difficult first time. She said, 'Relax. Let's talk about it.' We lay in her bed, draped by a sheet and nothing else. Pretty soon, we were snuggling. And talking. Having telephone sex without the telephone. Problem disappeared. So did the sheet. I'm on a roll, I thought. Getting lucky in sex, while getting reamed by everything else.

And then, all barriers seemed to come down. It was as if, trusting each other as sex partners, we were ready to open up to what otherwise mattered most. For me, it was the agony of my divorce, and the separation from my children. For Diane, it was an inability to love anyone appropriate.

'There were several guys early on who just fell back. I'm working sixteen, eighteen hours a day, traveling all over the world – unless you're part of that, it seems crazy. People who'd rather do it than be with their lovers get dumped.'

'Not necessarily by other people who do it,' I said.

'Others who do it – males – have a tendency either to be womanizing shits, or to be married with children. And don't think I haven't tried the latter.'

'They wouldn't leave their wives?'

'Oh, yes. They were going to. For me or someone else. And by now have.'

'You didn't really love them.'

'One of them, I did. Not a great love, but we got along extremely well. It was the kids. I don't get along with kids. I don't have the knack.'

'You'd like mine.'

She shook her head. 'You see, that's why you're safe, Rick. Safe sex. No danger of anything more. I'm sure I'd like your kids. I'm sure they're terrific. From a distance. Another household distance.'

'You'd have to see them close up,' I said.

She mashed her face in my chest and rolled it side to side. I took that for denial.

'The thing about kids,' I said, 'what they think about is interesting, but it's more the *way* they think. They zone in, they're specific. Mine are.'

'Example?' she said, her face still mashed against me.

'OK. In Central Park, there's a place called Safari Playground, that's the official name. It's full of steel sculptures of animals, all kinds. My kids love the hippos, so to them it's Hippo Park.'

I felt her shrug.

'And they're constantly surprising.'

'OK,' she said dubiously.

'OK,' I said. 'I'm in a movie theater with Sam. He's six. We're watching one of the Harry Potters, which he's already seen twice. Twenty minutes into the film he yanks on my sleeve and warns me, "Scary part's coming." When it gets on the screen, he says, "Don't be frightened, Daddy. It's only a movie."'

She pulled her head away. 'See, that wouldn't happen with me. That's my point. I don't relate to kids. They don't get me, and they clam up.'

It had already dawned on me that this lovely, smart and successful young woman somehow, for no evident reason, lacked the assurance she usually tried to project.

'Clam up, you say? Really? So here's another example,' I said. 'Molly. At a French bistro, one Saturday afternoon, just the two of us.'

'Eating clams.'

'Mussels actually. Molly's eight, and she loves mussels, so that's what she orders. Then this gigantic bowl of them gets set before her, and everyone in the place – other diners, waiters, staff – gawk. How's this little kid going to deal with this mountain of shell fish? Usually, in a Manhattan restaurant, no one looks at anyone else. But here, Molly's meal is the prime attraction. Only she's oblivious, she's lost in the wonder of this glorious food. And when she finishes the plate, she rips off a big slice of French bread and sops up the broth. Then she looks up. Sees everyone gazing in amazement. Is she embarrassed? Absolutely not. She's triumphant. She gives them this huge grin. And, would you believe it? They applaud. And my Molly – like royalty – inclines her head in acknowledgement. She's very special.'

'Maybe it's you.'

I forced her to look at me.

She said, 'You gave her leave.'

'How so?'

'It's what you do with kids, I'm sure. That I can't. It's what you did with me, Rick.'

We finally talked about her acting career, or, at least, why she didn't pursue one full time after college.

'I didn't fit in,' she said. 'Still don't.'

'You don't like other actors?'

'They're lovely, the ones I know.'

'So?' I said slowly.

'I just . . . can't hang with them.'

My look persisted.

'OK,' she said, sitting up. 'My problem? Not jumping on every bandwagon that swerves to the left. Insufficient hugging of trees.'

'And all actors . . .'

'Huge majority. The others pretend. Until they're successful enough to come out of the closet.'

'Are you right-wing?'

'*No* wing! That's what I'm telling you. I don't like running with herds.'

'How do you feel about small ones?'

She hesitated.

'Family size,' I said.

A long unreadable silence ensued.

She got out of bed. 'I told you, man.'

The Eighth Victim

Arriving on her landing at about three thirty in the morning, Emma could tell there was someone in her apartment. No cats stirring, for one thing. Normally she heard them scratching on the other side of the door, ready to fly at her legs as soon as she opened it. The air conditioner for another thing. It was whirring, although she'd turned it off before she'd left. And the scariest thing – no mistaking it – a footfall inside that was a lot heavier than a cat's.

This really pissed her off, this invasion. She'd been to a lousy party in Brooklyn, was way tired, did not want to cope. So who was inside? A thief? Some former john? An addict scrounging for drugs or something he could barter for drugs? 'What the fuck,' she said aloud, turning the key and busting the door open.

Bad move, she thought, going down, strong hands and foul odors gripping her. Wham! – pancaked to the carpet. The door slammed. This thing – *a gun?* – pressed to her cheekbone. Then his Darth Vader voice, as his weight lifted off her. 'You stay on the floor, you stare at the carpet!'

'Oh, *shit*! What the hell do you want?'

'What you have, which is next to nothing.'

'Just take it, then.'

'You're in a rush,' he said, amused.

'*I'm tired!*'

'I've just killed one of your cats. I did it slowly. With a knife. I could start on the other one now. What do you think? Or maybe you.'

In the dim light coming in from the street, she saw the source of the smell. Her tabby, three feet in front of her, a bloody mop. The sight numbed her fear. Panic did that to Emma; it worked like a drug.

'Get to your feet,' he said. 'No sudden movements. Then remove all your clothes.'

She said wearily, 'So that's what this is.'

He shot a hole in the carpet, a foot from her head. A big thump from a silencer and a geyser of dust. The next hole's in your skull, was the message.

'You have five seconds to start. Five, four—'

'OK!' she said, bouncing up, terrified. 'I know how to do this. No problem.'

'Do not turn around.'

'Whatever. Great.'

'Everything off.'

'Hey. Gimme a sec. You're gonna love it. I've got a terrific bod.'

'Fast now! Strip! Fast!'

'You got it! You got it!' she said, leaping about to get naked.

'I said, don't turn.'

'I won't. Sorry.'

'Now just stand. Be still. Calm yourself.'

'I'm calm!'

'You're moving.'

'No. No, that wasn't moving. Twitching, I think. You're scaring the shit outta me.'

He stood right behind her, his breath on the back of her neck. His gloved hand curled under her armpit to show her the blade of a knife usable to scale fish. He pressed it flat on her right breast, blade up, directly under her nipple, then used it to push her breast upward.

'You got a knife *and* a gun?' she said, gulping air to steady her breathing.

'It's quite sharp,' he said. 'Worked very well on the cat.'

'Don't do this, please,' she said, shutting her eyes, hating the fact she was begging.

'I want you to talk. About yourself. I want you to tell me the things about yourself that most embarrass you. Physical things, intimate things, fantasies. I think you know, the sort of thoughts you've never confessed having to anyone . . . because they're too embarrassing. If I suspect you're not being genuine, I'll kill your other cat. As a last warning. Before I start cutting you. Do you have any questions?'

He released the knife and waited. After a moment, she half turned to face him. 'I know who you are,' she said.

He let out a sigh, as if lamenting a great loss.

'I know who the fuck you are!'

FORTY-THREE

When I awoke, Diane was returning from her morning run, raising the shades, glistening with good health and perspiration. My suggestion we shower together was greeted with a derisive grin. We had breakfast instead.

'You left last night,' she said in the middle of corn flakes.

'Yeah. Sorry. Did I wake you?'

'For a while. Then I woke up again, and you still weren't back.'

'I do that,' I said. 'I'm not a great sleeper.'

'You go out?'

'For a bit.'

'Walking?'

'Yeah.'

'Thinking?'

'Yeah.'

'Your Betsy theory.'

''Fraid so,' I said.

'It wasn't her. Not with me.'

'OK.'

'You think, maybe I'm wrong.'

'It's possible.'

We ate in silence.

Diane said, 'I don't see Chacon giving you much of a hearing.'

'I thought, first I'd talk to Luis.'

I filled her in on the strange behavior of my former doorman. 'Someone scared him into lying about me. Only three people knew I was relying on him: Betsy, Ali and Carter.'

'All right,' she said. 'Take my opinion out of this. Take *me* out of this. All these women, the other victims – *including* Helen Cassenov – identified you the same way: walk, mannerisms. But if Betsy did Cassenov, how could she have impersonated you? Cassenov was attacked before you even met Betsy.'

'I know,' I said.

'And?'

'It's been troubling me too.'

'Rules her out, don't you think?'

'It's not a plus,' I said. 'But she might have seen me someplace. I noticed *her* on the running track around the park reservoir. She's there every morning, and she—'

'Does stand out?'

'As you would, for the same reason,' I said.

'Gorgeous sexy body.'

'Exactly,' I said.

'You're so full of shit.'

'Maybe . . . she noticed me too?'

'For the same reason,' she said.

I laughed. 'No doubt. The point is, the opportunity was there. And maybe she knew who I was. Or maybe she saw some physical traits she could imitate, like my walk being lop-sided.'

'I thought you were running.'

'Well, sure,' I said. 'Most of the time.'

Diane said nothing for a moment. Then, 'Why didn't she imitate you with me?'

'You were apparently the first. Maybe she hadn't thought of doing it yet. Or noticed me yet.'

'I don't know, Rick. This is pretty thin.'

'It is. I agree. But we'll know for sure if we can talk to Luis.'

'OK,' she said, without enthusiasm. 'Where is he, and what's his last name?'

I spread my hands in a gesture of ignorance.

'Good start,' she said, getting up to refill our coffees.

'My guess is he still works for the same managing agent.'

'Who will be happy, no doubt, to give you – or any other dangerous fugitive – whatever information you want about one of their employees.'

We looked at each other and said it at once, 'Leon?'

Leon said on the phone, 'I'm beginning to feel guilty about taking your money.' He called back almost immediately. The managing agent's system security had slowed Leon down, he told us in a deadpan voice, 'almost two minutes.' Not because it had required that much time to break into, but because it had made him laugh that hard that long. 'Can you believe these idiots? Paying good money for this crap.'

The agent's employee list included no fewer than thirteen Luises. Only one of whom, however, once worked in my building. He was now employed elsewhere. Park and Ninety– third Street, to be exact, for which we set off that evening. The plan was for Diane to promise Luis a hundred bucks to meet her at a coffee shop during his break; then, when she got him there, promise him another hundred to talk to me. I'd appear, and we'd sit down together.

It didn't quite work out like that.

We found a parking garage between Lex and Third. Diane walked back to the building and had no difficulty persuading Luis to join her later – the pretext being she had something to ask him that was better discussed away from his post; the incentive, the waving of the hundred dollar bill. They'd settled themselves into a booth when I materialized from the men's room. Before Diane could calm him, Luis sprang up and struggled out into the aisle. Diane threw herself at his chest, and I grabbed the sleeve of his uniform. Diane laid five hundred dollar bills on the tabletop. Luis reassessed his situation. Reluctantly, he sat again, facing the cash.

We were in the rear of the shop which was otherwise empty. The fry cook/manager, perusing the sports pages near the front window, had looked up briefly at the skirmish, got bored and resumed reading. The waitress, a short Mexican woman, drank her own coffee at the counter and never looked up at all. Diane had already tipped her twenty dollars to leave us alone.

I launched a frontal assault.

'Luis,' I said, putting my thumb on the bills. 'Why the hell have you been lying about me?'

Bad tactic. I saw him lurch back in the seat as if preparing, after all, to bolt. Diane lifted my thumb, resting her other hand on Luis's.

'Could you use this money?' she asked with a smile.

His look said, *what do you think?*

'If you help us,' she said, 'there's this and even a bit more.'

He nodded. He understood. And his eyes never left the long green.

'What cop interviewed you, Luis?' she asked in a sympathetic tone.

'Blonde woman,' he got out sullenly.

'A police woman?' Diane asked.

'*Si*. Yes.'

'Did she threaten you in any way?'

'Threaten, yes.'

'Immigration status?' I queried.

He nodded tightly.

'What did she ask you to say? About me?'

His swarthy complexion appeared to get darker. 'She asked me when you came home.'

'And you told her ten fifteen, right?'

He shook his head.

'Why not?' I demanded. 'That *is* when I got home that night.'

Luis's eyes darted as if he were searching for an escape route.

'Luis!' I persisted. 'You're going to get me thrown in prison for life for something I didn't do.'

He glanced at Diane, his face pleading. She picked up the bills and began folding them. Then she added another hundred so Luis could see. 'What did this woman say specifically about your immigration status?'

'Not just me,' he said to Diane, eyes riveted on the money in her hand.

'I see,' she said. 'Who else?'

'My family. Everyone we got here. Seventeen people. And my wife, who is trying to get here with our children.'

'She knew this,' Di said, 'before she interviewed you?'

'She knew this. She knew all about me.'

'Ah,' said Diane. 'And did she threaten to have all of you deported if you didn't answer her questions the way she wanted?'

'You don't understand,' he said mournfully.

'What don't I understand?'

'She surprised me. She just was . . . there! Suddenly. She showed me this badge. She started talking about immigration. Me. My wife, my family. That's a threat. She don't have to say *nada mas*. Telling me what she knew, that's a threat. Telling me she had taken the trouble to get all this information, that's a threat.'

'I do see, yes,' said Diane. 'She said all this before she asked you about Mr Corinth.'

'*Si*. Yes. Right off. Before anything.'

'And who first suggested that Mr Corinth did not return to his building until after midnight? Was that you, Luis, or her? This woman police officer?'

With Luis still staring at the money, Diane spread it on the table and sat back.

'It was her,' said Luis, shifting his eyes to Diane who gave me a look of acknowledgement.

'You knew he actually returned at about ten fifteen.'

Luis looked into his lap. '*Si*.'

'And two weeks later,' she said, 'did this police woman ask you to lie again? To say that Mr Corinth had left the building at nine fifteen at night?'

He put his hand on the money, Di nodded, and he took the bills.

'*Si*,' he said.

FORTY-FOUR

When Luis left the shop, I ordered a ham sandwich and a cup of coffee, and Diane asked for some herbal tea. That interview had not been my finest hour. It's always the case; a lawyer representing himself has a fool for a client. But Diane had been splendid. I told her so.

'Thank you.'

'And now what do you think?'

'Beyond the obvious, that she's trying to frame you?'

'Yes,' I said, 'beyond that.'

'She was not the person in my house,' said Diane.

I thought she'd say that. And if it were true, who the hell was Betsy trying to protect? And why? I realized I knew damn little about her, like whom else she knew, what other men, for example. But the facts from her file, and from Carter and Tucker, formed a fairly consistent picture that also jibed with the one I now had in my head. And Luis's story plus Betsy's history were evidence enough to convince anyone. Except maybe Diane.

'OK,' I said. 'Should we listen to what we've got?'

'Sure.' She took a tiny recording device from her handbag. 'But it's there. I've gotten a lot of serious shit on this thing.'

'As serious?'

'No, although money's pretty serious to me.'

I pressed the 'play' button, and Luis's voice could be heard as if he were still sitting in our booth. We looked at each other for a moment, and I laughed with relief.

'Let's hope it brings you what you want,' she said.

My cell phone rang. Flashing a 'sorry' expression to Diane, I dug it out of my pocket. Ali had this number, which was why it was on. But she'd obviously given it to someone who I'd have preferred didn't have it.

'Rick! Bob Hayden. I need your help. Now! *Please!* It's Emma.'

I didn't want Diane anywhere near this. I left her right there on the street, despite her pleading with me not to go alone.

Why rush off at all? Hayden was hardly a friend of mine, let alone anyone to whom I owed anything. But my going wasn't about him, or even anymore about Ali. Though Hayden was almost incoherent on the phone, it was apparent Emma was in trouble, and whatever had happened, he was obviously unable to cope.

Hayden had managed to blurt out the address, but, of course, I knew it. Cross-town traffic was light; I got there in fifteen minutes and bounded up the steps. The door to her apartment was locked. It opened at my pounding. Hayden stood inside looking like hell, his face ashen, old, smeared with tears.

The place stank worse than before. Emma was dead, naked, lying on her side, legs splayed, hip bone to the carpet. Blood caked in her pubis, down her thighs and the crack of her ass. Her head was twisted toward me at an angle I'd never seen outside of horror movies. I thought her neck must have been broken. She looked like she'd been lying there for days.

Hayden stared at her, then me, unsteady in his lovely pinstriped Dunhill suit, heavy eyebrows mussed and bushy. 'I got here, saw this, called you. I haven't even . . . covered her.'

'You haven't called the police?' I could feel it coming, that sensation I get before blacking out. I fought it.

'I . . .' He looked faint, then tried to steady himself. 'Odd, isn't it? I don't suppose I was thinking very clearly. Walking in here, seeing this.'

I braced myself to look at Emma again. I felt my own tears coming with a spasm of grief. And there was something wrong about the shape of her head that I couldn't quite make out from my angle of vision. I moved to get a better view. Took me a moment. Oh, God, there was no back to it. Then I did black out.

I awoke to find Emma's cat on my chest. I brushed him off. Hayden sat in a corner, smoking. Emma's body remained on the carpet. So did mine, not five feet away.

'You OK?' asked Hayden, stubbing out the cigarette in a cup he was holding.

I was staring at her, feeling unbearably sad, and sick again. 'Yeah.'

'I felt I couldn't call the police with you here.'

'When you called me—'

'I shouldn't have,' he interrupted. 'It was stupid, selfish and unpardonable. You're absolutely right, call the police. I should have done that immediately.'

I sat up and rubbed the back of my head.

'No man should ever have to see his daughter . . .' He covered his face, couldn't finish the sentence. 'Jesus Christ! It's macabre, unimaginable!'

'Calmly,' I said. 'We have to get cops here, and you out.'

'Absolutely right,' he repeated. 'Cops.'

I felt a chill in my gut. 'Bob, are you worried about being blamed for this?'

'I'll be a suspect. How could I not be? I found the body. Someone will blame me. People get blamed unjustly. Look at you. That's how your name came to mind. Then I thought, I need help, who better to give it? So I called you. I shouldn't have, and I'm sorry.'

'You should call a lawyer who does this sort of thing.' I thought about it for a moment but then put it like a question on cross. 'How well do you know Doris Strickland?'

Total blank. 'Who?'

'Never mind. When I leave, the guy to call is Joe Stein.'

'Joe Stein. Yes, thank you. I think I've heard of him. And Rick, if you need some place, you know I'm deeply in your debt. I've got a house in Putnam County miles from anywhere. In fact, if you want, I can get you out of the country.'

The guy who will get blamed for this is me.

I was on my feet, and another thought struck me. 'After nine one one, first call should be your step-daughter.'

He looked at me curiously. 'You know Betsy?'

'Sure. We've worked together.'

Half way out the door, I turned back. 'What kind of terms were they on, Betsy and Emma?'

'Oh, my word, they could scarcely tolerate being in the same room.'

FORTY-FIVE

I knew of P. J. Sullivan by reputation. We'd never met. And I wasn't clear why Joe Stein had felt the need to invite Sully to join the session Joe and I had scheduled for that afternoon. Sully's meter ran at six hundred bucks an hour. I thought a five-minute phone call at the end of our conference might have been enough. Joe had simply said, 'You'll see.'

I did, ultimately, along with the irony of the occasion. As a lawyer, my time had always been billed by the hour. The team now working for me also billed by the hour, but their fees were coming out of *my* pocket.

And the pocket was bare. Joe knew this, so I assumed the others did too. It gave me some bounce that they believed I'd ultimately free myself from this horror, get re-employed and be able to pay them.

We all gathered in Joe's office at four thirty. Overnight, everything had changed. The murder of Emma Hayden had monopolized the morning news. Putting that story together with the manhunt for me left little doubt as to who was responsible. So dealing with that dominated this meeting.

Under ordinary circumstances I'd have had problems accusing Betsy of the crimes they were attributing to me, even with Luis's statements on tape. Now I'd be accusing her of killing her own step-sister. And the full story would make that accusation not only less plausible, but ghoulish. According to Joe Stein, who'd somehow gotten a preview of the coroner's report, Emma's body had been sexually abused *after* the back of her head had been blown off.

Sully asked Diane to play the tape and sat there concentrating with the stillness of an egret. He was an ungainly older man of surprising height, with a narrow forehead and formidable nose that hooked leftward. When the recording ended, he merely nodded with some secret cognition he had no evident disposition to share.

Nona said, 'That's pretty good.'

I'd hoped for more enthusiasm.

Joe said, 'Not air tight. You don't have the words she used. Only his conclusion.'

'Her words, from *Luis*? You've got to be kidding,' I said.

'I didn't say it would've been easy to get,' said Joe. 'Only that you didn't get it.'

'Look,' I said. 'I'm not suggesting we have the evidence here for an indictment. But I thought we had enough to lift suspicion from me. I mean why in hell would Betsy Spaeth have gone to the trouble – and the risk – of bullying Luis into lying about me unless she herself is implicated? Are you guys disagreeing with that?'

'I'm not sure,' said Joe. 'What's your thought? We take this to Seaton?'

'Of course,' I said. 'Frank should hear this tape. Why not?'

'And what about that weird meeting you had with Hayden?'

That stopped me for a moment. I hadn't thought it through.

Sully broke in. 'May I inquire,' he said, 'whether there was any cash involved in this transaction with the doorman? This interview?'

A bothersome point, yet it annoyed me that it bothered him too. 'We wouldn't have gotten him to the table without cash.'

Sully rolled his eyes.

I said, 'OK. Not perfect. But the facts are, Luis is now at last telling the truth – admitting that Betsy got him to lie – and as for the rest of it, let the cops sort it out. If I get my life back, I'm happy. Relatively.'

Sully's look was sympathetic, not encouraging. 'Let's break this down. I don't minimize the importance of the tape. I simply note, going public with the tape is an accusation. The person you'd be accusing happens to be a young woman from an influential family. The series of acts you'd be accusing her of having committed – well, to say the least, the *apparent* likelihood of her having done these things is not high.'

Although he'd said nothing yet we didn't know, he had our full attention.

'So war is about to begin,' he said. 'The fit will hit the proverbial shan. Everything – and I do mean that word – will come out. Including the fact that you have, in effect, paid for this doorman's, Luis's, testimony.'

I audibly exhaled and said, 'It gets . . . more complicated.'

Attention swung heavily to me.

'If, as you say, all the linen's getting hung out?' I tried not to look at Diane. 'Betsy and I had a brief thing going. As it now appears – pretty dumb. On my part.'

In the silence that followed, Diane emitted one long, sardonic, single-syllabled laugh. Sully finally said, 'Let me ask you. You said you wanted your life back. What exactly does that mean to you?'

'Ideally? What I said. To return to what I had before this

thing began. Before someone – Betsy, it now seems – got the idea of setting me up as a serial rapist.'

He shook his head sorrowfully. 'Your life will never be the same. I think you probably know that.'

Yes, I knew it. Having him say it just made it worse.

At my look of frustration, his eyelid fluttered. 'Everyone who knows you, Rick, and millions who don't, have this new fact in their heads about you. You're the fellow who's been accused of raping six women – and now raping and murdering a seventh. This fact will never be removed. So now, reputation building is no longer a natural process. It requires art. And the art involved is to associate this fact in everybody's head with another fact that converts it to something positive or, at least, palatable. You understand?'

'Of course,' I said.

'It must be clear you've been framed. It is *that* with which people can empathize. They don't care about you. They care about themselves. To be made to feel any emotion on your behalf, they need to empathize. They need to think, when they hear your name, Ah! The guy who got framed. *That* might have happened to them. *That*, they can empathize with. But the key word is 'clear.' The fact that you were framed must be clear. Confusion on this point will leave you almost where you are now, not even close to where you say you want to be in restoring your reputation.'

I glanced about, catching Diane's now somber expression.

'And the tape isn't clear?' I said.

Which was greeted by silence, because the question answered itself.

'Suppose I confronted Betsy with the tape? Not Seaton or Chacon, but Betsy herself?'

Joe said, 'You'd wear a wire?'

'Of course.'

'She'd suspect that, certainly once you'd played her the tape.'

'My wire,' said Diane, 'is sufficiently small that it would readily fit into . . . how might I put this delicately . . .?'

'Wouldn't work,' I said. 'Not with Betsy.'

'First place she'd search?' said Diane, her blue eyes flashing.

When I blushed, Nona exclaimed, 'Oh, la, Ricky!'

Joe said, 'Is that really likely?'

I shrugged.

No one said anything.

'I'll tell you. Next time I see Betsy? I'm going to have a real hard time not wringing her neck.'

Joe said, 'Unless you've been training, buddy, she'd probably kick your ass.'

'Sounds to me,' said Diane, 'that's not what she wants to do with it.'

'All right,' I said, passing on that remark. 'Is this a good idea, or isn't it? Confronting Betsy with the tape?'

Nona said, 'You give her information she doesn't now have – the existence of the tape. And nothing may come of the meeting.'

'Yes,' I said, 'but, if we're not now otherwise going to use the tape . . .'

'I think it's worth a shot,' said Joe.

Everyone looked to Sully. He nodded. Seemed to make it a decision.

Driving home with Diane, she said, 'So, tell me about you and this Betsy woman. I mean, since you were still screwing her until, what? Last week? Bit odd you hadn't mentioned it, don't you think?'

'Yes,' I said.

'And it's not as if it's irrelevant to what we're doing. Our investigation.'

'You're right,' I said. 'I should have mentioned it. I'm sorry.'

We drove another mile.

'So what's the thing with you?' she said. 'Do any woman who's not half horrible? Any warm body who moves?'

I didn't answer.

'You resent the characterization?' she persisted.

'It's a pretty pejorative way of describing a normal male dynamic.'

'Which you share,' she said.

'No doubt.'

'End of story?'

'No. OK. You go into something like that – sometimes you think, maybe this can work. With someone else, you don't have to think about it. You know.'

'Someone else?' she said.

'You,' I said.

'Hmm,' she said non-committally. 'As if there's still reason to believe anything you say.'

FORTY-SIX

The following afternoon, Diane dropped me at Ninth Avenue and Forty-seventh Street. Our evening meal had been strained; our sleeping arrangements separate. As I cranked out of the car, she gave me an inscrutable look. I had her miniature recording device, which, of course, also operated as a player; on it, I had a tape of our conversation with Luis, which was one of several copies we'd made. And I had a new, even smaller device Diane had stuck with adhesive at a place 'this girl, on this visit, shouldn't want to get near to.' She mouthed one tight 'good luck' that got lost in the rumble of traffic. I understood the nature of my crime, but the punishment seemed excessive.

Had I not been so angry at Betsy, I doubt I'd have had the balls to do what I then did.

The first part was easy. I rang her downstairs bell. No one home, or at least answering, which was what I expected. So I waited outside for someone to leave. A delivery boy, as it happened, who could not have cared less whether the intruder was me or a bomb-throwing terrorist.

Inside the building, I took the stairs to Betsy's landing. She'd bolted her door, but there were four other apartments in this brownstone; one on the second floor had been left unlocked. I walked in, imposed calm over a pounding heart, called out to establish no one was there, went to the kitchen, opened the window, crawled out to the fire escape and climbed one flight.

Amazing, I thought. Nowhere in the world are people more obsessed about the possibility of break-ins than in New York City. But I doubted there was an apartment in Manhattan you couldn't get into if you were really determined.

Betsy's windows on the fire escape were locked. No big deal.

One broken pane of glass was the least she owed me. I took off my sweater, wrapped it around my fist and waited. In Manhattan, the intervals between sirens are relatively brief. As soon as I heard one begin its wail, I smashed the glass. Then looked behind me. Back windows of loft buildings, apartment buildings, office buildings, brownstones with scruffy, empty, backyards. Hundreds of windows, glistening and lifeless. I unlocked Betsy's, pushed it up and climbed inside.

I searched the drawers first. Bedroom drawers. Then the medicine cabinet in her bathroom. The two most intimate places. An invasion of privacy, but then she'd sent a team to do me.

I'm not sure what I was looking for, yet you do learn by looking. For example, three different types of sleeping remedies, prescription and non-prescription. Insomnia or guilty conscience? One drawer for ordinary cotton underwear, another for silk and fancy. Nothing too exotic, but it did imply a certain premeditated approach. Also, everything was in its place, according to a system. No random stowing here of anything, including clothes. And no surprises. The usual assortment of female hygienic and beautification products. Birth control pills. No vibrator. Well, she wouldn't have needed one, would she? And no papers. None of any kind. No memoirs or diaries, unfortunately.

I found a large cardboard box in the back hall behind her kitchen area, sliced it open, used one sheet to pick up the glass and, after disposing of shards, tacked the whole of the flattened box on to the frame of the open window. I wanted her as calm as possible when she got home. But it was odd, I thought, after finishing the job. I should have been trashing the entire apartment for what Betsy had done to me – and worse for what I'd suspected she'd done to her sister – and there I was cleaning her place up. In the living area, I plunked down on her sofa, stretched out, then waited with the lights off. About an hour, as it turned out.

She must have taken the stairs; I could hear the front door locks being opened one at a time. Three of them. A lot of good they had done her. Lights came on. She went right to the kitchen area with a bag, probably of groceries. What set her off, I assume, was the cardboard covering the window. She came in running, armed, spotted me on the sofa and started screaming obscenities and commands.

'Easy,' I said. 'It's me.'

It took her a moment to stop shaking and quiet down. 'Godamnit, Rick. You didn't have to smash my fucking window.'

'Actually I did; the street's crawling with those blue-coated colleagues of yours.'

'We could have met somewhere,' she said, laying the gun on an end table – now seemingly easy, relaxed.

'Dicey,' I said.

'Like breaking in here wasn't? Shit. You gave me a scare. I might have killed you.'

'I know. It was a risk.'

She gave me a look, as if to say, *Then why did you take it?*

'I wanted you to hear something.' I laid the small tape player on her coffee table.

'What is this?' she said, suspicion no longer disguised.

'Just push the button.'

'You pushing mine?'

'Maybe,' I said.

With a mordant twist to her lips, she reached toward the tape player and made it work. The conversation with Luis, Diane's and mine, resonated with a quality unimaginable from anything that small.

When it stopped, Betsy said, 'Who's the woman?'

'Does it matter?' I pocketed the device.

'I don't know, Rick. Why'd you want me to listen to that? I mean, you broke my window so you could play it for me – what's your point?'

'I should think the point's pretty obvious.'

She squinted and shook her head. Then she sat on the end of the sofa. With the gun on the end table at her back. For a moment she just studied me, as if she'd never seen me before. 'You're accusing me of framing you?'

'On the night Doris was raped, I know when I got home. It was ten fifteen. On the night Jane Hentchoff was raped, I never left my apartment. Luis lied about both nights. Now he tells me you suggested it. Is there something else I should think?'

'And why would I do that?' she said, as if being patient. 'Frame you? Something that stupid? What the hell do I get out of that?'

'Right. What? You tell me.'

Her expression went from disbelief to derision. 'You think *I rape women*?'

'More like tormenting them, isn't it? And only women of a certain type. I think you might have the motivation for that.'

'Y'know, Rick,' she said, twisting back for the gun. 'I think you ought to get the fuck out of here.'

'I thought we might talk about Emma.'

'*Get out!*'

'And the tape.'

'Really? You want to talk about the tape? I'll talk about the tape. You deserve to know how stupid you've been. I went to see Luis to help *you*. You told me what he'd said to you. I went to see him.'

'Right away?'

'Same fucking day.'

'You came to my building, then?'

Only the slightest hesitation. 'That's right.'

'And how about the second time?'

She laughed. 'You're wearing a wire, aren't you?'

'Do you care?'

'Yes, I care. I hope you are. So we have on record what an asshole you've been. Now get the fuck out of here.'

I hung, she didn't move, not a single muscle of her face. There was in me a stab of doubt. In her? I thought I saw regret. In the eyes, I was thinking. But I couldn't be sure.

FORTY-SEVEN

I took off. Down the stairs, out into the street. Betsy didn't try to stop me. Or, as far as I could tell, call to have me picked up. About Luis, she had almost made me believe her. And who the hell knows? I thought. How the hell do you ever really know?

Diane was waiting three blocks away. I got in the car; she motored off; I told her what had happened.

'So how does that feel?' she asked.

'Like shit,' I said.

'Not very expressive.'

I gave her a look, as if to say, what more do you want, but she kept her eyes on the road. We settled for silence.

On the kitchen phone in Di's house that night, we had a conference call with my brain trust, and I played the new tape for them.

Joe Stein, still in the office, said, 'You planted the bug?'

'No, I wore it,' I said. 'Took a gamble.'

'So did she, then. Letting you leave like that.'

And a mystery to me. I puzzled over it: her sitting there watching me go.

'Well, we don't have much,' Joe said, 'but it's something. She identifies herself as the woman Luis met. As for who said what, it's still her word against Luis's. We could use corroboration.'

A thought had been troubling me since I'd left Betsy's apartment. Really, since I'd left Emma's. 'There are other suspects,' I said.

I had the floor: silence on the phone; a stare on me in the kitchen.

'A guy who I'd once thought of as a close friend who's a Federal judge. And Bob Hayden.'

'He killed his own daughter?' Joe said.

'I don't think the relationship was wonderful, at least from her standpoint.'

'So he raped and killed her? Although it would seem in the opposite sequence. And what is Betsy doing in this scenario? Protecting her dad?'

'I agree, there're loose ends no matter—'

'And a Federal judge? Rick, I know you're stressed—'

Sully broke in, speech slightly slurred. He was at Le Cirque with a client, and they were probably on their second bottle. 'Aren't we getting a little ahead of ourselves? We have a lead on this Betsy woman. Shall we nail that down first?'

Obviously the right approach, and we all said so.

'As I recall from the file,' Sully continued, 'Luis left a wife in whatever South American backwater he comes from.'

'That's right,' I said.

'He's still a young man. I wouldn't be totally surprised if he were cohabiting up here.'

'We have his home address,' I said.

'If there is such a woman, we should certainly interview her,' said Joe. 'The question is, who on our team is best suited to nose around there and gain the confidence of such a woman?'

The pause lasted only a second.

'OK,' said Nona. 'I hear you.'

'We could hire someone,' I said. 'A trained private investigator.'

She said, 'No, I'll do it.'

'I owe you, baby,' I said.

'Yeah, man. I'll take that.'

When we got off the phone, Diane, slumped on a kitchen stool, said, 'Do you really suspect Hayden, or are you just pissed off at him for sleeping with your wife?'

'Both.'

'What's the suspicion based on – he was there?'

'Maybe I should have let you come with me. I'm not a great judge of acting.'

'You think he may have *been* acting?'

'His grief seemed real, but, like I said . . .'

'So you're just going on instinct.'

'Which you don't trust.'

'The man's got no motivation,' she said, 'unless he's a complete whack job.'

'Which you don't think he is.'

'I don't know him that well, but he certainly gets along in society all right.'

'Not necessarily inconsistent.'

'What about Hazzard?' she said. 'That cologne smell – he must know he reeks of the stuff. And there are ways one could deal with that, remove it, disguise it.'

'I ruled him out too fast?'

'He's the one guy we know hates you. The fact that he has no reason to only makes him more suspect, as far as I'm concerned.'

'And you don't like him.'

'And I don't like him. Now that I know what I know about him.'

'We have evidence on Betsy. As Sully says, let's focus on that.'

Diane heaved a sigh; then: 'How come you call her baby?'

'*Betsy?*'

She gave me a look.

'Right,' I said. 'Nona. We do go back.'

'And we go where?' she said.

'Up?' I returned her look fondly.

'Up?' she said, sitting up, tilting her head inquisitively. 'This is what? A word you're floating out there metaphorically?' In her form-fitting camel hair sweater and black slacks, with her frizzy curls and no make-up, she might have been taken for a skinny teenager.

'I thought maybe literally? As in upstairs. Together. For tonight.'

'Y'know, it's funny,' she said. 'You've still got the hots for your ex-wife, and she wants to treat you like a platonic friend. I, on the other hand, do relatively little for your heartstrings, whereas you – for reasons I don't even begin to understand – kind of ring my bell. Then there's this babe we're talking about, Betsy, whom you lusted after. And she wants nothing more than to nail your ass to a prison cell. Are human relationships *necessarily* that fucked up, or do I just happen to swim with a strange school of people?'

'You're wrong about the heartstrings,' I said.

'Don't start.'

'We've already started.'

'Started what?' she said. 'That's the question I'm putting.'

I draped my arms around her shoulders. 'You and me? We like each other. A lot. More than a lot. We give each other great comfort and pleasure. We may damn well be a perfect fit. And—'

'I'd say we had serious problems.'

'Anything we can't deal with?'

'Yeah. That's what I'm saying, Rick.'

'Diane, listen to me, please. We're here. Alone. We have at most a few days, maybe just a few hours. Any time now, the cops could come marching in, throw me in prison, break us up maybe forever.'

'What's there to break up?'

'Plenty. OK? And besides, what *I'm* saying, why waste the opportunity?'

'Because of the pain, darling. The pain that comes later.'

'It's not a given,' I said, 'that there'll be pain.'

Her laugh had some bite. 'There's always pain. When you care, you can count on it.'

I said, 'You can't believe I don't care.'

She said nothing.

'And, if there's going to be pain, why not take the pleasure too, *darling*?'

'Ah,' she said.

'Right thought?'

'Right word.'

'And?' I asked.

'I'm thinking on it.'

'You've got to *think* about it?'

She smiled.

'Baby . . .?'

Her smile broadened.

'No,' she said, then leaned her skinny frame against me. 'I don't. At least for tonight. Let's go to bed.'

FORTY-EIGHT

I t took Nona two days. Two of the best I can ever remember. Lots of take-out, mainly sushi, lots of movies, mainly old, and several attempts at chess. Diane had a battered copy of *Waiting for Godot*. We read it twice aloud, switching roles. We'd both done it in high school, it turned out, and it seemed to fit the occasion. More than anything else, however, we talked – hours at a time – learned a lot more about each other, and I liked what I learned. I hoped she had.

Despite my weakness at chess. Playing a six-year-old boy

hadn't prepared me. After three games with Diane, she announced there was no point. I said, 'Do you ever lose?'

'Not to someone below my rank.'

'Oh, you're ranked,' I said.

'Of course,' she said.

'So you take this game very seriously.'

'It's not a game,' she said.

I thought, as I had often during those two days, I could be happy with this woman. Get real attached. Though I knew we still had a few miles to go here.

'There are things I take seriously,' I said.

'Oh, yeah. What?'

We were in bed, and I pulled her to me, scattering the chess pieces.

She said, 'You take *this* seriously?'

I said, 'You ever throw a chess game?'

'Never.'

'Not even to make someone feel good?'

'It's not in me' she said.

'Well, it's the same for me . . . with . . .'

'W*hat?*'

'Making love.'

'That's what we're doing, making love?'

'We're getting there,' I said.

'And you're honest, always,' she said.

'I try to be.'

'But you don't always know, do you?'

She sat up. Then I did too.

'The thing about love,' she said, 'is that it blindsides you both ways. You don't see it coming in the first place. Not all the effects of it, certainly. And then, once you're afflicted, it blinds you to everything else.' She thought about that. 'Every*one* else, I mean.'

I said nothing. I didn't have to. The point was self-evident. With Ali, even after fourteen years, when I saw her, even thought of her, my blood coursed. I felt it moving. Because, given an image of her, I felt everything. It sent my body into some rarefied state of sensitivity. What I felt for Diane was surprisingly close to that, after a very short time, and growing daily, but Ali – intermittently – still stood in the way.

'Don't worry,' Diane said, seemingly reading my thoughts again. 'Crossing that line – committing myself to someone – is huge for me. I don't do it lightly. There's a big emotional wrench. And, frankly, darling, as we *have* talked about' – she did it sing-song, to take the edge off – 'you are not the ideal candidate for me.'

'Being a fugitive, and all.'

'Being a father, man. I keep telling you. Two kids. I'm not equipped to deal with kids.'

'Mine are easy.'

'Great.'

My comment was thoughtless. Hers meant, she thought it unlikely she'd ever find out.

Nona's call, when it came, was anticlimactic. In fact, it ushered in a sustained period of anticlimax, most of which seemed surreal. At the time, of course, I had no way of knowing what it truly was: the calm before a storm – one of unpredictable violence.

Nona called from Joe's office. The news was almost too good, so naturally it worried me. There was in fact a young woman living with Luis. She had been present when Betsy arrived, and didn't like Betsy 'no how.' She even remembered the dates of the visits, because she and Luis, 'who never fought,' had 'big fights' then. Betsy had lied on my tape when she'd said she had interviewed Luis the first time at my building. She had actually gone up to his apartment in the Bronx. And, more importantly, she had lied when she said she had seen Luis *after* I had questioned him following Doris's incident, and *after* Chacon had interviewed Jane. Both times Betsy had gotten to Luis earlier. Both times she'd manipulated him to implicate me. Nona had the whole interview on tape.

Nona was as breathless to tell as I was to listen.

'Baby,' I said. 'You really done good.'

'Yeah,' she said with a great exhalation of breath. 'I make a pretty good gumshoe. Who'd have thought?'

'So, Joe?' I said. 'OK? Finally? We got enough now?'

'To take to Frank?'

'Who else?'

'Absolutely, Rick, sure. But you realize Betsy will deny the story. The woman living with Luis is an illegal alien. Luis's status here's confused, to say the least. The two of them may be gone tomorrow.'

'All the more reason to move now.'

'Of course,' he said. 'I'm just warning you not to get your hopes too high. I'll call Frank, set something up, let you know.'

Approximately an hour later he told me, 'I'm going over there this afternoon.'

A little past six that evening, Joe called again on his way uptown. 'No real news. Frank listened. He heard me out. Very non-committal. Kept saying this whole thing was a "sorry business." Kept repeating his fondness for you, how disturbed he'd been personally even to think of you in this light. But no promises. Naturally. He's got to hear her out, and then he'll call me.'

So once again I was waiting. I thought, this is going to strain our relationship, Diane's and mine. But she was too smart to let that happen. She kept away most of each day; she even went back to Goldman Sachs to begin the process of re-entry, a huge step for her. I looked forward to her coming home. Like a house-husband.

FORTY-NINE

When the call we were waiting for came, it was to me, not Joe. And it was Chacon on the line, not Frank. I thought, *how the hell does he know where I am?* What he next said was so stunning I forgot to ask.

'You can go home now,' he said. 'Travel freely. No one will stop you. One thing though –'

They brand me for life, and now back off? Just like that?

'– this afternoon,' he continued. 'Two o'clock. Would you join me for another walk in the park?'

'A *what*?'

'You won't regret it.'

'You setting me up?'

'Since I know where you are, Rick, had I wanted to bring you in, it would have been real simple to have the New Jersey cousins come and get you.'

I called Joe Stein and waited ten minutes for him to call back. When I told him of my conversation with Chacon, Joe immediately asked the question I should have. 'How'd he know where you were?'

'You have no idea?' I said.

'I sure as hell didn't give it to him.'

'Maybe he intercepted your cell phone call to me?'

'I suppose it's possible,' he said. 'Barely. Anyway, apart from that, it's good news, right? Of course I'll call Frank, confirm, see what they're putting out to the media.'

'What do you think of this walk in the park business?' I asked.

'Ah. You mean whether it's just an easy way for him to pick you up in New York, rather than fool around with extradition?'

'That's the question.'

'Pretty big risk on his part – risk of flight, once he calls you – if he really just wants to collar you.'

'Yeah,' I said. 'That's what I thought.'

'On the other hand, you're under no legal obligation to see him.'

'I know.'

'But you're curious.'

'Wouldn't you be?'

'I'd probably be more cautious,' he said. 'Why not wait for Seaton to tell me you're in the clear?' Joe laughed. 'That fucking Chacon. Just his kind of stunt. He wants to tell you something, why can't he simply spit it out on the phone? No, he's got to stage a scene.'

I called Di at her office. 'Sorry,' chirped her secretary. 'Ms. Nethersong's at a meeting.'

I left a message and called Ali. Same result. Meeting. With people who wished to meet her. Making things happen. Everyone was gainfully employed, except me.

At least I was going home. I wasn't waiting for any call-back. That very night I'd see my kids. There was no need to pack anything. I walked out the door on a damp fall morning, thrilled by the feeling of freedom.

FIFTY

Frank never did call back, and Chacon arrived as promised at two p.m. He probably realized that I'd have agreed to meeting him in Sadr City, to find out what the hell was going on. Were they indicting Betsy? Would they publicly exonerate me? Maybe even apologize for fucking up my life?

In the lobby of my building, Vincente Chacon was brooding, pacing, bundled up in a trench coat that was too obvious a cliché to be accidental. He greeted me silently, heading for the park. Dodging the traffic on Central Park West, we took the same path he'd selected on our previous walk. It was a day much cooler, however, and a sky more leaden, than before. The trees were barren, black, the grass brown or yellow. To my questions, I got clipped responses that seemed deliberately ambiguous.

'You know the painter, René Magritte,' he finally asked, sniffing the clean cold air.

This guy could be infuriating. 'Magritte? What about him?'

'Do you have a favorite image? The man in the bowler hat, for example? With the apples floating around him? No. Too common. You see it on ashtrays. Maybe the houses shrouded in nighttime darkness under a bright mid-day sky. You like that one? I do. I think what he's saying is, we see so little of reality.'

I stopped walking. I'd had enough. My face said so.

'Especially,' he added, ignoring my look, 'about ourselves. Right?'

'Where is this going?' I said.

His lips pressed together, his melon-shaped head nodded. 'Look down the path,' he said, pointing. 'About eighty yards down there. See? The woman on that bench has something to tell you.'

Ali. From eighty yards away, I still recognized her. And panicked. 'My kids?'

'Everyone's fine,' he said hurriedly.

'Then what is this?'

'Let her tell you,' he said.

Ali on a wood-slatted concrete bench, probably freezing her ass off, watching me approach – *this* was surreal. She wore that expression, the one she gave Sam, when she knew she might hurt his feelings or thwart his plans.

'Hi,' I said, sitting next to her.

'Hi, darling.' Her cheeks were red from the cold. She looked like an actress trying to remember her lines.

'So what are you doing with this guy? Consorting with the enemy?'

'I don't think he's the enemy.'

'Ah,' I said. 'You've gone over to the other side.'

'I'm still on your side,' she said. 'I think he'll help us.'

I was wrong about the sky being leaden. It was pewter glossed by a bit of sun somewhere. And I'd overdressed for this excursion. I opened my leather jacket, feeling the air move through the weave of my sweater.

'You call him?' I asked.

'I did, yes.'

'What's going on, sweetheart?'

'Oh, God, what do you think, Rick?'

'I'd rather not games-play this.'

'I know it was you, baby.' Her nose started running.

I'd no need to ask what she meant. 'Why do you think you *know* that?'

'You're thinking, my eyes were taped – but *I recognized your scent!* You understand? What I wasn't sure of was, whether *you* knew.'

'I saw him,' I said. 'My eyes weren't taped.'

'No, baby. Believe me. You imagined it. There was only one man in that room. And it was you.'

'This is crazy.'

'I knew you'd think that.'

'How could I think otherwise?' I said. 'And this is what you've told that guy – Chacon?'

'Please accept help, Ricky.'

Everyone experiences dreams so real we tell ourselves inside them we couldn't possibly be dreaming. This was real, and I was telling myself it was a dream.

I got up. Did not look down, for fear she'd still be there. Careened down the path, and did not look back. Chacon was waiting, his breath fogging the air. He joined my stride, although he was chugging.

'You said I wouldn't regret this. I already do.'

'Long term,' he said, 'you won't regret it.'

'I thought you were straight.'

'And you'll think so again. Talk to Professor Cassenov.'

'Oh my God. Where is she on this canvas? Next bench?'

'That's right,' he said, as if where else would she be?

The absurdity of it made me laugh, but there was Helen Cassenov seated not fifty yards away. As we came near, Chacon drifted off.

'Sit, Eric, please.' Imperious as ever in a thick down coat.

I placed a foot on the front slat of her bench. Did a slight knee bend. 'Chacon enlist you for this, or was the whole idea yours in the first place?'

'We cooked it up together, actually. He's a rather surprising man. As, my dear, are you.'

'You know my scent too?'

'I do now.'

I sat, numbed by accusation.

'When it happened,' she said, 'I had this feeling you get when you hear a slightly familiar voice and yet can't quite place it. When I saw you in the line-up, I had it, I absolutely had it. I've never been so sure of anything in my life. I also had another insight. It's prevented me from wanting to kill you. It was that you might not be aware of what you were doing.'

I tried to think about that without laughing out loud. I couldn't.

'Well, you can laugh,' she said, 'but I assure you it's entirely possible. And not funny. I've had three such cases. Same syndrome. In the first, a young man killed his lover, then dashed out into the street chasing the presumed assailant, screaming, calling attention to himself. And it wasn't a ruse. I'm still treating the man. I've had him under the deepest hypnotic therapy. The other cases are almost identical. I assume – we'll deal with this more during treatment – but I assume you suffer from what appear to you to be blackouts? There was a time when GPs, or pediatricians, listening to their patients complaining of blacking out, would misdiagnose the ailment as narcolepsy, even though that almost never occurs before the age of thirty. And a narcoleptic episode simply leaves the victim where he passes out. He doesn't travel.'

'Helen,' I said. 'Listen to me. If I were the guy who molested you and these other women? The memories that would have to have been blocked out! Not only of the incidents themselves, but think! All the preparations! This guy has broken into, what? Three houses. Four apartments. He had to plan all that. I didn't.'

Throughout she shook her head. 'How much planning did you do to break into Betsy Spaeth's apartment, or Ali's?'

'You know about that?'

'Of course.'

'It wasn't me, Helen. You're wrong. I'd remember it.'

'Counter-intuitive, right? Sounds implausible. Selective erasure of any memory that, for a person of conscience, is intolerable. I simply note, it's a rare phenomenon, but a real one. It exists. There are several documented cases in addition to the three I'm treating. Living people. And there are many historical accounts of other such cases. Not multiple split personalities, but two very different identities. It's called DID, dissociative identity disorder. You travel wherever you want, and do what you want, because you turn into somebody else. I don't know you well enough to know the cause in your case, but . . . sorry Eric . . . I have very little doubt you suffer from this affliction. And the State, I gather, is willing to accept my testimony on the matter. In mitigation. As part of a plea.'

That was it. This elaborate set-up staged by Chacon was to get me to agree to a plea bargain. I was up and walking without a farewell.

So there I was again, back on the path. I did not believe the conversation I'd just had. I was laughing uncontrollably. Then I stopped.

Chacon. 'One more person,' he said. 'Next bench.'

In a sense, it was the worst of all. Doris Strickland. When we got there, Chacon once more disappeared.

'You too?' I said to her. 'A member of this cabal? Am I going completely insane?'

Her bruised eye, swollen mouth and chin contrasted oddly with the designer coat and scarf she was wearing. 'I'm sorry, Rick. Which is kind of funny, when you think about it. You raped me, and I'm the one feeling sorry for you.'

'It wasn't me.'

'Yeah, it was. I didn't think so at first, and then, knowing, I didn't want to.'

'You say, "knowing." How can you think you *know*? You didn't *know* when I visited you in the hospital.'

'Yes, I did. By the end, when you left. That's when I knew for sure.'

'How?' I demanded.

'It's complicated.'

'I've got a lifetime, Doris.'

She looked away. 'I'm kind of bi, y'know . . . sexually.'

'All right.'

'Once in a blue moon . . . some guy comes along . . . I feel something. It's entirely instinctive. It's got less to do with what the guy looks like, how he talks, than his . . . presence. I can't really explain – but, if I feel it, I can feel it in a dark room.'

It was pretty clear where this was heading. 'It wasn't me,' I repeated.

'All right, Rick. I'm going to tell you something. In the first few seconds, before the punching started, I was into it, OK? It felt scary *and* familiar. Like . . . a fantasy I had, OK? When Helen Cassenov called me – what I felt? Relief! Really did. I had wanted to kill you. Because the whole goddamn thing had hit me as you were walking out that hospital door. I didn't have the slightest doubt then, and I don't now.'

'You're wrong, Doris.'

'No, I'm not. Listen to me. Listen to all of us. When Helen told me what Ali had said, I called her. We had quite a conversation. Then I called Frank Seaton. Behind your back. I thought – Rick, I hope to God this was right – that it would be best for you. Frank's now offered Joe a deal. Two, maybe three years at worst, in a hospital. You won't even be disbarred, he thinks.

All you've got to do is accept the deal. Please, Rick. Accept the deal.'

I was walking again. Back toward the exit. Chacon stood in the path, looking at me sympathetically. As if now I would understand how helpful he was trying to be.

'Where's Diane?' I said. 'She isn't a part of this?'

He gave an ambiguous grimace.

'What are you saying?'

'She harbored you,' he said. 'And we're not charging her.'

'You're suggesting what? She helped you in some way? Told you where I was?'

I looked at him hard, got more sympathy and warmth.

'I don't believe you,' I said.

As I tried to get past, he thrust a card in my pocket. Then I heard him call after me, 'Keep in touch.' As if I were going to have a choice. 'And don't worry,' he said. 'We won't let you do it again.'

The two cops following me out of the park gave explicit meaning to that statement.

In my apartment, I went right to my daughter's closet. I'd no idea why. One of those moments when you stop at the place you've just walked to and say, what am I doing here? There was the ladder. I climbed it, and above the top shelf was the secret hiding place I'd kept waiting for Molly to find and use. I removed the panel. Small tools fell out. Wire-type things, mainly. For picking locks. Then real ugly things. A forty-five with a silencer and a box of shells.

I got down off the ladder and sat there, on the floor of the closet, for about ten minutes. I thought with wry amusement, Betsy's people had done a lousy search – unless they'd planted it. Then I put the gun and shells back and started calling Chacon. But his people were already banging on the front door.

FIFTY-ONE

In my life, I had fantasized lots of things, good and bad. Being institutionalized for a mental disorder wasn't one of them. I was certainly having trouble accepting reality – the reality of my confinement, with everyone there telling me I was crazy. I didn't feel crazy. I felt disoriented, because of what everyone was telling me. It's amazing how easy it was to have doubts.

Of course I said – shouted, screamed – my accusers had the wrong man. The fact remained, as was repeatedly pointed out to me, they were all smart women, had no motive to lie and were very sure of their accusations. And of course I told the government shrinks that other, perfectly competent doctors had earlier attributed my blackouts to narcolepsy. They came back with brain scans showing no physical cause for that condition. In fact, every psychiatrist with whom I talked fell in with Cassenov's diagnosis.

I argued it out with Chacon. I got him to listen twice to the taped interview with Luis. The detective was condescending, and unshakeable in his belief that I killed Emma and raped those women. I thought something more was influencing these people, and I'd no idea what it was.

I had had one long talk with Joe Stein in his office before taking the plea. Just Joe and me, not Nona. Frank Seaton had given me a few days to decide, and that time was about to run out. Joe said, 'They're being awfully smug, Rick. I've got the sense they're sitting on facts they haven't told us about.'

'Such as?'

'Something out of the ordinary. I mean, they've got a strong case without it – five women, maybe more, willing to identify you—'

'None of that will stand up on cross.'

'It's a goddamn parade, Rick. I can break down each one, but the cumulative weight – if all these women keep coming, the jury'll start thinking it's our side that's playing lawyers' games; it's the prosecutors with the truth.'

'Why do you think there's more evidence?' I said.

'Frank's certainly implied it.'

'How?'

'Well . . . last meeting, I'm about to leave, he says, "Joe. You and I go back, and we're both friends of Rick's." Then he gets up, walks around that huge desk of his, and grabs my arm. "I'm telling you," he says, "friend to friend, take this deal." And then, like he's announcing the deliverance, *"Take this deal!"'*

'So, you're saying, take the deal.'

'I'm not sure you have a realistic choice. We could get disclosure of their evidence, if they proceed against you, but then you've got the publicity circus of a criminal indictment. And a trial in these circumstances is a crapshoot. You know this. You're a trial lawyer. With the deal – it's a brilliant deal – in six months you could walk. They'll talk about a minimum period, but that's, at worst, presumptive. If you can show you're no longer a danger to yourself or others, they have to let you out.'

'If their case against me is such a lock, why's the deal so lenient? They're saying I raped eight women and killed one. And for that, they're offering some indeterminate stretch in a hospital?'

'Well, it's not a lock. The case is as iffy from their standpoint as it is from ours. The women will all testify to what they believe you did. But Cassenov has everyone believing you lacked *mens rea*, the criminal intent to do it.'

'The man-who-believed-his-wife-was-a-grapefruit defense.'

'In a sense,' he said. 'And if the jury buys it, you know what you get.'

'An indeterminate stretch in a hospital.'

'Right,' he said.

'So take the deal,' I said.

'I think you have to. And all of them, the women, are willing to drop their own charges against you if you do. Even Delfine whom Helen has talked to. It's extraordinary, Rick, but these women, despite everything, really seem to have some sympathy for you.'

'What about Diane?'

'I assume she's part of the group.'

I stood thinking about the unreality of that. 'You realize,' I said, 'I'd never met Diane before any of this happened. I'd no idea of her existence.'

'You sure?'

'Oh, Christ!' I said. 'You too?'

'I just want you to be sure.'

'You're coming around to their side.'

'I'm not, Rick.'

'Just agnostic.'

'I'm on your side. But they could argue you knew who Diane was, even if she didn't know you.'

'You believe that?'

'No. But still . . . what we've got here, on the one hand, a three-ring trial, sensationalized in the press every day for weeks, with a substantial risk of conviction, the stigma of that and life in prison; and, on the other hand, an enforced vacation in the loony bin for some unpredictable period of time, probably less than two years.'

'With the stigma of that.'

'Yes, but more erasable.'

I laughed with some bitterness, but I took the deal. I went into their institution to be treated for a mental disorder I wasn't convinced I had, to avoid conviction for crimes I was far from believing I'd committed.

And they gained ground on me. Helen Cassenov and her team could not have been more supportive. They understood, they said, how difficult it was to accept the fact of such a disability. But nonetheless they persuasively stated the case, as well as the benefits of accepting their conclusion.

They said you can do this like a jigsaw puzzle, starting with the easy pieces at the corners. The easiest piece for me was the chain on the back door of Ali's apartment. I'd put it on as soon as I got inside. I remembered counting on Ali's not having affixed that chain and doing it myself immediately. When I left in the morning, I checked it. The door was still chained. So was the front door. There was no explaining that.

Other pieces also fell into place. Memory flashes I'd never had before that left me questioning my identity. Quirks and habits that were probably neurotic. And, of course, the blackouts. Who the hell knows what you do when you black out, or, for that matter, why you go off? I'd been given as many opinions on my own condition as the number of doctors I'd seen. And now I had another one. I couldn't dismiss it simply because it didn't feel like me. If, in fact, I was hosting some murderous personality that wasn't *me*, I wouldn't necessarily know or feel anything about it.

In a sense, I had the right mind-set for what was happening. If I'd totally bought into their diagnosis, the guilt of these crimes might have shattered me. But if I hadn't thought they *might* have been right, the injustice of being incarcerated might have driven me into exactly the sort of state for which people are legitimately institutionalized. So I just floated in a limbo of agonized uncertainty. I railed at them for proof. They offered none. They tried hypnotizing me twice, which just struck me as funny. Helen, of course, believed she had witnessed me exhibiting my alleged other personality, but that testimony was just Helen reasoning from conclusion. Without their admitting it expressly, I guessed they had access to the additional facts Chacon was sitting on and withholding from me. They kept saying, 'Trust us, Rick. We know more about this than you give us credit for.' Or words to that effect.

If they were right, I was certain I didn't want to recover the memory of whatever had split my persona, and, I learned, on this issue shrinkdom itself is divided. The classic Freudian view is open it all up like a boil. A more modern, dissenting opinion is, not if you don't have to. If the original trauma was so horrific as to beat your brain into suppressing it, resurrecting the memory may not be such a great idea. If you can redress the aberrant behavior without restoring that memory, do so. Such a case, we at Stony Brook were all hoping, was me.

As institutions go, this one wasn't intolerable. Food lacked originality or seasoning, but I got used to it. Even looked forward to some dishes I knew were coming, such as the steamers brought in from clam beds five miles away, or the flounder when they didn't steam tray it to death. There were rolling hills, lots of trees and greenery, and a big old stone mansion on the top of a moraine. I had my own room, a small but remarkable

luxury, with a glorious view of the grounds. I was even something of a celebrity – not on the outside for what I had allegedly
done; Sully managed to keep that almost entirely insulated from
public attention – but here, at Stony Brook, for being this case
study of an exotic form of mental derangement.

I hadn't much common ground, however, with other inmates.
These were seriously troubled people, routinely drugged into
placidity. Whatever my condition, Helen spared me the lithium.
I thought I might strike up something with a fortyish school-
teacher who once commented wryly on my celebrity status. It
turned out the man in fact suffered from multiple personalities,
only one of which was wry, the others vacant or abusive. Two
of the women there, kitchen staff, I genuinely feared. Stella, a
large brooding dark cloud of a person, and her companion,
Steph, slight, shifty and mean. Apparently, they didn't like what
I was celebrated for, and Stella, I suspected, was spitting in my
soup.

My first visitor, surprisingly, was Roger Hazzard. He owned
a house nearby on the North Shore of Long Island, and simply
arrived one day, a week before I was officially allowed to have
any visitors. Since he had good news to impart, they let him
in.

A brief visit. It was spring, and we sat outside on lawn
chairs watching the shuffleboard. Roger simply wanted me to
know, when I was ready to return to the firm, I'd be welcomed
back. He said it without fanfare. Gave no explanations or
embellishments other than saying this was something he'd
'been working on.' It should have been a momentous piece
of news. Acceptance by the firm meant the world would accept
me too. Yet, on my part, instead of jubilation and euphoria, I
felt what? Unequal to the challenge? Fear? I'd gotten rather
clinical in analyzing my emotions. None of the foregoing, I
concluded. What I felt was indifference. Couldn't muster the
energy for an expression of gratitude. It wasn't there, and
Roger knew it.

'When you're ready,' he said. 'Don't push it. No need to.'

There was something else involving Roger that still troubled
me.

'That time I came to see you in the office,' I said. 'Someone had called you about my having to leave my new job. Was that a cop named Chacon?'

Roger gave this his professional look of deep thought. 'It was a cop. Don't remember his name, but it wasn't Chacon.'

'Well, he probably had someone else call.'

'Can't help you there, Rick, but about returning to the firm?'

'I'll think about it, Roger. I will.'

After he left, I speculated a bit about his motives. Gratitude to me for not turning on him? Fellow feeling for a fellow psychotic? A demonstration of the firm's liberality? Did it matter? I decided not. It was a down day. In my mood swings, getting deeper, doubts of innocence were routing resistance to guilt. So, as for Roger's offer, what I thought was, I didn't deserve it. Didn't deserve anything, really.

FIFTY-TWO

With a cold front the following weekend – air chilly but dry, sky resplendent – Ali arrived, dressed for the country: corduroys, quilted jacket and sensible shoes. A thrill, as always, on seeing her enter the room. A shock to the system. Even though I sensed there was a new element for me. A welcome bit of distance. I didn't seem to care quite as much. Or was it just waffling? As if waffling on my own guilt had made me indecisive as to everything else.

She said, as we walked out on the lawn, 'I thought you'd never forgive me for turning you in.'

'Some days, I thank God you did,' I said.

'Really?'

'Look at me,' I said. 'See the mental health flourishing?'

'I see you've put on a couple of pounds,' she said. 'Doesn't hurt.'

Although it had rained before the front moved in, the morning sun and breeze had acted on the grass like a great hair dryer in the sky. I suggested we walk down near the edge of the property line. I knew of a bench there within a small grove of apple trees just beginning to bud. We strolled in silence and, arriving, stood for a moment in front of the bench, she in her corduroys, I in sweater and jeans, as if we were posing for an L.L. Bean catalog cover. A brief awkward moment, until Ali opened her arms.

Serious hug, no restraint. The fact that this gesture seemed in no way spontaneous bothered me less than the thought of what was probably coming next.

'So,' she said bluntly, when we took our seats. 'We have lots to talk about.'

Had I not been wary, I might have said something stupid. Like, how about resuming our marriage? Like, the chief shrink here, an authority on my peculiar disorder, thinks what brought it on in the first place was your splitting us up. As it was, I said simply, 'Molly and Sam.'

She looked down. 'I've told them you've been ill, are in the hospital, but that they can see you soon. I'm especially worried about Molly. She's had another episode.'

'What does the doctor say?'

'He thinks it may be related to . . .' She looked away.

I gave out a great sigh. 'What they teach you here, the big thing they teach you, is to get over the guilt and the shame. It's the hardest part. With other people, what I've learned here will help. Just don't think about their judgments. Day to day, do the best for people you can. But with the kids, I owe them . . . more. An honest explanation at least. And I can't begin to imagine what to say.'

'It will come to you,' she said. 'It will arise out of the situation. It will.'

'I'm sure that's right,' I said with no conviction. Then caught her eye and held it. 'Ali. You all right about money?'

Only the slightest hesitation. 'I am, Rick, yes.'

'I haven't been able to send you any.'

Her look confirmed my suspicion.

'You ought to just tell me what you came here to tell me,' I said.

She lowered her head and took my hand, which I allowed, though I knew what was coming. 'I love you, Rick. But . . .'

Bad beginning.

I said, 'But not enough to excuse what . . . you believe I've done.' I thought I'd make it easier for her. Hadn't; only left her confused.

'I'm past that,' she said.

Not likely, I thought. 'I wish I were.'

Her head snapped up. 'Look. Darling. You've done bad things. No doubt bad things were done to you. You've had a shock now. You've been made aware of the problem. Like you just said, don't dwell on the past so much any more. OK?' She looked at me hopefully.

Simple sound advice. Couldn't be repeated too often. Big difference between receiving and taking, however. Even bigger difference between swallowing tonics when one is certain of guilt, and digesting them when one is still dangling on the subject.

'Why do you love me?' I said. 'I realize that's a dumb question, asked out of pathetically reduced self-esteem, but what's the answer?'

Her eyes closed for an instant. 'Because you don't deserve to be loved, right? That's what you mean?'

'Exactly.'

'Rick, I do love you, but I also . . .' Her face contorted; her eyes filled with tears. 'You're not going to like this, but I feel . . . with Bob Hayden . . .' Then she lost it, couldn't talk for a moment, although she tightened her grip on my hand.

She cried, 'Even when you were making me unhappy—'

'I wouldn't do that anymore. At least I'd be a lot more careful.' Instinctively, I was fighting for her. Even when I hadn't thought I would. Even when I knew I'd lose.

I did, and maybe wanted to.

'I'm sorry, baby' she said. 'I'm so sorry.'

'Makes sense,' I said, surprised how right it felt. 'This makes sense. Our being separate.'

'Oh God!' she said. 'It does.'

FIFTY-THREE

Carter, coming next – the following day, in fact – took the brunt of Ali's visit, which may have been why he came. In a brown plaid jacket, heavy plum-colored sweater, gray flannel slacks. As if he were parodying the Rye country club style. Or maybe I'd become overly conscious of style, wearing, as I did, much the same kind of clothes every day. His manner and dress created a picture of self-assurance – success with a clear conscience. Since I seriously doubted that was his state of mind, I envied his ability to project it.

In the past – the pre-nightmare past – I'd meet up with Carter, dinner, ballgame, whatever, it was a rush. A guy you respected and liked, great company. Not now, knowing what I did about him. On the other hand, I thought, who the hell was I to judge? Carter at least understood his problem, was addressing it intelligently, had it under control. Whereas at that stage of my hospitalization, I was a nutcase talking to walls.

Compared to those, however, in terms of responsiveness, Carter offered modest improvement.

We did a walkabout. All over the grounds. I was restless. With Carter it was habitual. I was arguing with myself, and he got to hear it.

'The objective facts are there,' I said. 'Only a lunatic would dispute them.'

'So not being one, you confessed.'

'In a fashion.'

'And apologized.'

'Abjectly. On occasion. And yet, as of yet, no memory. Not a clear one. But still I feel guilty. I feel sometimes like I did these things. But you would think—'

He broke in impatiently. 'What about hypnosis?'

'They can't do it. I'm not a good subject, it seems.'

'I don't know, man.'

'Look. I'm not trying to say I didn't do it. Half the time I think I did.'

'Without remembering it?'

'Well, I remember something. An impression. Enough to make the whole thing plausible. And these facts. Both doors in Ali's apartment were not only locked, but chained from the inside. Front and back. I had to remove the chain on the front door to leave in the morning. There was a doorman and a cop out front all night. And the gun was in my goddamn closet, man. It's just not clear.'

I looked out over the lawn. 'And they apparently have some other proof.'

'What *proof*?'

'I don't know,' I said.

'Whatta you mean, you don't know? Find out!'

I'd stopped walking and stretched my neck.

He said, 'You don't want to find out.'

I said nothing.

'You prefer the uncertainty.'

'I guess so,' I said.

'Let me tell you,' he said. 'When I was a kid, a teenager, I did some real bad stuff.'

I was far from sure I wanted to hear this. 'And you remember it all,' I said quickly to discourage him from revealing the details I already knew.

'You're damn right. Every rotten move. Every breath I took. I'm still paying back. Always will. You've got a conscience, you don't forget these things. And *you've* got a conscience.'

'With a powerful eraser, it seems.'

'That's what the shrinks tell you?'

'That's what they say.'

'Hell of a thing to live with.'

'Could be worse,' I said. 'My wife might have moved in with another guy. Taken my kids there.'

Carter frowned, which cut deep ridges under his cheeks. 'Yeah, I heard. Kick in the ass.'

I laughed. 'One thing about sinking this low.'

'You're wrong,' he said. 'Things can always get worse.'

'She was here yesterday. I thought of saying, what do you see in this guy? But it's obvious. Nice guy. Built an empire. And the best thing about him? He's not a convicted murderer and rapist.'

'Rick.'

'Yeah?'

'Got to stop this, man.'

'This feeling sorry for myself shit.'

'Right,' he said.

I laughed again. 'Yeah, it's pretty bad.'

'Awful.'

'So you know this guy?' I said. 'Bob Hayden?'

'You starting again?'

'Of course not. You know him?'

'Sure.'

'And?'

'He seems all right. Kind of guy, though, who not only grabs your upper arm when he's giving you a hand shake, but massages it.'

'You think he's gay?'

'Probably not,' he said. 'Probably just wants to be liked. Like all of us.'

'He's apparently supporting Ali and my kids. You know how much I hate that?'

'*Rick!*'

'You think he's capable of raping and killing his daughter?'

'*What?*'

'Forget it,' I said.

'Where the hell did that come from?'

'Nowhere sane, I'm sure.'

He nodded slowly as if he might be agreeing with that.

We each looked elsewhere for a few moments.

'You think Betsy Spaeth could murder her own sister?' I asked.

'Whatta you doing, man? I mean, you got something, or you just flailing around?'

I turned away.

'Ricky, boy! Talk to me!'

'On Betsy, yeah, I got something. It's complicated. Forget I said anything.' In earlier days, I would have told him. 'So what do you think she sees in him?'

'Who? Ali in Hayden? Jesus. How the fuck do I know? Probably the same thing she saw in you – some extreme form of it. You're probably like him in some way neither of you would see, but she does. That's what we do, repeat ourselves. We're always attracted to the same traits.'

I was getting sick of the subject too.

'By the way,' he said. 'Before I leave. That woman who helped you, what's her name?'

'Diane?'

'Right. She still thinks you didn't do it.'

'You got that wrong. She's the one who turned me in. She told Chacon where I was.'

'I don't think so. That's not what Nona says. She's been talking to the woman and thinks she's totally in love with you.'

At my dumbfounded expression, he said, 'See, you never know about people. Look at you. You don't even know about yourself.'

I love that expression, 'The scales fell from his eyes.' When I first heard it, as a kid, the only scales I knew about were those you weighed yourself on, so it was a difficult image.

Ali, for me, was finally over. Inevitably, I now think, from the moment I met Diane. A complete displacement like that – it can happen fast or, at least in my case, take an inexcusably long time to make itself known. If Carter hadn't said what he said, I might have continued not getting it.

Chacon had implied she'd turned on me, and I'd believed it because it seemed everyone else had. I finally realized how stupid that was. Diane had taken me in, protected me, fed me, clothed me, dressed my wounds, both mental and physical, routed Ali right out of my life. I'd been missing her terribly. I wanted to call her immediately. I wanted her there with me right away.

I went to the phone – the coin phone patients used – put a quarter in, began to dial, and hung up. I couldn't do it. Couldn't risk it. I was sicker than I'd thought.

FIFTY-FOUR

The surprise visitor was Betsy. Two weeks later, out of the blue, unannounced, and two days after the big decision had been made to spring me.

'You're about the last person I wanted to see,' I said bluntly, as she came striding into the visitor's lounge on the first floor. 'And I'd have thought that feeling was mutual.'

'Because you broke my window?' she said.

'Yeah. Right. It's about the window.'

'I did try to nail your ass.'

Now she had my attention. 'You want to go outside?'

'In that humidity?' she said. 'Hell no! Let's stay in, watch the inmates out there from the comfort of this air-conditioned room.' Settling down on a corner sofa, she managed to show off her lavender Chanel suit. 'Speaking of inmates,' she said, peering at the shuffleboarding on the lawn, I hear they're letting you out of this place. Like, in days.'

'I'm no longer dangerous, couldn't you tell?' I said, sitting on the opposite end.

'Quick cure.'

'They're very clever here.'

'Well, I wish you the best, Rick.'

'Oh yes? That's a charitable line.'

'And why not?'

'Indeed,' I said.

'And how about you?' she said. 'The line you're taking? We OK?'

I looked at her.

'When you get out?' she said. 'We going to be all right?'

My expression said, *What the hell are you getting at?*

'Relax, darling. I'm not suggesting we resume our torrid love affair.'

I laughed. Then we both watched the shuffleboarding. For a while.

'So what do you think, Rick? Now that you've had the benefit of all this high-priced psychiatry? You do it? Didn't do it?'

'What do you think?'

'There hasn't been a single repetition,' she said. 'Not once since you've been in here. Pretty damning.'

'Well, I was framed,' I said, wanting to believe it. 'No doubt by the perp. So it's what you'd expect.'

'Which leads one to speculate: what *will* he do when you get out?'

'He?'

'Of course,' she said, 'he might let things sit. No more risks, just leave you with the guilt in everyone's mind.'

'*She* might.'

'What are you going to do about that?'

'About her? Nail her. Eventually, I'll get her.'

'No let up?'

'None at all,' I said.

'Your new life's work.'

'Can you think of a more worthwhile pursuit?'

Silence, except for the noise outside muted by the air conditioning and window.

'Heard you met an old friend of mine,' she said. 'Guy named Tucker.'

'Friend?'

'I know what you're thinking. Tucker does talk.'

'Why are *we* talking about Tucker?'

'You understand what happened?'

'I now understand why you're so down on lawyers.'

'Only one,' she said.

'The guy who defended Tucker.'

'Defended all of them, yes. But it wasn't a guy,' she said.

I felt it coming.

'Doris Strickland,' she said.

I sat there quietly for a moment, absorbing the shock.

'You OK?' she asked.

'Yes, I'm OK.'

'I wouldn't want anything I've said to upset you.'

I said, 'Why are you telling me this?'

'I haven't told you anything.'

'You ever know Jane Hentchoff, the sixth victim?'

'Jane? No. Not before the incident, of course.'

'The incident in prep school,' I said.

'That one, yes.'

I looked at her hard. 'Her brother there with you?'

'That's right.'

'Play lacrosse?'

'I believe he did.'

I stared at her again, this time for more than a minute. She suffered it in silence until finally returning an inquiring glance.

'You didn't have to do this,' I said.

'I haven't told you anything,' she said again with more emphasis.

'Why have you come here, Betsy?'

She slid to my end of the sofa, opened my buttons and caressed my skin, under my shirt, front and back. Nothing romantic or sexual. She was looking for a wire. Satisfied, she said, 'There are people you get tangled up with in strange ways. You and I, for example, are not only star-crossed, we're star-fucked. Totally. I've no idea what it means, or whether it means anything but coincidence. But I take no chances. I like to be square with such people. Whatever guilt you may have, you can reduce it by two. Strickland and Hentchoff.'

I said, 'So you did what, as to those two? Take a free ride?'

Her look was intense. 'There's not a single shred of evidence connecting me to either crime.'

A surge of anger blocked my ability to talk.

'Easy, Rick.'

'And the others? Diane Nethersong, Helen Cassenov, Caroline Lambeth, Solange Delfine?' I had to stop for a moment. 'My wife? Your sister?'

She said it squarely in my face. 'Not me, Rick. I had absolutely nothing to do with any of those six. Except for Emma, I never even met them.'

I tried to take the resentment out of my voice. 'You just did Strickland and Hentchoff.'

She resumed her interest in the activity outside the window.

'OK,' I said. 'Clears things up a bit.'

'Good. So I guess I'll be going.'

I thought about how to keep her talking for a while and realized I didn't really want to. She'd just dropped a bombshell. Her stated reason for doing it was so thin on its face, I doubted she herself expected me to believe it. What she did make plausible by implicitly confessing to two of these crimes was that someone else had committed the others.

She got up. We shook hands. I asked, 'If not you, who?'

She gave a shrug and a head shake. 'I've been thinking you, Rick. Which is what everyone else thinks. And the file's now closed. It may be a shame, but you'll go to your grave with that rap.'

We exchanged a pair of strained farewells. Then she strode off with a slightly exaggerated lop-sided walk. Mine, not hers – except, it would seem, on special occasions. She turned to give me an overdone smirk. 'See you around,' she said. But neither of us really wanted that.

I called Ali three times before I caught her. At her office, as it happened.

'I want you to tell me,' I said. 'I know you're living with Hayden now. How are the kids with that?'

Silence on the line as she probably fought down an impulse to complain about the abruptness of the question.

'They're fine with it, Rick. With him. I wouldn't have gone there if they hadn't been.'

'They like him?'

'They like him fine.'

'But?'

'There are no buts, other than those in your mind. We are happy. All of us. As happy as we can be . . . in the circumstances.'

I accepted it. Not that I had much choice.

'When I get out of here, get back to work, I expect to pay for the kids again.'

'Sure, Rick, whatever you like.'

I accepted that too. I'd broach resuming joint custody when I felt stronger.

What I wanted was to see Diane.

Naturally, I continued to think about calling her. I also thought about calling Nona – but I know why I didn't do that. Shame. No doubt Betsy was right. Everyone believed I'd committed these crimes, and not even I could be sure that I hadn't. Which is probably, at bottom, the reason I didn't call Diane. Betsy having reduced the number by two mattered, really, very little so far as my own feelings were concerned and actually increased my confusion.

Then, on the day I was to leave, my most surprising visitor showed up: Tucker, the banker-sexaholic. I was packing a small canvas bag and dropped a shirt on the bed when I saw him.

'You remember me?' he asked, thumping into my room like a shotputter, with his keen glance around.

'I remember you . . .' I started slowly.

'And you're thinking, what the hell is this guy doing here?'

I gave a look of resignation, prepared to listen to what he might tell me.

'I've been seeing a friend of yours,' he said. 'Diane Nethersong. We both do M and A, you know, mergers and acquisitions. And, would you believe it? We ended up on the same deal about two months ago, and I asked her out.'

With control – because I was furious – I said, 'You came all the way out here to tell me you're seeing Diane?'

'It may not be the best time. Maybe we should meet for a drink sometime when you're back in town.'

'Say what you want to say, Tucker.' I sat on the end of the bed. 'You drove a long way to say it.'

He scraped under him the one chair in the room. 'OK. Here it is. Plain and straight. I'm in love with this woman. I can't get her to take that in, value it, or act on it. The problem is not my past. I think she accepts my . . . atonement. And I think she likes me. I'm single, childless, successful in her world. The problem is you. How she feels about you. And she's not going to ask you, so I am. And don't say it's none of my business.'

I said nothing.

'Are you going to tell her?' he persisted. 'I mean, you obviously don't give a damn about her.'

'Tucker,' I said, rising, ready to hit him. 'Plain and straight? Get the fuck out of my room! I'm trying to leave this place, and you're in my way.'

When he departed – stunned, double taking, muttering to himself about me – I had to sit down again. Where had that rage come from? I barely recognized myself. No blame on Tucker, I was the one going nuts.

FIFTY-FIVE

So, finally, I did leave. No celebration. No one to leave with. Hauling a gym bag of clothes, I took the LIRR back to Manhattan. And eventually I went back to work at my former firm. Was treated kindly. Resumed my life. Tried to pick up again with the people I cared about.

With Sam, when I had him, I slipped easily into the old routines. He was shy at first, as if I were a distant relative. Within a week, however, he was telling me things, when I collected him in the morning to take him to school, or when we tossed a ball around in the park or played chess or video games the way we always had. Small things, he began to confide, that mattered to him. Nothing basic had changed.

My relationship with Ali was to be a larger project. There was still a reserve. She once said to me, 'You know the kind of movie I really hate? The sci-fi flick where people you think you know aren't who they seem. They've been taken over by aliens or whatever. Like *Invasion of the Body Snatchers*.'

I said, 'I'm not like that anymore.' And to myself said, if I ever was.

'I know,' she said. But it was obvious what she meant. For her, I was going to have to prove it.

Molly was something else entirely. For almost a month, she scarcely acknowledged my presence. Children know how to hurt you. Molly certainly did. Her standoffishness was as deliberately intended to get back at me for the hurt I'd caused her as it was an expression of her own confusion about who I was.

And she chose her moments.

I picked her up from school one evening, as I often did. It meant leaving the office early, but it gave us a walk down Fifth

Avenue together to her new apartment, fifteen blocks away. About mid-way, Molly, who had until then been silent, said, 'Lissy told me what you did.'

'Lissy's a girl in your class?' I said.

'Yes. She said you broke into women's apartments and made them take their clothes off.'

I had nothing to say for a half block. People went by – with God knows what concerns. My fragile hold on the world was slipping.

'Is that right?' she insisted I tell her.

'I wish I knew,' I said. 'It might have happened. I just can't be certain.'

She stopped walking. I looked at her face, saw tears streaming. 'I don't understand,' she said.

I bent down to get on her level. 'I don't either, baby. I was in a hospital for ten months so the doctors could figure it out, and they couldn't.'

'Everybody wants to look at everybody naked. Why?'

'Human nature, baby. Not to worry.'

'But it's nasty to force someone.'

'Very.'

'*So?*' she fairly shrieked at me.

I drew some breath and said, 'Millions of years ago, there wasn't much on this planet but reptiles. They evolved into monkeys. And monkeys evolved into people. So in our heads we have reptile and monkey brains, as well as our own. In some people sometimes one of those other brains takes over. That's as close as I can get to an explanation. It's an illness, a lot worse than the flu. If I had it, I'm better now. Fully cured.'

As I rose, she gave me a red-faced look of agonized indecision. With a brief hesitation, in which her face curled into a pitiable sob, and my own heart stopped, she threw herself around my legs, right there on Fifth Avenue. No doubt we were a spectacle, but I hardly cared.

The thought came into being on the way to my apartment, after delivering Molly to her new home. It was roaring by the time I got upstairs to the phone and punched in the numbers.

'Chacon.'

He was in, answering his own telephone. I was absolutely certain he would be.

'Vincente, it's me.'

'Hello, Rick.'

'I need you to tell me this! No reason not to. The case is over. It'll never be tried.'

'Tell you what, Rick?'

'What evidence did you have? That you were holding back, saving for the trial?'

'I've been wondering why you never asked me.'

'I'm asking now.'

'We probably would have turned it over earlier.'

'So what the hell was it?'

'A photo, Rick. Night shot. You coming out of Emma Hayden's apartment. The photographer said he was tipped off by one of the street girls who recognized you. According to the lab, it was taken the night she was murdered, the night before her father found her and called nine one one.'

FIFTY-SIX

I entered into a state of mind I'd never experienced before nor have since. I remember rage so hot it hit a realm of calm. I had this odd serenity built of anger and certainty. Climbing the ladder, getting what I needed, there was an intense, and even pleasurable, concentration on the job at hand. I reflected calmly that the gun still being there strongly suggested it hadn't been stashed by Betsy or Chacon. Downstairs, no trouble about a cab – one rolled up right in front of me. No traffic. The driver's gibberish on the cell phone – I barely heard it.

The doormen to the building waved, they knew me as the father of Ali's children whom I'd often picked up and dropped off. And Ali herself was there, in the lobby, waiting impatiently for the elevator. It was a coincidence which, in my weird state, I took for granted. She didn't. We stood for a moment, speechlessly, in the opulence of that hall.

'Where's Molly?' I said. Barked at her really, right over her inquiry as to what I was doing there.

'Upstairs. Why?'

The elevator came; we got on it.

'Who's babysitting?'

She glanced at the board as we ascended. 'Bob.' Trying not to make it sound defensive.

'You trust our daughter to Bob?'

'He's probably reading her a story,' she said, troubled by my tone but not comprehending.

The elevator door opened. I stormed past. Made straight for her bedroom. Burst in.

'Rick!' Shock on the smooth famous face of Bob Hayden. Molly standing with her nightie off, and Bob on the pink canopied bed, in his gray suit pants and open shirt, hands just lifted from her. Molly's face wet with tears.

He didn't move as I strode toward him. I jammed the barrel of the silencer into his mouth, smashing his gold teeth, smashing his skull against the headboard. 'You put this gun in my closet? Yes?'

A muffled response, at which I yanked out the gun and got the admission.

I gestured Molly out of the room, and Ali arrived screaming. I ignored her and addressed Hayden. 'How you answer the next question will have a direct effect on whether you live to answer the one after that. You understand?'

That affected look of distraction. 'Yes.'

'You paid a paparazzo to snap me leaving Emma's apartment and lie about the date?'

'Rick . . .'

I smashed the gun in his cheek. 'Yes or no?'

'Yes.'

'You guessed I'd go to Diane Nethersong's house, and you waited. Probably in a parked car across the street. Yes?'

'Yes.'

'You saw me black out and dragged me over two fucking walls to deposit me in her backyard. You thought she'd report me. You wanted me to think I'd moved myself.'

Ali stopped screaming. Her silence was worse. Hayden looked

at her as if he were about to explain a misunderstanding. I
started squeezing the trigger.

'Yes,' he said, almost relaxing.

'That night when you threw us around – the both of us,' I said,
pointing at Ali, 'you had a key to her apartment, and you came
up the front elevator because the night doorman knew who you
were. And you didn't leave! You chained the front door and hid
out until everyone else left.'

He started offering an appeasing smile, the expression of one
about to set matters straight.

I said, 'You even bought my brand of deodorant to imitate my
scent.'

'Rick, if you would just listen for a moment . . .'

I said, 'And you've been systematically abusing my daughter.'

Ali now commenced a low moan.

'I would never do that, Rick. I couldn't. I myself was the
victim of abuse, I could never—'

I aimed at his eyes. His mouth became a soundless pleading
rictus. There was the same shock on his face when I shot him.
In the belly, to make the pain last.

Robert Hayden died on the way to the hospital. I felt no sorrow
that I killed him. Or ultimately got away with it by dint of the
exercise of prosecutorial discretion.

On the contrary, I thought he deserved worse. Must have
been that reptilian part of my brain.

FIFTY-SEVEN

Another two-week sensation. Sully knew how to make
stories burst into print and how to smother them. On his
advice, I gave one press conference, said that was it,
and kept my word.

The terms of Hayden's will never reached the papers but
were certainly of interest to me. He left half his estate to Ali.
It provided for her and the children far more handsomely than

I'd ever likely be able to do. The other half he left to Betsy.

Regarding Betsy, I had unfinished business with Chacon. I tracked him on his cell phone, said I wanted to talk.

'You'd like to thank me?' he said. 'It's OK, no need.'

'Thank you?' Not what I had in mind.

'For weighing in on your side. On Frank Seaton's decision. Not to prosecute.'

'I didn't know you had.'

'Well, there were a number of factors. Your wife's testimony was certainly important.'

'Ex-wife,' I said.

'Of course. And you'd probably like to know what I added,' he said. 'It was about the gun. I made a point of the fact it was Hayden's.'

'You knew that?'

'I found out,' he said. 'Worked it.'

'You mean, you conducted an investigation.'

'I did.'

'And what? The gun was registered in Hayden's name?'

'That's what you thought?'

'To tell you the truth—'

'So you're saying, not much of an investigation.'

'I thank you, Vincente, for whatever you did.'

'The fact is,' he said, 'the gun wasn't registered at all. We had to dig. We had to find the guy who confessed to selling it to Hayden.'

'You went to that trouble?'

'Not huge. We had some leads. The shells in Emma's apartment. Other things. And, of course, since it was Hayden's gun, that implies you had to take it from him in a struggle, maybe. Self-defense likely. Very difficult case for a prosecutor, given that and those other factors.'

'Vincente, he planted the gun in my apartment. I brought it to the scene.'

'That's one interpretation. Not one I personally favor, nor should you.'

'Whatta you mean, interpretation?'

'No offence, Rick, but, in this case, your recollection's not entirely trustworthy, is it? You being in an altered state at the time. And my people, the ones who searched your apartment, before and after you took off for New Jersey, even after you went to the hospital, they're very experienced police officers. They don't miss things like that. Guns, stuck in some secret wall compartment? They'd look ridiculous.'

I suggested we do this face to face. I still hadn't gotten to the reason I'd called him. He invited me to his office at eleven the next morning.

I climbed out of a cab at five minutes of. There on Police Plaza, as if I had conjured it, Betsy stood talking to a group of plainclothesmen. She couldn't help but see me looming ten feet away, staring openly. She nodded at me, smiled and turned back to her peers. Until the pressure of my not moving caused her to break up that conclave and come over.

'Hi, Rick. You wear celebrity well. What are you doing here?'

'Last time I looked the Federal Courthouse was around the corner.'

'Well, well, you're a lawyer again! You're going to court! Lovely. So why stop a block away?'

'Saw you.'

'How flattering.'

'One thing, though. That call made to Roger Hazzard—'

'Oh no, Rick! Jesus! Drop it! It's over.'

'Not quite for me.'

'So what is this? You asked me – no, practically begged me to call Hazzard.'

'Different call. The one you had someone make before that. The one that told him what I was suspected of.'

The glimmer faded from her smile. 'Who told you that?'

'You did. Just now. Another big question. You said you did two of the victims, but not why.'

She squinted at the sun, glanced around swiftly, then gave me a hostile look.

'I think I got half the story,' I said.

'What story might that be?'

'The motivation story. Getting even with those women, revenge – pretty extreme for just a grudge.'

She looked away, deciding whether to walk away.

I wasn't going to let her. 'So why else did you do it?'

'Let it go, Rick, OK?'

'Were you after Hayden?'

She blinked.

'You said it yourself once,' I prodded. 'The more often the perpetrator is seen to strike, the greater the pressure on the investigation, the more likely he'll be caught.'

Her arms folded with a show of impatience.

'Two birds with one stone,' I said. 'For you.'

Her expression said, now why the hell should I answer that?

'You still owe me,' I said.

'Why do you care, Rick?'

'Because, if you were also gunning for Hayden, you had to know it was Hayden. Almost from the start. At least from the Caroline Lambeth video. I'd really like to know how you knew that.'

'Because you didn't?'

'Because I didn't,' I said slowly. 'And because, *had* I known—'

'Right,' she agreed with reluctance. 'Why I owe you.'

'Hardly the only reason.'

She took a moment. 'Go on.'

'I did what you wanted done most in this world. What you came to Stony Brook to maneuver me into doing. The only thing is, you didn't expect me to come out of it with any credibility, did you? Big chance you took, telling me that stuff.'

'I told you nothing.'

'If you like. Why did you suspect Hayden?'

She rocked in thought before deciding it couldn't hurt her to tell me that. 'Same M.O.,' she said.

Not unexpected. Nonetheless, hearing it rocked me. After a moment, I said, 'Emma too?'

'Oh, yes,' she said, with a groan from deep in her throat.

'He actually told me once that some older man had debauched her.'

'Did he really!' she said. 'That bastard.'

'He had a distinctive patter, a ritual . . .'

'You heard it on the Lambeth tape.'

'That's horrible!' I said. 'You and Emma went through that?'

She laughed, I think, at the pathetic insufficiency of that comment.

'Yet,' I said, 'you let me be the fall guy. You watched my life crash, let me get put away. You allowed him to do it to others. And to kill. Your own sister.'

'There was no certainty,' she said with anger. 'I couldn't prove it. It could have been anyone.'

'And suppose you had taken what you knew to Chacon? That same patter, the ritual? You, your sister?'

She said very quietly, 'I couldn't do that.'

It took a moment, but the penny dropped. 'Frank Seaton once told me,' I said, 'they thought child abuse victims were too emotionally crippled to do this work.'

She looked away again.

'You knew that,' I said.

Her laugh was bitter. 'It's hardly a secret.'

'So you let it all happen,' I said. 'Because of a job? A fucking job?'

She said nothing.

'Without your job – all that need for vengeance with no place to go?'

She wanted to leave. Her eyes darted in every direction.

'But there's something more, isn't there?' I said. 'Much deeper. You said this too. Abusers abuse. You enjoyed it.'

She tried to leave, but I held her by the arm.

'Look,' I said. 'This is how it's gonna be. Your boss is waiting for me upstairs. We have a meeting at eleven. My thought had been, lay out the case against you. Now I'm going to give you a chance. To stop that. First, you go to Strickland, tell her what you did. Once you've confessed, you offer her whatever part of your inheritance she'll take as compensation – and yourself. You be her sex slave, if that's what she wants, although she'll probably take the money and kick your ass. If she turns you in, too bad. Then you go to Hentchoff. Same offer, although she's strictly hetero as far as I know.'

Long pause.

'Fuck you.'

'See ya,' I said, heading off.

Now she held *my* arm.

'Tell Chacon what you want. We'll laugh about it together.'

'I don't think so,' I said.

'Even if you testified – I never admitted those crimes. You'd have to exaggerate what I said, lie.'

'And what makes you think I won't do that?'

'Your word against mine.'

'True. But I still have the tape of Luis. And even if they won't prosecute, how long do you think you'll keep that job you love so much? Or that some evidence won't turn up to get you? Now that they'll be looking for it?'

Long stares.

'And we'd find the cop who you got to call Hazzard. Now why else would you have done that if you weren't squeezing me? And why the pressure on me, if not connected to Hayden?'

'OK,' she said.

'You better mean that.'

Tight nod.

'I'll know,' I said.

'Right.'

'And you don't have forever.'

'Gotcha.'

'It may be the other way around.'

'Funny.'

She didn't really think so and took off. I watched her body move, her graceful walk as she turned the corner, and the frame filled with other people. I figured she'd take the deal, and I hailed a cab.

FIFTY-EIGHT

When the notoriety died down, I called Diane, finally, and suggested we meet the next day.

'You sure?' she said, on her mobile, walking between meetings.

She proposed Battery Park; it was near her office.

'I'll be at the railing of the sea wall,' I said, 'just south of the monuments.'

A hurried cell phone conversation, crammed with detail, static and sharp silences.

We chose a good day as it turned out. The air was a bit gusty, but soft, even if salty, with the sun blazing out now and then from behind clouds big and fluffy like pillows. With my back to the rail, I picked her out of the crowd. She sailed down the path in her cream and tan outfit with white pearls – lovely in my eyes, but too thin again. I wanted to feed her. When she saw me, she stopped for a moment, then advanced slowly.

'Hi,' I said.

She came to the rail, gazed out at the water, then quickly at me. 'You look OK. Not as haggard.'

'I look like hell, love. You're the beauty.'

'Oh sure!' She scrunched her eyes up, glanced away again, held her hair back against the wind.

'We should talk,' I said.

Her glance back to me said, I'm not really here for the view. Three backpacking tourists vacated a bench, and we crossed the path to take it.

I watched Di sit stiffly.

'It's your meeting,' she said.

'OK.' I sat next to her, let a moment go by. 'You didn't visit me. At the hospital.'

'And this is what? A complaint?'

'You were busy?' I asked.

Her slight weight shifted with impatience. 'You think if I thought I should be there, I wouldn't have come?'

'So what made you think you shouldn't be there?'

'Lots of reasons.'

'Yes?'

'I was *told,* for one, your treatment was going very, very well. Because – I had to piece this together – you were convinced you had done the things they were accusing you of. I wasn't buying it. And I wasn't going to buy into it, if I saw you. I told *them* that.'

'Then why did you tell Chacon where I was?'

'*Why did I what?*' She came off the bench, blue eyes radiant.
'You didn't?' I smiled with relief.
'I damn well didn't! He'd known for days. Maybe from the
outset. He'd traced your calls to your wife, and knew exactly
where you were. The way this guy operates? It's just too fucking
clever!'
'When did you learn all this?' I asked, now bemused.
'He called me,' she said, sitting down again. 'The day they
grabbed you. He got me out of a meeting, and tried to convince
me to participate in some crazy plan he was hatching supposedly for your benefit. I tried to reach you immediately. First
the phone was tied up, then no one was there, and you were
not answering your cell. Next thing I know, you've gotten
yourself institutionalized without a word to me. And they're
telling me – your shrinks are – leave you alone. Don't visit.
Don't confuse you. Treatment's going great. And then you're
out – still no call – and then it all gets revealed, you're a public
hero for killing that maniac.'
'Well, it hasn't all been revealed.' I related what I knew about
Betsy and the deal I'd offered her.
Diane thought about it. 'Have you talked to them since,
Strickland, Hentchoff?'
'I have. Strickland's initial reaction was to call Frank Seaton.
Frank, of course, never takes calls. She told his new Chief
Assistant she wouldn't discuss the matter with him or on the
phone, had to be Frank in person and alone. A week later, Betsy
and Doris were an item in the clubs, and Doris told Frank to
forget about it, false alarm.'
'Jesus,' Di swore. 'That witch's going to get away with it.'
'Jane just took the money. From what she implied, more than
ten million.'
'Not what I would have done.'
'I know. Me neither. But I thought it was more their choice
than mine.'
'I don't disagree,' she said.
We both looked away, letting a hot dog vendor go by.
'You said there were lots of reasons,' I said, finally. 'For not
visiting me.'

'Did I?' She sniffed the air. 'How's your wife?' she said with false cheeriness, and not really changing the subject. 'You two back together?'

'No,' I said.

'Oh?' She nodded, as if reflecting more deeply. 'These things take a little time to mend.'

'There's no mending this, Di.'

For the first time she looked at me steadily.

'I'm sorry for you,' she said. 'For you both.'

'You're kind to say so, but it's really over.'

'Great. So you're in love with a woman you can't have.'

'That'll be true,' I said, 'only if you won't have me.'

I got an expression of frank disbelief.

I thought for a long moment. 'When you walked into the park,' I said, 'the sight of you . . .'

She blew out her cheeks.

'. . . thrilled the hell out of me.'

Stony face.

'We should be together,' I said.

She put her hands over her eyes and sat back.

'You're worried about the kids? OK,' I said. 'Let's talk about the kids.'

'I'm worried about *you*,' she said, thrusting her hands to her lap. 'My feelings have been on display here. Too long, too clearly. But you! In love with one woman, then the next day it's someone else?'

'You. And hardly the next day. It took almost a year. In fact, now you know something about me. I commit, I don't leave. I'm not a leaver.'

Slowly she rose, and I reached for her arm. 'Are *you*?' I asked her.

Momentarily held, she looked tired. 'I have to think about this,' she said. 'And you're not really helping me now.'

She moved determinedly through the park until I could no longer see her.

FIFTY-NINE

thought, I told her what I had to, even if it was a bit clumsy. She's a smart woman; she'll see behind my awkwardness, she'll get it. She either believes me, or she doesn't. We either have a chance, or we don't. Putting pressure on her now isn't wise, or kind. Maybe I'll call later, I thought. Let it go a few weeks.

About three and a half, as it happened. Then, I called her cell phone, hoping to get her voice mail, which I did. I'm not terrific at leaving messages. I just said, 'Hi, it's me. Wanted you to know, just in case, I'm going to be with the kids this Sunday afternoon at that playground they call Hippo Park at West Ninety-first.'

She showed up. I saw her watching from outside the gate in her black tee shirt and white slacks. I'd no idea how long she'd been there. We locked eyes for quite a while before she came in.

'Molly, this is Diane.'

Molly shook Diane's hand formally, and I introduced Sammy who openly appraised this new woman up and down. 'Smart outfit,' he said, which made everyone laugh. Where did he get those lines?

'I know who you are,' said Molly. 'Daddy talks about you.'

'Oh, yes?' said Diane. 'Horrid stuff?'

'Oh, no,' said Molly. 'You're the heroine of the story.'

'Really!' For the first time in my experience, Diane blushed.

'Should we get some ice cream?' I said.

'Don't know,' said Diane. 'Being inside here is kind of special for me. You can't get into this playground, you know, without a kid.'

'Now you've got two of them,' I said.

She gave me a questioning look edged with anxiety. A trace. I saw it.

It hoarsened my voice. 'Up to you.'

Diane's white slacks got pretty grimed up, before we all trooped off to Broadway for sodas and ice cream at Sweet Shots. We felt the newness of including her in our routine, but doing so felt right. It was Molly who invited Diane back to the apartment. I eavesdropped on their conversation as Sam and I led the way to our building several blocks north.

'You know what happened?' I heard Molly say. And then in a hushed voice, 'To Bob?'

'I do, yes,' said Diane.

'It's OK to talk about it, y'know.'

'I think that's right,' said Diane. 'With the right person.'

'I think . . . you're the right person. Bob hurt you too.'

Long pause.

'He did, yes.'

'I'm glad he's dead. I know you're not supposed to think that, but I am.'

'Molly, I am too.'

Upstairs, Sammy challenged Diane to a chess game. I said, 'She's out of your league, sonny boy. She's a black belt.'

He let out a scoffing sound. 'You don't get a black belt in chess. You get a ranking, like Master.'

'Well, that's what she is, then.'

He looked uncertain.

'Come on,' Diane said. 'Let's give it a try.'

They marched off to the dining room where Sammy set up the board. Molly and I conferred about dinner, meaning which of the various take-out restaurants we might call. We picked Japanese. The kids loved sushi; so did Diane. Hanging up after placing the order, I heard a whoop from the other room. Sammy ran into the kitchen beaming rays. 'Checkmate in ten moves!' he proclaimed. Diane's grin on entering was sheepish. 'He's going to give me another chance.'

SIXTY

One likes to think there was a point. There were certainly consequences.

Maybe I would've met Diane anyway, but it's not likely. She's a full-time actor now, and gets lots of jobs, mostly in other cities. I hate her going, every time. And every time, as she heads into the elevator with her bags, I stand in the vestibule watching the doors close, feeling so sharply how much I'll miss her.

The children love her too in their own ways. She's not their second mother; she's their best friend. She's turning Sammy into a chess shark. It's a little excessive, but I'm going to let it go for a while. He's still at an age where his school work and sports schedules are light enough that the time he spends working out chess strategies doesn't interfere. With Molly, Diane's influence is more pronounced. They get lost for hours together in Molly's room. Neither will say what they talk about. Diane asks me to trust her, says she basically just listens, and she thinks it's healing. And I do trust her, especially because Molly seems much the better.

The consequences at work have been surprising. The people I relate to, day to day, don't normally deal with notorious fugitives, suspected rapists, or someone who's killed a man. Being all three, I confuse the hell out of them. On the other hand, I'm also the guy who shot the bastard who did it. Which, after the initial confusion, seems to generate awe. Gives me a weird kind of gravitas. Doors open, new clients line up, partners don't poach on my associates, invitations and appointments flow in.

Last year, Frank even offered me my old job back. As it turned out, he never got his appointment as Chief Judge; the governor changed his mind at the last minute. So it looks like he'll be DA for life. He took me to lunch at that Greek coffee shop he likes near the courthouse. 'No reason we can't pick up were we'd left off,' he said. I just laughed. Not a polite response. He meant well.

I think now, what a world! The dice bounce one way, you're a hero, another, an outcast, a third you stay where you are, frustrated at what looks like a treadmill. What you do is react; to sudden events, to unfolding developments. And I have to live with that, the particular way I reacted.

My father would have said that I was as bad as the guy I shot, even before I shot him, and that my being blamed for his crimes was not accidental. My dad was a big believer in people, especially me, bringing misfortune on to themselves. Which is easy to credit if you think, as he did, there's someone up there quick-triggered on punishments, not willing to wait even for you to drop dead.

Of course, we never agreed, and I think, on this, the evidence favors my side.

Just last Friday afternoon, when we were all driving up to Rhode Island, we had a blow-out on I-95. In the summer, we go up there every weekend we can, to a house we bought in Matunuck, a seaside resort too far from New York or Boston to be fashionable. Since it's a long haul on a cruel road, I bought a new car with, of course, new tires. Didn't help. Some sharp object, having missed thousands of other speeding vehicles, caught mine and blew out the back left tire.

When it happened, I was doing about seventy, just keeping my place in the fast lane. I thought at first we'd turn over. The initial impact, the racket of an unraveling tire, the frantic wobbling of the car, pushed everyone's screams down their throats. Cars on the right might have blocked my getting over, but there was an opening to the breakdown lane that I shot through before the disintegrating tire left us driving on the rim. We skidded to a stop. And sat there. Silent for almost a minute. Sammy said, 'Geez, Dad! Someone shoot out the tire?' Diane said, 'We're members of triple-A, right?' Molly said, 'Can we get out of here?'

The side of the road on this part of the highway was a grassy embankment. It might have been a concrete wall, or a sharp drop to nowhere, since much of the highway is narrowly bounded. And at the top of the embankment was a large shady elm. Our eyes went right to it, given the fact that the temperature had climbed to one hundred and three, with the sun frying everything not shaded.

So the four of us huddled under the branches of this fortuitous tree while I spoke to the AAA lady on my cell phone and we waited for the truck to arrive. They're not that fast on a summer get-away day, when there are likely to be several rescue jobs ahead of you. So the wait went on, but no one complained.

It took the triple-A guys forty more minutes to get there, then ten to change the tire. While Diane and the kids stayed under the tree, I joined the mechanics – a beer-bellied white guy and a slack-jawed bearded black fellow – in the breakdown lane, with the cars whipping by us, still at seventy or eighty miles an hour. The two of them did a comedy routine as they worked, like Mel Gibson and Danny Glover.

'You stickin' your ass out into the traffic again?' said Danny.

'You worried about my ass or the traffic?' said Mel.

'I couldn't care less about your ass.'

'Then why you keep lookin' at it?' said Mel, while rolling the damaged tire to his partner.

'Because you walk around with your head up it – that's quite a sight.'

'How'd you like this finger revolvin' up yours?'

'Promises, promises,' trilled Dan.

I gave them each twenty dollars, which they hadn't expected. Apparently, most people don't give them anything. The service was supposed to be free.

All back in the car, heading smoothly up the coast of Rhode Island, Diane said, 'That wasn't so bad.'

I glanced around at three lovely faces and had what amounted to a small epiphany: how most everything is interaction between the randomness and you.

'What?' she said, sensing something.

I told her.

'And this is news?' she said.

'One of those things most everyone knows or should, and doesn't appreciate enough, I haven't.'

'Well now we do,' she said.

'And what do you think?' I said. 'How we doing?'

She laughed. 'Now?'

'We're on a roll,' I said softly. 'On a roll.'

She gripped my arm high up, so as not to interfere with the driving, and held on, as if to tell me once again how it really was with us.